When Stars Fall

Cora Blacksen

Copyright © 2023 by Cora Blacksen

All rights reserved.

No portion of this book may be reproduced in any form without written permission from the publisher or author, except as permitted by U.S. copyright law.

This is a work of fiction. Unless otherwise indicated, all the names, characters, businesses, places, events and incidents in this book are either the product of the author's imagination or used in a fictitious manner. Any resemblance to actual persons, living or dead, or actual events is purely coincidental.

*"True love stories
Never have endings."*

Richard Bach

Chapter One

Charlotte

The ninth circle of hell would be more appealing than being in Los Angeles right now, this late August heat *is killing me.* By now, what passes for a summer back home in England will nearly be over. It will be all gunmetal skies and punishing winds again. Here, my shirt is sticking to me. As much as I discreetly try to pull it away from my bra, it goes straight back to being stuck. I keep flapping the front in an unsuccessful attempt to cool down which makes me look like a giant bird trying to take off. To top it all off, the car that I borrowed for the next couple of months—a 1996 silver Mercedes—has broken down. It came with the flat I'm subletting. "*The old girl's a bit temperamental, Darling,*" the owner said. What I think she meant to say was, "*It's an absolutely useless piece of shit, Darling.*" Still, at least whilst I'm frying to death, I get to ogle the mechanic working on it. He must be around 6ft 2, and he has that dark brooding look going on. He has a five-o clock shadow and a mess of black hair that keeps falling in his face when he leans forward. He looks like he belongs in one of those Diet Coke commercials they used to run on TV in the nineties, where women in offices went crazy over a hot guy in blue jeans. This one unfortunately isn't shirtless, though. He's wearing a white T-shirt, and I can see the tight contours of his body underneath it. Every time he reaches into the engine bay to tighten something, his sleeve rides up and I get a glimpse of a fish tattooed on the top of his tanned arm. The scales seem to move with his muscles as if it's swimming upwards. Watching it shift so fluidly has a calming effect on me. He hasn't said much. Though he did smile at me when he came out. I noticed that one of his front teeth is ever-so-slightly crooked. The tiny, inconsequential flaw is barely even noticeable, but it does serve to make this demi-god of a man seem somewhat human. He probably thinks I'm some dumb blonde who knows nothing about cars. I mean, it's true, I do know nothing about cars. I did lay on the ignorance a bit too thick when I came in, hoping they might feel sorry for me and give me a cheaper price. However, so far, I don't think it's working out in my favor. This guy has barely acknowledged my existence, apart from that initial smile. The other mechanic did—the one with his stomach poking out over his pants and the sweat patches under his arms. He seemed to appreciate my existence a little *too* much. I was glad when he had to take a call and Mr. Cool here took over. I only caught sight of his face briefly before he disappeared into the engine, but just that glimpse triggered a memory of a painting I saw once in the national gallery in

London. It was titled, "*The Lost Boy.*" The artist was unknown, but they had painted a boy with eyes so melancholy and dark, it was as if they had pulled them from a moonless sky.

Damn. Thinking about those commercials has made me thirsty; suddenly I'm desperate for a can of Coke. "Have you got a vending machine here?" No response from Mr. Doe Eyes. Is he just ignoring me, or can't he hear with his head under there? "Is there any chance of a can of Coke, or something cold to drink?"

He says something but I can't hear what. I move closer to him, "Sorry, I didn't quite catch that."

He pulls his head from under the hood. The memory of that painting flashes through my mind again. He pushes back his hair; and it immediately flops back into his eyes. His lashes are willow like, and he has a piercing in the perfect arch of his left eyebrow. I have the urge to bite it. He grabs a cloth from his pocket and wipes engine oil from his hands; there's something mesmerizing about the way he does it. For a moment, I lose myself in the fantasy of those fingers peeling down my bra strap.

What the fuck is wrong with me? He must be in his early twenties, so much younger than me. Here I am, a thirty-five-year-old woman, lusting after a freaking kid.

"I said we're a mechanics, not a Starbucks."

How bloody rude!

"Just anything cold would suffice. I'm sure that you have something here." I fold my arms and stare at him. I refuse to let him intimidate me, even if he's possibly the most gorgeous man on planet earth.

He doesn't say anything, just indicates that I follow him into the garage. I'm 5ft 9 in heels and feel short next to him. He puts his hands in his pockets and I notice how his blue jeans fit nicely on his ass. There's an ease to his walk, as if he's leading me down to a cool swimming spot on a lazy summer afternoon. Instead, he leads me to a rusty old fridge and opens it, pulling out two cans of coke. He hands one to me and I notice there are still traces of oil between his fingers; for some reason, the sight of it makes me squeeze my thighs together.

"Thank you." I press the can he just gave me to my forehead. I watch as he cracks his can and tips his head back. His Adam's apple moves up and down under his stubble as he swallows. There's something weirdly sexy about it—god*damn* those Diet Coke commercials. He wipes his mouth with the back of his hand as I open my can and gingerly sip, aware that he's watching me now. I suddenly feel self-conscious in a skirt that is probably too short for my first day at work and my white blouse that has now become a second skin. His eyes are fixed on me, but he's still not saying anything. I feel like I am in danger of losing myself in those liquid eyes of his. I turn to face my hopeless car.

"Do you think you can fix it?"

"Yep."

"Like, in half an hour?" I cringe-smile hopefully.

He tips his head back again and finishes the last of the can, before crushing it and throwing it into the bin.

"Nope." Perhaps he's Monosyllabic Man

"Well, how long do you think it'll take? I have to be at work soon. I was hoping it was just gonna be a quick job." I'm sure I sound like a demanding bitch, but I'm hot and tired and I have to teach my first class in less than an hour.

"Do you want it done right or do you want it done quickly?"

Wow, what a jerk.

"Is it too much to ask for both?"

He walks off ahead of me across the garage floor, and I scramble in my heels to keep up with him.

"Where are you going? Aren't you going to keep working on my car?"

"No, Ma'am, not right now. I've got somewhere else to be."

Ma'am, did he just call me Ma'am? Great, this shit storm of a day just keeps getting better and better.

"You can't just leave me here stranded, I've got to get to work, it's my first day!" I'm still following him, clip clopping behind him in my heels, like a demented pony. He goes into the office and grabs some car keys off a hook. When he turns around, I'm so close I bump into him, nearly spilling the rest of my coke on my shirt.

"Shit, you nearly got this all over me. This shirt is silk."

"Of course it is."

"What's that supposed to mean?"

He looks me and up down, "Nothing."

I put my hands on my hips, "Go on, tell me what you mean."

He shrugs his shoulders, "I dunno, you just seem a bit...uptight."

I sigh heavily. He's only just met me and has made his mind up who I am. It pisses me off.

"You don't know anything about me. For your information, I'm actually quite easy going. I'm..."

Why the fuck am I even explaining myself to him? He's just a dude fixing my car, an incredibly good looking one - but I haven't got time to think about that.

"All I need to know is that my car will be fixed, that it won't cost a fucking fortune, and the number of a cab company. I need to get to the community college on Ocean Drive. I'm teaching an English Lit class in less than half an hour and I cannot fuck up my first day." I brush away some straggly hairs that are sticking to my face. He raises an eyebrow—the pierced one. The metal bar catches the light, it glints at me like a tiny star.

"You're a teacher?"

"Professor of English Literature. It's my first day, not as a professor obviously. That was years ago. I mean it's my first day teaching at this college." I take another sip of my drink to stop myself from rambling. He doesn't say anything for a moment, then puts his hands back in his pockets.

"Well, I'm going that way, I can give you a ride."

I wasn't expecting that. I'm not sure I want to get in a car though with a man I want to simultaneously punch in the face and have pin me up against the filing cabinet.

"Your choice, I mean the seats aren't made of silk or anything." He grins at me as he says it.

Asshole.

"Non silk seats will do just fine, thank you."

"Great."

I stand there awkwardly for a second and feel like I need to fill the void with something.

"I'm Charlotte by the way."

"Ethan."

"Ethan, strong and wise."

"Excuse me?"

Shit! Did I say that out fucking loud?

"Ethan, in Hebrew, means strong and wise."

"Okay...good to know." He smirks at me, and I pray for the earth to swallow me whole.

"I'll just get my wheels and meet you out front." He heads out the back of the workshop, and I make my way to the front entrance. I'm nervous about getting in the car with him, I can't seem to behave like a normal human being in his presence.

He has a convertible Ford Mustang. It gives a throaty roar, like a panther, as it rolls up in front of me. He reaches over and opens the passenger door, aviators now shading his eyes. He flashes a smile at me and my stomach flips. I lower myself into the car, trying and failing to do so elegantly. I misjudge the height of the seat and land hard on my ass.

Classy Charlotte, real classy.

"That was impressive." He grins at me cheekily, before putting the car into gear. Of course, he drives stick. He can force the Mustang to make all the annoying, throaty noises he wants to that way. *I hate him.*

He pulls out onto the Pacific Coast Highway, and the wind messes with his hair, tousling it into a wild thing, as if even the elements want his attention. *My* hair threatens to strangle me, so I take the hair tie from my wrist and secure it into a ponytail.

The leather seats are hot. I repeatedly tug the hem of my skirt down as it appears to have a mind of its own and keeps riding up my thighs. Part of me enjoys flashing a little skin, hoping he notices my legs. He doesn't seem to, though. Even when he reaches across me to the glove box for a packet of cigarettes and his arm brushes against my knee, he doesn't react. I, on the other hand, can't ignore the reaction the contact elicits in me as a shiver races from the crown of my head to the soles of my feet. He doesn't look like an Ethan, more like Raphael, or Gabriel or a fallen angel. He *must* have been in God's good graces at some point—there is just no way beauty like this is created by accident.

"Do you want one?"

"Hmm?" He's offering me a cigarette and I'm so wrapped up in thinking about him, that I don't even notice.

"No, thanks. I've given up." *Such a lie.* It's more like pretending I don't smoke in public, then sneaking one or two in the evening on the balcony with my bottle of wine. But he doesn't need to know that.

He shrugs his shoulders and slides one for himself out of the pack with his teeth, before leaning forward and pulling out a lighter from his back pocket. I can't stop myself staring at his mouth. The sexy way his lips wrap around the end of the cigarette, and how he bares his teeth when he grabs it. Is that how he'd take off my panties? With his *teeth?*

Why the fuck am I even fantasizing about this? I don't even like him.

We stop at the traffic lights, and he cups his hand around the cigarette and lights it, blowing the smoke in the other direction. It still wafts over, and I sit on my hands to stop me reaching for the packet that he drops in the console.

"How long have you been a mechanic?" I shout over the noise of the traffic and engine, eating pieces of my hair as I do.

"Long enough." He doesn't take his eyes off the road. I take advantage of the moment to study his profile. I mean, why not? I'm just *looking.*

He has a roman nose—something I have always loved on a man. His jaw is razor sharp. There's a jagged scar on his chin, like a small lighting strike. It's just visible under his stubble. *"Every scar, every scratch, every mark tells a story."*—that's something I always tell my students. He catches me looking at him and knots his brow before turning his eyes back to the road. I keep sitting on my hands and face forward, determined he won't catch me watching him again like a crazy person. I lean back and inhale the salty air as we weave along the highway. The vibration of the car purrs underneath us and it feels good. He's clearly a good driver, which I suppose goes along with being a mechanic. I'm not sure that *my* car will last the rest of the summer. Mind you, if this heat continues, I'm not sure I will either.

We pull off the highway into a tree lined street and into the college parking lot. As soon as I see the school's sign, my stomach lurches. Out of nowhere, the reality of teaching at a community college in Los Angeles hits me. It's all very well romanticizing this from across the other side of the world, but here I am on my first day, sticky and nervous. Ethan pulls the car over to the side and lets the engine idle, before turning to look at me. It's as if he's searching for something. It's disconcerting as hell, having those intense eyes boring into me; perhaps he knows all the names I've been calling him in my head. I grab my bag from the footwell and reach for the door. "Thanks for the ride." I go to open it, but the handle won't move. "I think it's locked."

"No, it's just stiff." He leans over me, and I inhale his scent. It's earthy and pine-smelling, as if he'd been rolling around on the forest floor right before I showed up. The door swings open, and I get out, pulling the hem of my skirt down as I do.

"Shall I give you my number, so you can call me when my car's ready?" Unashamedly, I lean over *way* too far. *Boobs, Ethan. Check out my* boobs*, damnit. They're magnificent, I know they are.*

Nothing.

God, the guy is completely immoveable.

He puts the car into gear. "No need, just swing by the garage when you're done. Rob will have it ready for you."

Seriously? *Nothing?*

"Rob, right." The over-friendly guy with the protruding stomach. Great. "Okay. Well, thanks again, Ethan."

"You're welcome, Ma'am."

I freaking wish he'd stop calling me that.

As soon as I close the door, he drives off. "Bye!" I shout after him and wave. "Hope to see you again." He doesn't acknowledge me; he just turns the corner around the building and out of sight. I'm left standing in a pool of my own sweat.

Once I've found my way inside the college's main building, I'm directed to the classroom I'll be teaching out of, personally, by the Dean. He spends far too much time looking at my legs, and nowhere near enough time looking over my lesson plan. Wearing a short skirt was definitely a mistake today. I make a quick pit-stop to the restroom, whilst the Dean hovers about outside. A speedy retouch of my makeup is necessary - my foundation's melted half off my face in the sun. Did I mention it was hot? My hair is doing all sorts of strange things after that car journey; I look like I've stuck my finger into a power outlet. I twist it into a bun and pat it down with water. A quick blast of my shirt under the dryer also helps. Once I slide my glasses on, I actually look like a semirespectable professor. Hah! Take that, morning from hell!

When I exit the restroom, the Dean, *"Call me, Frank. Y'know, just between us,"* informs me that I have a full class. He leans in close to whisper this to me, and I can tell he had some sort of garlic sausage for lunch. There's also something green sticking out from two of his front teeth. Is it polite in America to point out these things? I don't know, so I just smile back at him. I note how different his scent is from Ethan's. Frank's is garlic, rubbing alcohol and that inescapable school smell which has clearly ingrained itself into his skin after thirty years working in the system. He gives me a quick run-down of his career as we walk to the classroom, even though I hadn't asked for it. Does the man ever draw a breath? He's overweight and unshaven, the guy looks like a freaking Yeti. My class is a mixture of ages, he tells me, walking so close to me down the corridor that his arm keeps nudging against mine. Students range from eighteen to sixty. Some are working towards their G.E.D, some for a new career, others because they just want something to fill their day. It'll make a pleasant change from just teaching young undergrad, though I haven't even done that in a while. Casting my mind back, I shudder at the person I became over those couple of years, when I left my university post.

Don't worry about that right now, Charlotte. That was then, and this is now. A fresh start. A way to return to yourself, after far too long. You deserve this.

"Well, here we are." We stop outside a classroom door painted orange. "Are you ready to meet your students?"

My stomach flips. I smooth down my skirt, "As ready as I'll ever be."

Frank opens the door and ushers me inside. "Everyone, this is Professor Charlotte Rose. She will be teaching your class this semester and if we can convince her to stay, the next one, too. We're very lucky to have her." It's like Frank's presenting a speaker at a conference; I half expect a round of applause from the students, but of course, they just shift in their seats, unimpressed.

"Thank you, Fra...Dean Fletcher, I'm honored to be here." I nod at him, giving him the signal that he can leave, but he shows no sign of vanishing, so I open the door for him. "I think we can take it from here."

"Right, yes, good luck!" Embarrassingly, he gives me a wink and a thumbs up. I resist the urge to roll my eyes up to the ceiling. God, I will have to get a handle on him.

I have a hard time taking in a room full of people at first; they all sort of merge into one. If I meet someone in a restaurant or bar, everything sort of swims in front of me. It's the only time I suffer from face blindness. Typically, I'll ask whoever I'm meeting to wait for me outside to save the embarrassment of not recognizing them in a crowd of people. Now, I must sit down, get my bearings, and then take my time getting to know my pupils individually—a scary prospect. I put my bag on the desk, then sit and smile at all my new students in the vain hope that it will put them at ease. Some smile back, others look bored, probably regretting signing up for English literature on a hot August afternoon.

"Well, I know we're all here for different reasons, but the one thing I hope we can share once this semester is over is a love of story, and of language, and how both these things shape our lives." A sea of faces just stares back at me. "Let's start by talking about some of the stories we've read that have stayed with us or affected our lives in significant ways."

I stand to go to the whiteboard and it's only then that I see *him*, sitting at the back of the classroom. His flop of midnight hair; the white t-shirt clinging to his taut body; the nonchalant look on his face as he leans back in his chair with a pencil dangling from his mouth. I was so discombobulated when I entered the classroom, that I didn't notice him. Trickles of sweat instantly run down my back. My chest tightens. Whoa! How the fuck can a man I just met—no, a *boy,* even—have this effect on me? I stand up and my legs buckle a little. How the hell am I supposed to teach a class with Ethan in it?!

Chapter Two

Charlotte

Class is over, Ethan is loitering and I'm pretending not to notice. Damn it, my hands are shaking.

He's a student, just like the others Charlotte. Get over yourself. Shit, he's coming over. I don't know what to say. I'm angry, I'm...'

"Professor Rose." He holds the word 'Rose' in his mouth until it comes out in full bloom.

"Ethan."

"Are you mad at me?"

"No." Now it's my turn to be monosyllabic.

"Doesn't sound like it."

I take off my glasses as if in a serious manner and sigh. "Ethan, I have no feelings towards you at all. I only met you an hour ago. Why you felt the need to hide the fact that you're my student, I can only assume." I put my glasses back on and continue to ignore him. I attempt to look official by making a tick on a piece of paper.

"Okay, all good then." He's being sarcastic. He *must* be. He starts to leave as I get up from my desk.

"Is that it, Ethan?" *Oh yeah, here I go, I can't contain myself apparently.* "You only failed to tell me you were going to be one of my students and you let me..."

"Let you what?" He looks genuinely confused; he obviously didn't pick up on the fact that I was flirting with him earlier. He probably feels completely asexual towards me. I mean I'm thirty-five years old; that's probably ancient for him.

I don't want him to know how badly he's gotten under my skin. I feel like I should just dismiss him coolly and walk away—that would be the smartest thing to do—but it seems that all common sense has fled me today.

"What were you hoping to accomplish by hiding the fact that you're my student? Did you think I wouldn't notice you the moment I walked into the classroom."

He shrugs. A small smirk plays over the corners of his mouth. "I've been told I have a very forgettable face."

"*Bullshit.*" The word leaps up my throat and out past my lips before I can even think about trapping it behind my teeth. With a sinking feeling tugging at my gut, I watch as that tiny little smirk of his develops into a full-blown, incredibly boyish grin.

"What, Teach? You think my face is *un*forgettable?"

I blush hotly. "I didn't say that."

I shuffle papers on my desk to bring back some sense of decorum. "My point is that it was childish." I purposely peer down my glasses at him. "But then I suppose you are barely an adult."

He winks. "I'm adult enough."

I'm not sure if we were still talking about the same thing.

"If you say so."

He looks at me for a minute, and I can't read what he's thinking. Then he throws his bag over his shoulder, his sleeve riding up again, the fish swimming up his arm, it's scales silvery and wet.

"Why do you have a tattoo of a Koi Fish?"

"Cause I like them." He rolls the sleeve of his shirt up to reveal the rest of the fish's head diving up over his shoulder blade. "In the Koi fish waterfall legend, the carp swims upstream over a waterfall and turns into a dragon."

Well, damn. Guess who's a smart ass, as well as an *asshole*.

"Then you should also have a tattoo of a dragon to complete the story."

He puts his bag down and takes hold of his T-shirt. He slowly pulls it up, revealing a tight stomach and the black tail of a dragon, flicking just above his belt. It can only be headed in one direction. The burning sensation in my cheeks intensifies to blistering proportions.

"I'd show you the rest of it, but you're my professor," he says slowly.

I feel my cheeks get hot. He's *teasing* me. We stare at each other for a moment, and I swear the room starts to spin. I feel like I'm going to faint. I take a giant step back, overcome with the impropriety of the whole interaction—on my first fucking day, at the end of my first fucking *class!* —and what does the arrogant son of a bitch do? He takes a giant step toward me, undoing the space I put between us. In fact, now he's even closer than he was before. Close enough for me to smell him again; earthy and addictive, and *real*. I can't stop breathing him in. I—

Holy shit, I'm leaning in and smelling him! What the hell is wrong with me?

"If you insist, I could be persuaded to show you the rest of..."

I need him to stop talking. I need him to *not* finish that sentence. I do the first thing I can think of, and I reach up and trail my fingertips along the scar he's sporting along the knife edge of his jaw. The skin there feels slick and smoother than it should.

"How did you get that?" He opens his mouth like he's about to say something, but then shakes his head.

"I can't remember."

There's a knock on the door. The sound snaps me out of the weird reverie that's pulled us in. I turn and quickly walk away from him.

"Charlotte? Ahem. I mean...Professor Rose?"

Oh, great, just what I need: *Frank*. A darkness flashes across Ethan's face when he sees him, like something nightmarish has just disturbed the surface of a lake.

"I trust everything is okay, Professor?" Frank looks at Ethan when he says this.

"Yes, everything's fine, thank you. I was just going over the homework for Ethan."

Frank hesitates. "Well, I wouldn't want to disturb you."

"You're not. Ethan was just leaving, *weren't you?*" I daren't look at him as I say it. I sound snappy; I didn't mean it to come out so abruptly, but I don't want Frank to think anything is going on. Not that anything *is* going on, or ever would have. I pick up my laptop from my desk and put it away. I'm hoping that Ethan gets the message.

He picks up his bag again and slings it over his shoulder. "*Fletcher.*"

"*Delaney.*" Frank puffs his chest out as he says it and watches Ethan leave the room.

"I hope he wasn't giving you any trouble?"

That's an odd thing to say. "No, why would he?"

Frank wrinkles his nose as if smelling something foul. "Nothing. He's just that type."

Something has obviously gone on between them, and Frank isn't about to tell me what.

"I'm just going to finish things up here and I'll be leaving, too." I turn to the whiteboard to wipe it, hoping he gets the message. I just want to get home, to open some wine and enjoy that cooling breeze off the ocean. I need to get all thoughts of Ethan out of my head. I don't know why I'd reacted like that, as if the floor was about to fall away. How embarrassing. I can feel Frank's eyes on me as I reach up to wipe the top of the board—no doubt he's enjoying the sight of my skirt riding up.

"Charlotte, I was just wondering if you...uhm, never mind."

"What is it, Frank?"

He runs his fingers through his thinning hair, then hitches up his belt to try and cover his belly that's spilling out over the top like pudding. I suppose he could have been handsome once, before thirty years in the school system got to him. He looks down and pats the back of his neck, swatting at something.

"Well, as you are new here, I was wondering if you'd like me to take you out this evening and show you the sights. Just as colleagues, of course, I'm a happily married man. Though my wife is away right now, not that that means anything. I'm not implying anything."

He's squirming. God, men like Frank are *so* predictable. I feel a bit sorry for him, he's obviously lonely. I guarantee that there's a bottle of bourbon tucked away in a locked drawer under his desk that his assistant pretends not to notice. I'm going to have to handle this delicately. I walk over and put my hand on his arm. He's wearing a tweed jacket with patches on the elbow that are fraying around the edge. I can see now that his eyes are bloodshot, and the collar of his shirt has a thin line of dirt around the rim. Yes, his wife is definitely away.

"That sounds lovely, Frank, but I really am quite tired after my first day. I could do with an early night. Why don't you ask me again next week?" I smile at him and squeeze his arm. I try to soften the blow, but I can tell he's offended.

"Okay, yes, next week then." He begins to back out of the class, eager to go now that he's been rejected, but he stops and turns around just as he gets to the door.

"It's important Charlotte, that we do establish a good working relationship if we're to look at extending your contract, going forward." There it is; the kind of thing I'd expected from a man like Frank. I give him my most dazzling smile yet.

"Of course, Frank. I'm looking forward to getting to know you better."

"Good, good, me too. Getting to know *you*, that is! I know me."

I indulge him with a giggle and stop the minute he's gone. Ugh, just what I need: two men at work that I now need to avoid, but for vastly different reasons. I finish wiping the board and collect my things. My feet hurt, I'm sticky with sweat and I have a headache brewing. I pull my hair loose from its bun and rub my fingers through it. Ethan comes to mind, unbidden. *He storms back into the room, and for a second, I think he's going to taunt me with another clever little barb, but he doesn't. He grabs me forcefully by the neck and simply engulfs me. His tongue in my mouth. His hands in my hair. His chest, a wall of hard packed muscle, pressed up against mine, my breasts smashed up against the heat of him. He lifts me on the desk and tears at my clothes like a wild animal. I am consumed by him. I reach down to his jeans and tug at his fly, my fingers scrambling in their desperation to...*

No, stop it Charlotte! It might have been fun to flirt with him earlier, but now you know he's your student you must put all those thoughts out of your head. Just get home and start fresh tomorrow.

Oh shit, how the hell am I going to get home?' Ethan was my ride here. Perhaps he waited for me? Not that I should be getting in his car again. I clearly can't be trusted not to embarrass myself when I'm alone with him. I practically swooned earlier like a character out of a Tennessee Williams play. I'll have to call a cab.

I keep my head down as I walk along the corridor and out to the parking lot. I feel like I'm one giant slick of sweat in this heat. What I wouldn't do for a crappy English summer's day right now. For a minute, I look around half hoping to see a black mustang or hear the rumble of an engine coming towards me. But no, Ethan hasn't waited. I mean, why would he? I need to get a grip on myself and act professionally around him. An affair with a hot younger guy is out of the question for many reasons, not least of all because he is my student.

Chapter Three

Ethan

"Fuck Frank Fletcher!" I slam my palm against the steering wheel and instantly regret it. I shake my hand out, using my knees to steer as I grab my cigarettes with my other hand. Should I have waited for her? I don't know what just happened, but I don't want to fuck up this class. I should've told Charlotte that I was a student, but I thought she'd see the funny side of it. I guess not. As usual, I've probably messed things up already, I just can't help myself. I pretended not to notice her shirt sticking to her, or her little skirt riding up in my car, those smooth thighs parting. If she wasn't my professor I'd go there, but I can't. It's lucky that Fletcher came when he did. He definitely would've filled her in on my past by now. I probably deserve it - though fat old Frank is certainly no angel. My plan when I signed up for class was just to avoid him. Now, I expect he'll be waiting for me to slip up. Even more reason to keep my head down and not entertain any inappropriate thoughts about my English Lit

Professor. I also have Gina to deal with, and that's one headache I can do without. I was hoping she'd be out when I got home, but I can see her car is in the driveway. When we broke up, I said she could stay until she got herself a new apartment. I had no idea she'd given up the lease on her place. I didn't think she'd still be here six weeks later. Mo, my sister-in-law, said it was a mistake letting her stay, and she was right.

I open the front door and gently put my keys down on the kitchen counter, hoping Gina won't hear me come in with the TV blaring. Sounds like she's watching some trashy show again. I just have time to open the fridge and grab a bottle of beer before she saunters through. I press it against my head; I have a vision of Charlotte doing the same thing today with her bottle of Coke, and I shit you not, my dick twitches in my pants just thinking about the sweat dripping down her skin. The first thing I noticed about her was her tits and the way her shirt clung to them. Those long legs in that tiny skirt did things to me. Her full lips smeared with gloss, look like they want to be bitten, *hard*. Her eyes are huge and green and there's an innocence in them that I want to ruin. I can just imagine my hands through that soft blonde hair of hers and...

"How was your first day at school, Babycakes?" Here's Gina, right on time to interrupt my dirty thoughts about my teacher. She's wearing a bikini; every day she wears less and less around me. As much as I don't want to go down that road again, she isn't making it easy for me. The consequences, though? Holy shit, they would *not* be worth it.

"Going swimming?" I take a swig of my beer; it feels nice and cold in my throat.

Gina puts her hand on her hip. "No, I'm just hot and you didn't answer my question."

"That's because it's not school, it's college and I don't answer to *Babycakes*."

She pulls herself up onto the countertop. "Okay, college then. How was it? I hear your new professor is pretty hot."

I jerk back, shooting her a sharp look. *The fuck is wrong with this girl?* "Who told you that?"

"I have my spies."

Of course, she does. "Well, your spies are wrong. She's not that hot."

"Liar."

She's right, I am a liar, but Gina's the last person in the world I would tell I want to fuck my professor. I down the rest of the beer. "I'm going to take a shower."

"Save me some hot water!"

"Yep, will do."

"Unless you want to share?" she shouts at me up the stairs. I act as if I haven't heard her and slam the bathroom door.

It feels good to finally be in the shower, soaping the city and the garage off my body. I need to wash Charlotte off it, too. I would never have pegged her as a professor when she showed up at the garage. I should just get her out of my head, but my thoughts keep going back to her leaning over the desk, slowly sliding her glasses up the bridge of her nose. Her accent made the words seem as if they were written specifically for her to read out loud. Now I find myself plagued by mental images of all the other things I'd love her to do with that talented mouth of hers. My dick hardens at the thought of it. God, maybe she'd tease me with filthy words in between licking and sucking me. I move my hand to my shaft and begin to stroke myself. If I had her in the shower right now, I'd take the soap to her tits and circle her nipples with it, then take it down her body. I'd have her bent over; hands planted against the wall. I'd spread her legs, then bring the soap between them. I'd have her move on it, to slide back and forth whilst I pressed myself against her. I begin to stroke myself faster.

"Are you sure you don't want company?"

Its Gina, on the other side of the door. *What the fuck is she doing*? Can the woman not take a hint? Even as I think this, I know it's a stupid question. She categorically, absolutely can*not*; if she could, she'd have moved out when we fucking broke up. I remove my hand from my dick, all thoughts of Professor Charlotte Rose's tight little cunt vanishing from my mind. "I'm fucking sure, Gina!" I turn my face to the shower and run the water cold, opening my mouth, let it run onto my tongue, praying the ice-cold downpour will stop me from saying something I might regret. The frigid temperatures help ease my raging boner. Once I feel like I can touch myself again without wanting to fuck my own hand, I grab the soap and wash the fantasy off my body.

Gina is sitting on the kitchen counter when I go downstairs. I grab another bottle of beer out of the fridge.

"You were made perfectly to be loved and surely I have loved you, in the idea of you, my whole life long." She's reading from one of my textbooks from class.

"So romantic."

"That's not yours to read." I snatch it out of her hands and put it down next to her. Fuck, she's annoying.

"Geez, I was just looking at what Miss Hottie Professor was teaching you."

"Don't call her that. It's disrespectful, and can you get off the worktop? We have to eat off that."

Instead of getting down, she wraps her legs around me. "Gina, don't."

"Why not? I'm single, you're single," she whispers into my ear, "We both know what each other likes."

"I'm pretty sure you have no idea what I like." I pull her forward and down onto her feet.

"You haven't changed, have you? Still the same selfish Ethan Delaney—" Venom drips from each word.

"What the *hell* are you talking about?"

"—Only ever thinks about himself…"

"If that's how you feel about me, Gina, then why are you still here?"

"Because we both know, Babycakes, that what you want...what you *need*, is here, right in front of you."

"You mean my beer?" I go to take a sip, but she snatches it from me and takes a big gulp. She hands it back to me, nearly empty. *Bitch*.

"Oh, by the way your brother called when you were in the shower. I answered your phone for you. He said to tell you that you've got to pick up that English client in the morning, because her car still isn't ready. I wrote her name and address down for you."

God-fucking-*damn*it, I swear this woman was sent to Earth solely to test my patience. "How many times have I told you not to answer my phone?"

She shrugs her shoulders, attitude pouring off her as she swings her hips, sauntering back into the living room, presumably to rot her brain with more reality TV. I'm going to have to tell her to move out, but not tonight. I'll probably wind up murdering the woman, and we can't have that now, can we? Not when I have to pick up my English professor in the morning.

Chapter Four

Ethan

"Hi."

"Oh, I thought the other one was picking me up."

"The other one?"

"Yeah, the big guy,"

"You mean my *brother*?"

"Your *brother*? Sorry "

"He's been called much worse, believe me." I grin at Charlotte, trying to put her at ease. Clearly, she wasn't expecting me at her door at 8 am. I'm not particularly thrilled to be here either. Rob should've picked her up, but he knew after a late night of poker that he'd never make it. That's why he left a message for me last night. I'd just wanted to get to college, slip into my desk at the back and keep my head down. I can't afford to be distracted by anything, least of all by my *hot as fuck* English teacher.

"You're early. I'm not quite ready."

Her hair's still wet from the shower and its dripping on her silk shirt leaving big wet patches. It's turned parts of her shirt translucent, and I can make out the cup of her bra; it's lacey. I wonder if she's wearing matching panties. Perhaps they're a little white thong I can slip my hand down and...*Shit, Ethan. Get it the fuck together.* At least she's wearing linen pants today and not that fuckable little skirt. I'm not sure my dick would have coped with that *two* days in a row.

"Yeah, I wanted to beat the traffic. I can wait outside if you like." I fix my eyes on hers, ignoring the pull in my cock that's telling me to look at her tits again in that wet shirt. She's biting her lip and glancing at the patio behind me, deciding whether to let me in. I mean, I don't blame her; I wouldn't let me in.

"Uhm, are you sure? It's hideously hot out already, you'll melt."

She puts her hands on her hips and tilts her head to the side. Her lips are slightly apart, and I can see her tongue pressing against them. She wants me to tell her that it's okay, but I'm not going to make it easy for her. I say nothing and just smile at her. I can see in this direct sunlight just how green her eyes are. Her right eye is darker; like it is keeping a secret from the left. She taps her foot and still I say nothing. She's biting her lip again now. *Fuck, I want to do that, I want to bite her lip until it bleeds.* I can tell that she wants to be polite and let me in, but she's also uncomfortable that she's still not ready.

"Oh, just come in, I'll only be a couple of minutes."

I keep smiling and step inside, my arm brushes against hers as I go in and she catches my eye before quickly looking away.

"Cute place."

"Thanks, I'm just subletting it though. So, I can't take credit for how nice it is." She takes a towel from the kitchen chair and rubs her hair with it. I'm not sure what to do with my hands, I keep thinking about them sliding down her panties. I guess it wouldn't be polite to light up a cigarette in here, so I just put them in my pockets. There's a red bra slung over one of the chairs and seeing me notice it, she picks it up and tries to hide it behind her back.

"Sorry, that's embarrassing. I was deciding what to wear this morning and the outfit that goes with this bra didn't make it."

"Not its lucky day I guess." I grin at her and now she's blushing and backing out of the room with the bra still behind her back. She trips over her own feet and stumbles, and for a minute, I think she's going to fall. She does seem to get self-conscious easily. It's almost too easy to tease her, but I should stop. My plan had just been to pick her up, not to flirt with her.

"I won't be a minute!"

"No problem" I shout back, though if she's anything like the other women in my life, then getting ready will take longer than a minute. I pull out a kitchen chair and take a seat.

"Would you like tea or anything? I think you Americans mostly drink coffee though, don't you?"

"I'm good thanks and yes, I've had my coffee. Wouldn't be out of bed without it."

She appears in the doorway again, no more ready than she was a minute ago, rubbing her head with the towel again.

"Really? You're one of those who needs caffeine to function in the mornings?"

"Doesn't everyone?"

"Not me, caffeine makes me too wired, like one of those old-fashioned wind-up toys. I suppose you're too young to remember those. I doubt you even know what a CD is."

"A what?"

"Exactly."

"I was just kidding."

"Oh."

"I think I'll just wait outside."

"Alright."

She looks a little offended, but I've gotta get out of here. I feel like I'm overheating, despite the air conditioning. I go out onto the balcony and look out over the beach below. For a moment I take it in as any other person would, then I look at the ocean and that feeling of dread comes over me, a blackness creeps into my veins. I turn my back to it and get out a cigarette. I light it, using my hand to guard against any breeze. I see the cup on the table has ash in it, so she does smoke. Interesting that she said otherwise. I lean back on the wall and imagine her sunbathing out here in a tiny bikini.

"Ready!"

She jolts me out of my little fantasy. She's changed her shirt. She must've seen the wet patches in the mirror. This one has shorter sleeves and is tighter, her tits look fucking magnificent in it. I go to the table and stub out my cigarette in the cup.

"I found out your little secret."

"What?"

"The ash in the cup."

"Oh right." She suddenly looks pale.

"Are you feeling, okay?"

"Never been better. Shall we go?"

She doesn't wait for an answer and heads down the stairs. I'm not sure what all that was about, but I'm not the only one who's been spooked this morning.

Chapter Five

Charlotte

Class has finished and I'm waiting for Ethan on the college steps. I hadn't expected him to be standing at my door this morning. I thought the other one was going to pick me up. I never imagined that it was his *brother*. How could they possibly come from the same gene pool? One is a toad and the other one is a *God*. Perhaps the big guy has a winning personality. Though from what I've seen, I doubt it. Ethan looked a little rougher round the edges this morning, as if he hadn't got enough sleep. His stubble was a little thicker and his hair was swept back by the sea wind. He had that same amused light in his eyes that he had yesterday though, as if he's having fun at my expense. It's obvious that I make him uncomfortable, he couldn't wait to get out of my apartment fast enough. He's flirty with me too, which only confuses things. He made that comment about my bra, just like he made that one yesterday about showing me his dragon tattoo. Oh God, why did I go on about his fish tattoo yesterday.

Sometimes my mouth opens before my brain engages. It's not the best trait for someone who spends most of her career talking in front of people. I'm fine when I have something specific to talk about. It's when it seems like a great abyss has opened in a conversation, that my mouth begins to run away with itself to fill in the gap. *"You have no filter."* my mum liked to tell me *"It's terribly uncouth, you get that from your father."* God, forbid I get any traits from my dad, the man my mother thought was beneath her their entire married life.

I didn't even attempt to make small talk in the car on the way to work and Ethan seemed to have no interest in talking to me. The roof of his car was up this morning, and the engine noise was louder and so it just seemed easier to stay quiet. When we got to the college, he dropped me off like yesterday and went to park, then slipped into the back of class a few minutes late.

I wish I'd arranged for someone else to take me home or booked a taxi. Class finished fifteen minutes ago and still no sign of Ethan's car. At least I only had one class this morning and it's Friday today. It was a nice two-day week to ease everyone back into the fall semester. Next week will be full on with a couple of classes every day, and then there will be assignments to set and mark. I plan to spend the weekend devising them. I'm looking forward to the peace that comes with all that reading and researching. I can lose myself in it and shut the world out for two days. I can forget about what I've left behind in England and have time to empty all the dirty Ethan thoughts out of my head.

"Charlotte!" I turn to see Frank coming down the steps towards me. Great, I thought I'd managed to avoid him today. I can see as he comes closer that one of his shirt buttons has popped open on his belly, revealing a mountain of flesh underneath.

"Frank." I turn and beam at him as he grabs me by the arms and kisses me on both cheeks.

"That's how they do it in Europe isn't it?" I'm cringing inside.

"Sometimes." I hope he can't hear the sound of my skin peeling itself off.

"What are you doing out here? Were you hoping to see me, eh?" He nudges me and I really want to tell him to fuck off, but I can't. For many reasons, I need this job. It could be my ticket out of my life in the UK. So, I laugh and tuck my hair behind my ears, as it threatens to stick to my face in the heat like everything else does to me.

"Always hoping to see you Frank, but actually my car is in the garage, and I'm waiting for my ride." Something tells me that he won't be happy when he sees who is picking me up, and I'm not wrong. As soon as Ethan's car pulls up, his face changes.

"This is your ride, is it?"

I'm going to have to be careful with this one. Ethan hasn't acknowledged either of us. He's just waiting in the driver's seat, one hand on the wheel, the other draped over the passenger's seat, looking bored and effortlessly sexy.

"Yes, well you see my car is in the garage and Ethan, as you know, or perhaps you don't..." --Shit. I'm rambling. I only ramble when I'm seriously uncomfortable. "...is a mechanic. The other mechanic was supposed to pick me up, but he couldn't and as Ethan was here anyway...so yes, this is my ride."

I gesture to the car as if I'm a host on 'The Price Is Right,' and this is the grand prize. Ethan's looking at me with a fiendish grin on his face. *He seriously thinks this is funny?* I think the best thing to do is cut my losses and just get in the car. "Anyway Frank, let's go for that drink next week." I say it as I lower myself into Ethan's stupidly low and tiny vehicle. I swing my legs round and shut the door on my bag. "I've had such a lovely first couple of days here, you've made me feel so welcome." I open the door and retrieve my bag. I can hear Ethan laughing to himself beside me. "Goodbye Frank." I wave elaborately like I'm the Queen or something, expecting Ethan to drive off, but he doesn't. He just sits there; *the little fucker is enjoying this.* "I hope you have a lovely weekend!" I shout to Frank over the engine.

'Can we go now please?" I mutter to Ethan between gritted teeth.

"Are you sure you're done with all your goodbyes? Do you want me to circle round so you can do an encore?"

"Just fucking drive!" I fling back in my seat as he revs the engine. We fly out of the parking lot and Frank just becomes a blob in the distance. Shit, now I'm going to have to make up for all of that mess next week and go out with him for a drink. I still can't *believe* that, in this day and age, I still have to deal with men like him. I had enough of that back in England.

I turn to look at Ethan. "Enjoy that, did you?"

"Immensely."

"Well good, I hope you realize that I'm going to have to get back into his good books. He's already asked me out."

"It didn't take Fletcher long to get back to his old tricks."

"What do you mean?" He has the same dark look on his face that he did when Frank walked in the room yesterday.

"Nothing, just that he's a prick."

"What happened between the two of you?"

He shrugs his shoulders, "We have some history."

"Clearly."

He puts his foot on the peddle, harder than he needs to, and we spin round the corner. Just the mention of Frank has obviously got to him again.

"Can you slow down now please! It's making me nauseous. You're driving too wobbly."

"Driving too wobbly?" He laughs. "I think that's the most British thing I've ever heard. Apart from your name."

"What's wrong with my name?"

"Charlotte Rose, it's like someone plucked you out of a romance novel."

"No one plucked me out of anything, thank you!"

He looks across at me and I can tell he is enjoying teasing me.

Asshole.

"Anyway, isn't that an inappropriate thing to say to your English Professor?

"I think we passed that point yesterday when you asked to see my tattoo."

I can't even think about that dragon and where it leads. "I didn't ask, you volunteered."

"If you say so."

We stop at a red light, and I feel like my cheeks are the same color. He frowns, working his grip on the steering wheel as we wait at the light.

"Would you–" He stops himself short.

"Would I what?"

"Never mind."

'You don't strike me as the type to not say what's on your mind."

I'm taunting him. Like some fucking kid in a playground, I'm taunting him. What the hell has gotten into me?

Ethan shoots me a sidelong glance. "All right. Fine. Fuck it. You wanna get some lunch?"

"What?" *Did he just ask me out?*

"Lunch. With. Me?" He punctuates it as if he's talking to a child.

"Why?"

"You do eat, don't you?"

"You want to have lunch with your English teacher?"

"Not if you put it like that."

"Are you doing this for extra credits in class?"

"What?"

"Do you think that by being nice to me, I'm gonna give you a good grade in class?"

"What the fuck, Charlotte?" The car swerves suddenly to the right, and I grip onto the seat. He straightens the wheel and shifts the car into a lower gear. He puts his foot down hard on the accelerator and starts to weave in and out of traffic.

I've pissed him off, but seriously does he have to drive like a fucking maniac?

"Can you slow the fuck down, please?"

He ignores me and pulls in front of another car again. "I ask you a serious question, and you respond by driving like a *total twat?*" I shout the last part at him, hoping he hears me over the rev of the engine and the wind coming off the ocean. My hair is in my mouth, and I must hold it back with my hands. We drive in silence for the next ten minutes. I give up with my hair and let it just whip me in the face. My hands go back to being sweaty in my lap.

We pull up to the parking spot under my apartment. He doesn't turn the engine off, but instead just keeps one arm outstretched, with his hand on the wheel. He doesn't look at me. I get it, like all men, *he hates rejection.* It's not that I don't want to go to lunch with him, get to know him better. I'm afraid of where that might lead though.

"Well thanks for the lift, and for the offer of lunch."

He doesn't reply.

"Will you just *say something* Ethan? I've obviously offended you, but surely, you understand the position I'm in."

"It's just lunch Charlotte, I'm not asking for your firstborn." He turns to look at me, but his eyes are hidden by his mirrored sunglasses. They are *sexy as fuck*.

"I'm not sure you should be calling me Charlotte."

Yep, there I go, couldn't just respond nicely. It's like I'm genetically programmed to be a total bitch. I'm more like my mother than I'd like to admit.

"That's your name isn't it."

"Yes, but usually my students call me professor or Miss Rose."

"You want me to call you *Miss Rose*?" He laughs as he says it, it does sound ridiculous when it comes out of his mouth. I picture myself swanning around in a mansion, and he's my butler about to serve me tiny cucumber sandwiches on a silver platter. He shifts the gears into reverse and stares at me. Clearly that means *get the fuck out of my car*.

I pull hard at the door handle. I'm anxious to avoid having to ask him to do it for me. The door springs open, and I nearly fall out with it. *Why must I be such a damn klutz?* I recover myself and proceed to act as much like a normal person as I can muster.

"Oh and, Professor?"

"Yes?"

"I asked you out to lunch because I felt sorry for you. I thought you'd be lonely in a new country. I was just trying to do you a favor. I won't make that mistake again."

A lump forms in my throat. It stings that he said that, but I guess I deserve it. He rests his arm on the back of the passenger seat and turns his head. He reverses out into the street. I stand there, until the throaty roar of his car fades into the noise of the other traffic. I head for the mailbox under the stairs. My friend Lauren said she sent me a postcard from her trip down to Cornwall. Being so far away from home means that even small things like that feel comforting. The door to the ground floor flat opens and an old woman peers round it. Well, I'm not sure exactly how old she is; it looks like she's been festering inside for some time. She only ever opens the door to glare at me. I don't think I've ever seen her blink. Her eyes must be as dry as the desert. She treats me like a specimen to study. I've only ever seen her leave her apartment at nighttime. My bedroom window looks down onto her little garden. She's always out there after dark, watering her plants. It's full of nick knacks; plastic sunflowers with nodding heads, three fairies including one without an arm. Gnomes of varying sizes and a small, glazed horse and carriage with one of its wheels hanging off. She touches each one like they're pieces of treasure.

"Hello Mrs. Lebowski." She ignores me, as usual, then closes the door shaking her head. I'm not sure exactly what I've done to deserve such disdain. My mere existence seems to set her off. There's no postcard in the mailbox. There are some bills for the woman I'm subletting off and a free newspaper. I turn the little key in its lock and make my way up the stairs. A nice ocean breeze blows across the top of the stairs, and I pause for a moment to enjoy it. I love the smell of the sea and I take a big breath in to calm myself. The ride home with Ethan rattled me. A piece of mail slips out from between the free newspaper and bills. As I bend to the floor to retrieve it, my heart skips a beat. There's a British postmark, and it's addressed to me. I recognize the handwriting immediately. I grab onto the handrail to steady myself. No matter what escape story I've convinced myself of, reality just caught up with me.

Chapter Six

Ethan

"You're late."

The last thing I need right now is my brother in a bad mood. "Class finished late, and I had to take the client home; like you asked."

"I told you to pick her up, not drop her home as well. We're not a fucking taxi service." I ignore him and go and hang my car keys on their hook in the office. He follows me inside.

I wish he'd just fuck off.

"I didn't tell you to drop her home as well."

"Yeah, you just said that. We were at the same place, so it was cool." I just want to get on with work. I pull a clipboard off the wall and look through what needs to be done. The first job could be messy. I need to change into a pair of coveralls; but my annoying fuck of a brother isn't done badgering me yet. He sits down on the desk.

"How come she's at college? Bit mature to be a student, isn't she? Though, I wouldn't mind sitting next to that tight piece of ass in class." He licks his lips as he says it, and then stands for a second to hitch up the belt on his pants. They can't contain his stomach.

"She's my English professor."

"Lucky you. Did you work the Delaney magic? I mean I wouldn't blame you if you did. She's hot as fuck, and that accent...Damn, imagine that mouth talkin dirty and then sliding up and down your cock."

God, he's gross. Not that the thought hasn't crossed my mind. She's all I can think about. Even this afternoon when we were in the car, and she was being a *Grade A bitch*, I wanted her to lean over and unzip my pants. Doesn't mean I wanna hear that shit from my brother, though.

"Did you forget that you're married bro?"

"Oh, gimme a fuckin break, a man can dream, can't he?"

"That's all you can do."

I grab a pair of coveralls out of the cupboard and start pulling them up over my clothes.

"You're like my wife's little cheerleader, aren't you?"

"No if I was, I'd tell her she deserves better than you." I bring the coverall up over my shoulders and shake my legs; it shifts down my body. He squares up to me.

"You mean, deserves someone like you?"

"Don't be disgusting. Mo's like a big sister to me and you know that." I shove past him out of the office.

"Don't forget who pays your wages."

"Your wife pays my wages; you'd have blown them all on poker by now if she didn't."

"Yeah, but it's my name over that door; I can fire you whenever I like."

"Fire your best mechanic? I don't think you're gonna do that."

I finish doing up the buttons and look out onto the garage floor. This isn't one of those white lab coats, ultra clean car service spaces. This place is cold, dank, and dirty no matter the weather outside. The smell of brake dust and motor oil lingers on me long after I leave. Gina used to hate that. I was just a teenager when Rob took over this business. I'd come here after school, and he'd give me simple jobs to do at first. It was just assumed that I would become a mechanic as time went on. There weren't any other options for me as far as everyone else was concerned, and it kept me out of trouble. This place is in my bones now. It's in Rob's too. I guess that's why we keep working together, despite our mutual dislike of each other. It wasn't always like that. I looked up to Rob when I was a kid. He was like a dad to me when ours wasn't.

"I thought you were taking math, not English?" He's trailing behind me. He must've lost at poker last night and wants someone to take it out on. I'd rather it was me than Mo though.

"I'm taking math as well. Some of us can hold more than one subject in our heads."

His face goes red. I hit a nerve with that one. I'm at the car I need to work on now. I want to get it done so that I can spend time on the old truck I bought. It's sitting in the corner - getting rustier by the minute. Its blue paint half peeling off, the leather seats on the inside ripped. It pains me every time I look at it.

"Gina still living at yours?"

"Yep."

"Fucked her lately?"

"Jesus Rob, it's like you've got Tourette's." I open the hood to a Subaru and roll up my sleeves. "You ever thought about going into therapy for your issues with women?" I prop the hood open, grab a rag from the bucket and begin to wipe some of the grease off. Now I can see what I'm doing.

"You're the one that needs therapy for his *mommy issues*."

"What?"

"I'm not the one who lost his fucking mind when mom died."

Now it's my turn to go red, why is he bringing this up now? I figure the best thing is for me to just keep working and hope he runs out of steam. I'm wrong; seems like he's just getting started.

"I'm surprised your fuckable little English teacher hasn't jumped all over you yet. Another woman who wants to save you from yourself."

"Jealous?" I pull out the dipstick and check the oil. It's bone dry. I need to find where the leak is coming from. I'm going to need more light here.

"Shine the flashlight on your phone in here will you." For a moment I don't think he's gonna do it; but he pulls it out of his pocket and comes over. The only thing we can do together without arguing is fix cars. He shines it wherever I move my hand.

"By the way I was with you last night if Mo asks."

"Were you? I wondered who ate the last of the Chinese take-out."

"Just shut the fuck up and tell her that will you."

"I don't know how she puts up with you." I pull myself out from the engine. "You can take your phone back now."

"You need to get underneath?"

"Yep, I need to get it up on the lift."

"You know sometimes little brother I think you should have been the one who married Mo, seeing as you love each other so much."

This again? I need to wipe my hands. I shove the dirty rag in my coverall pocket and walk past Rob to the other side of the garage. I pull a handful of paper towels from the dispenser and try to rub some of the grease off. There's a ray of sun coming through the skylight. The glass is covered in creeping ivy; but a shaft of light always gets through. It's the only spot in this whole place we can see the sun. Charlotte stood directly in that spot yesterday. She lit up like a fucking Angel. I head back towards Rob, shaking my head in an attempt to remove all thoughts of her.

"Mo was like a mom to me when we lost ours. You know that."

"Oh yes, poor little orphan Ethan."

"She was your mom too." I look directly at him trying to find any bit of emotion in him. His eyes are smaller than mine and are increasingly sunken back in his head the heavier he gets. It's hard to read anything on him.

"Yeah, she was, but she's gone. I'm reminded of that every time I fucking look at you."

My hand is twitching to punch him. Instead, I head back past him to the Subaru.

"I don't know how you sleep at night. Oh, wait you don't. Had any nightmares recently?

Motherfucker. I slam the hood shut, start undoing my coveralls and head back to the office. The Subaru can wait. I just want to get the fuck out of here. Rob isn't done though. His hand is on my shoulder pulling me back, and for a second, I'm unsteady on my feet.

"Get the fuck off me." I manage to push him off and he stumbles back. He's heavier than me; but I'm younger and fitter than him and we've done this dance plenty of times before.

"You done?" I know he isn't, but I'll give him the benefit of the doubt just to get this over with. He comes at me then, his right arm swinging. I block it with my left and land one on his jaw with my other fist. There's a crack and his head spins and he loses his footing. He lands on one of the cars. I stand in one spot, catching my breath. Slowly he gets himself up, clutching his face. I go into the office and finish taking off my coveralls, taking the oily rag out of my pocket. I grab my keys and go back into the garage. I throw the rag at him, pointing to some specks of blood on the floor. "You might want to clean that up."

I know he's going to get me back for that, but right now I don't give a fuck. I turn and push open the door; glad to get some air in my lungs. I take a few deep breaths and get into my car. The evening is warm, but I can't feel the sun on me. I'm too full of the dark.

Chapter Seven

Charlotte

I set the wine and a glass on the patio table and sit back in my chair enjoying the sunset. It's all pinks and oranges and wispy clouds. I've been keeping myself busy with lesson planning since I got home this afternoon — anything to avoid opening that letter. I was lucky to find this place to stay in. A gorgeous apartment at this price overlooking the beach is unheard of here apparently. I'd posted on the "Brits in LA housing" page on Facebook that I was looking for accommodation and surprisingly managed to find this sublet. A woman called Lorraine had just got herself a three-month contract working in Rio de Janeiro. She needed someone at the last minute to rent her place whilst she was gone. She's an interior designer, and by the looks of her apartment she clearly has good taste. Big windows, soft furnishings, and well-chosen pieces of art. I'm sure she'll love Rio. I did when I went. Although, it was about fourteen years ago now. It was just after university with my friend Lauren. We went on a volunteer vacation and taught English for three months in a school in exchange for hostel accommodation. I've never been to a city quite like Rio; it's so full of contradictions. The whole place seemed to scream, look at me! Everywhere was alive with color and passion. We spent our Saturday afternoons exploring. New local friends showed us secret coves and the route to climb up the spine of Sugarloaf Mountain - bypassing the tourists and the cable car. Sundays were spent at the beach recovering from Saturday nights in Lapa. That was where everyone our age congregated at the weekend. It's a neighborhood of bars and nightclubs built around an aqueduct, 'Arco's de Lapa's', its tall columns standing like something out of ancient Rome. In the daytime we'd see favela kids waving and hanging off the tram that ran on the line above it. At night, the white arches were to party under. We used to go to this little nightclub made from corrugated iron and dance to the beat of tight skinned drums played by men with skin I wanted to lick. Lauren and I would walk back to our hostel at dawn, and I would climb into bed with Pablo. He was a Brazilian guy who worked and slept at the hostel. He was six years older than me and squeezed me like the watermelon they served for breakfast on the roof terrace. He taught me my favorite Portuguese word, *"Cafune."* It describes the act of running your fingers through someone's hair in a tender way. There's no equivalent of it in English; a word to describe a calming and affectionate gesture that you do to someone you love. He used to whisper it to me when we had sex, as he tangled my hair between his fingers and pulled me closer to him.

Fuck, that was hot.

I wanted to stay there with him. I even wrote to my mother to tell her I was thinking of putting off my masters and staying in Rio for another year. She wrote back, *"Over my dead body."* So, I went home and wrote to Pablo from rainy England. I sat in my bedroom looking out at the gloomy landscape. My English to Portuguese dictionary, hidden from my mother, tucked between Mary Shelley and Chaucer. We sent letters in each other's broken language for six months. Then one day he wrote to tell me that he'd met another English girl, *"He liked better."* I hoped it was the bad translation that made it seem particularly harsh.

I looked up the hostel online about six months ago. The pictures on the website showed it hadn't changed much. It looked a little more worn; like we all did. I clicked on the staff page and there was his photo. Underneath it read, *'Pablo Rivero,'* with the tagline, *"Happy to meet all your needs."* He was the manager now. That wasn't the life he'd dreamed of. The Pablo I knew wanted to become an archeologist and travel the world. I ran my fingers over his picture; trying to recognize the man I once loved. There were traces of the old Pablo, but his light seemed to have burned out. His face was puffy, and his olive skin had sagged a little under his chin; like he was keeping a small sack of something there. How different my life would've been if I'd stayed in Brazil and Pablo hadn't met *"Another English girl that he liked better."* Perhaps we'd have run the hostel together, or I would be a stay-at-home mum, looking after heaps of children.

Hmm. Would I have enjoyed that life? I already know my response to that question, and that answer is a resounding hell no! Nope. Absolutely no freaking way. I wasn't cut out for that then, and I'm sure as hell not cut out for it now.

I dreamed of running my own school in Rio for the kids from the Favela's. Either way, my life doesn't look like anything like I thought it would now. That's the biggest lie in life; that if you follow all the rules, it all turns out fine. The unopened letter staring up at me from the table is the biggest reminder of that. I can't bring myself to open it yet. I recognize the tight, neat writing on the front, with just a small flourish on the e of Charlotte that only I would notice. For a minute, I imagine I'm twenty-one again and it's Pablo who's written to me and the letter will be filled with incantations of desire in Portuguese and bad English. Then I'll cut out a love poem by my favorite sixteen century Sufi poet and stick it in an envelope and send it back.

I hope Lorraine is currently being squeezed like a watermelon, because then at least one of us is.

I light one of my secret cigarettes that I keep in my kimono pocket. It's the most expensive item of clothing I've ever bought. When I knew I was coming here, I wanted to bring something beautiful with me. I saw it in a lingerie store just off Sloane Square in London. I'd spent the previous two years shuffling around at home in cardigans and sweatpants. I'd given up my job at the university - yet another mistake in a whole litany of them. So, for my new life in LA, I wanted something luxurious. It feels as if it's made from juicy silkworms feasting on mulberries under a full moon. I took it home and kept it wrapped in its tissue paper in a box at the back of the wardrobe. Buying something like that would have aroused suspicion, so it was better to hide it.

Somewhere my life has taken a very wrong turn. Nobody should know where I am except Lauren; but now someone else knows. The one God damned person I'm running away from, and my sanctuary is pierced. I inhale and blow the smoke out in rings. It's a trick I learned as a teenager when I used to pick up the discarded cigarettes from my mother's ashtray. I used to sit in the mirror and practice forming my lips into an "O" like she did, thinking it made me look sophisticated. I uncork the wine that I bought at the liquor store across the street. I went straight there after seeing the letter and nearly stumbled down the stairs in the process. I still had the letter in my hand when I picked the bottle off the shelf. I wanted to take the wine and leave the letter in its place. My kimono falls open and I let it. The early evening breeze is welcome and feels good on my skin. No one can see me from here, unless I stand up and only then the odd runner on the beach might occasionally look up.

I pour myself a glass of wine and take a sip; savoring this moment of being free before I open that letter and reality comes crashing in again. There's a small part of me that feels wistful for the person behind the handwriting. When we met, I loved the preciseness of it. I thought that someone who was so meticulous could tame me. He could give me the kind of life I was repeatedly told that I needed if I wanted to be happy and successful.

What a fucking joke that turned out to be.

I didn't realize at the time that I was sacrificing a huge part of myself. I thought that part of me was dead. I couldn't relate to the Charlotte that traveled to Rio by herself, who threw caution to the wind and had a crazy love affair. There's something about Ethan that ignites that part of me, just because nothing can happen doesn't mean that I'm suddenly immune to the insane attraction I feel towards him. However, I'm not twenty-one anymore and can't just throw caution to the wind whenever I feel like it.

I take another sip of wine before I open the letter. This is going to need more alcohol to read. I open it slowly. I want to put this off as long as possible. As soon as I read the first few lines my heart sinks. I sit back in the chair and continue to read:

My Dear Charlotte,

I'm sure I'm the last person you expected to hear from, seeing as you left me like a ghost slipping out into the night. I woke up and felt the cold bed next to me where your warm body should have been.

Was he fucking joking? We've barely slept in the same bed these past couple of years, He was always late home from a night out, "with a colleague," and usually passed out on the sofa when he did come home. Though that was preferable to him getting in bed with me - stinking of alcohol and some woman's cheap perfume. I've got the shivers even now, thinking of his fat fingers on my skin -

pawing at me - trying to wedge his flaccid dick between my thighs from behind.

I take another sip of wine, but it's cold and metallic in my throat. I put the glass down.

I know that you haven't been happy in a while. I was hoping that taking a sabbatical from the University would help. It can't be easy always being in my shadow there, but you forget that if it weren't for me, you would never have got the job.

Bullshit!

You didn't for a minute think how your leaving might affect me. How do you suppose it looks having my wife run off in the dead of night? I have a certain social standing to maintain, and I will not be made a fool of. I have done my best to counteract any rumors but, nonetheless, it has been difficult for me to keep this quiet. The damage you are doing to my reputation is unforgivable.

Unforgivable? How about the time he locked me in our bedroom for hours because I dared to point out a tiny error in one of his stupid essays.

You are nothing without me. I have invested in you, and this isn't how I expect to be compensated.

What am I a freaking racehorse??

Rest assured; you will never work in a British University again if you continue to defy me. I demand your immediate return on receipt of this letter. Otherwise,

Charlotte, the consequences for you will be severe. I think you know by now that I am not a man to be toyed with.
   Your husband,
   Charles.

I can feel my heart pounding in my chest. Even at this distance the man frightens me. I pull my kimono tight, suddenly feeling foolish in something so frivolous. *What does he mean by consequences? How did he find me?* I was fastidious about everything. The only person that knows is Lauren and I'd trust her with my life. She's the one that drove two hours through a storm in the middle of the night to take me to the airport. I toss the letter onto the table hoping the wind will pick it up and carry it out to sea along with the man who wrote it. Charles Armstrong has found me. I'm an idiot to think he wouldn't. Even after having my lawyer serve him divorce papers and moving halfway across the world, my husband refuses to let me go. Not because he still loves me, but because a predator never let's go of its prey.

Chapter Eight

Charlotte

The week passes quickly. Ethan and I barely acknowledge each other's existence, he must think I'm such a cow for the way I spoke to him when he dropped me home last Friday. Though, I can feel the weight of his gaze on me as I plow through my classes. His eyes burn into me—the heat of his intensity feels like it's lasering through my damn clothes. It distracts the living hell out of me. On Wednesday, he passes me outside the classroom, his face a blank mask, as if he might be carefully controlling his expression, but his chest brushes up against my arm as he rushes toward the exit, and the visceral reaction the contact elicits in my body? It's fucking terrifying. It's as though my heart is sick and tired of being held prisoner behind the cage of my ribs and is attempting to stage a prison break. Needless to say, I haven't asked him for a ride again. I've been getting the bus to work all week. I called the garage and thank goodness it was his brother that answered the phone. He said that my car will be ready tonight. I just hope Ethan won't be there, the last thing I want to do is make small talk with a guy who makes my whole body feel like I stuck my finger in a socket. It was bad enough being in the car with him. Every part of me wanted him to reach across and put his hand on my thigh and trail it upwards. Instead, I acted like a dick, because apparently that's what I do now. God forbid I allow myself any pleasure in life. Years of being with Charles has turned me into a tightly wound coil. I'm afraid that should I let my guard down, the unraveling will never stop.

I still can't believe he found me. I set up a mail divert from a PO Box to my address as an extra security measure, but it still means he somehow managed to find the box number. Did he hack into my email account somehow? I changed all my passwords before I left. I was so scared of what he'd do, that I had my lawyer send him a very official looking letter stating that he wasn't to have any contact with me. What if he hired someone to find me; like some kind of P.I? Money's no object for him and a man like Charles will go to any lengths to get what he wants. I look down and my palms are sweaty, I drop my pen and pull out a paper towel from my desk. As I do, I see Ethan looking at me from his spot at the back of the classroom. His face is pensive, and his black hair is pushed back. He looks more brooding today than ever, like a dark cloud gathering itself into a storm. I attempt a tiny smile at him, but he doesn't respond. He just puts his head down and appears to be doodling in his textbook, rather than writing. He could at least pretend to be interested in this class. Why the fuck is he here if he isn't even going to bother? I pride myself on my students being engaged in my classes. I look around the room and everyone else seems to be focused. Is he just being a prick for the sake of it? I've never met a man before who can simultaneously turn me on and *fuck me right off*. If he doesn't want to be in class then fine, I can do without the distraction. I think I'll talk to him after class.

I watch him pack his stuff then stop him as he passes my desk. "Ethan, can I have a word?" He stands by my desk, and I make him wait as I finish up some notes. When I look up, I notice that his navy polo shirt is open at the neck. I follow the line of the open buttons to the top of his bare chest. I picture him on top of me, sweat dripping down his torso.

Fuck, I want to run my tongue up and down every inch of his body.

"Did you want something *Miss Rose* because I got somewhere to be."

His voice is dripping with attitude. I sit back in my chair and fold my arms. He will *not* rile me. I was thinking about starting by apologizing again for what I said to him last week, but his attitude *really pisses me off*.

"Do you think this class is working out for you?"

He shifts on his feet. "I guess so. Why?"

I'll be fine if I don't make eye contact or look at any part of his *goddamn sexy body. I will not allow his hotness to cloud my professional judgement.*

"It's just that you don't seem that focused, and it's my job to ask if there's anything I can do to help with that?

There's a tiny smile forming on his lips, and I instantly regret the way I worded my question. I wait for him to throw something sarcastic back. Instead, his face darkens again.

"Why don't you think I'm focused, Miss Rose?"

The little fucker is going to keep calling me that now isn't he, until the end of fucking time!

"When I looked up, you were doodling."

*"*Doodling?*"*

"Yes, the rest of the class were working hard, and *you* looked bored."

"I *was* bored."

I wasn't expecting that. I'd have thought he'd at least try to cover himself.

"Oh," I feel myself flushing as he stares down at me with those inky eyes. I'm startled again by the length of his eyelashes; beautiful spidery things adding another level of divinity to him. I wish I hadn't started this conversation. "I'm sorry that you find my lessons *boring*. Perhaps English literature isn't your thing and you'd be better off taking another class."

Please don't take another class, please don't - is all I can think as I stand and pull on my suit jacket from the back of my chair.

"I was bored because I finished the work you assigned."

I laugh, "You expect me to believe you finished that essay *twenty minutes* before everyone else?

"Yes Ma'am."

"Well then you won't mind handing it to me then, will you?"

I hold out my hand for it. He hesitates for a minute as if he's about to say something. Instead, he rips open the zip on his bag, pulls out his essay and hands it to me. I don't look at him as I take it. I feel bad, I felt for sure that he was lying to me.

"Frank Fletcher tell you I'm a waste of space, did he?"

I'm confused for a minute, what does Frank have to do with this? I mean, I know there's no love lost between them.

"No, why would he tell me that?"

He says nothing, just zips up his bag quickly and throws it back over his shoulder.

"Will that be all, Miss Rose?" His eyes are burning into me again, but not like they were before. Now there's a rage there.

"Ethan, I..." I try to stammer a response, but nothing else comes out.

"I'll take that as a yes." He storms out, taking long strides across the room and slams the door behind him.

Well, you handled that well didn't you, Charlotte. Ten out of ten for keeping it professional. I sit down with a groan and put my head in my hands. I think the best thing for me to do is to avoid contact with him as much as possible. I hope he's not at the garage when I get my car tonight. If he is, I'll just grab my keys and get the fuck out of there. I already have enough on my plate to deal with - I have a vengeful husband out there searching for me.

Chapter Nine

Ethan

"Delaney," My brother is yelling for me. Even though we have the same last name. He gets a kick out of calling me by it. It gives him a feeling of superiority over me at work. It's the first thing he's said to me since our fight last week, when I nearly knocked him out. I wish I had punched him out cold - he might have woken up with some sense and not continue to be such a *fucking asshole.* He won't talk about it because he doesn't want to be reminded that his little brother landed one on him. Mo called me last week to ask if I knew anything about the purple bruise on her husband's jaw. I said no. I know she doesn't believe me, just like she doesn't believe Rob that he walked into a door. He's not about to tell her what happened and I'm sure as hell not going to.

I don't want to be disturbed right now. I'm working underneath Old Blue; the truck I bought a few months ago. It's from the sixties and needs a complete overhaul, but I fell in love with it instantly. It's the same model my grandpa had when we used to visit him in Vermont in the summers as kids. Man, those summer vacations seemed to last *forever*. Even my dad seemed happy there - sitting on the porch drinking a beer, watching us chase the fireflies that as a kid I thought were magic. Those were the years my dad was making a semi decent living as an artist; when he didn't resent us or blame my mother for being the shitty person he was. Those few years when having a beer in the summer didn't turn into a whisky bottle a night, or a dark rage that grew wings and flew at us from across the room. I think Rob endured the most of it, that's why he was never fooled by those summer vacations. He's more like my father than he'll admit, and I know he hates himself for it. He's eight years older than me, so, it was usually just me and Grandpa in the truck whilst Rob was off chasing trouble somewhere, long before I learned to. I'd sit up front with the smell of leather and car wax filling my nostrils, riding alongside him on bumpy roads. My Grandfather taught me about engines, and how to drive stick when I was ten. He let me take the truck through dirt tracks and old forgotten trails that only he knew about. I never understood how such a great man could produce someone like my father; a drunk who wasted his talent and ruined my mother in the process.

"Delaney! Get your head out of your ass, I said you've got a visitor."

I don't want to see anyone, but I push myself out from under Old Blue just so that my brother will stop yelling. I come out at eye level with a pair of ankle boots and denim jeans. I follow my gaze up to see Charlotte standing over me, *great just what I need.*

"I'll leave you to your *schoolteacher*. I'm heading home. Lock up will ya."

"Dickhead," I mutter under my breath. I don't want to be dealing with this right now, I just want to work on my truck in peace. I haul myself up to standing. Why couldn't she have just got her keys and left? Does she want to give me another lecture?

"I'll get your keys." I start walking towards the office but can't help but take her in for a moment. She's wearing a light shirt tucked in her jeans and her hair is in a high ponytail. She's not wearing any make up and it softens her. Her cheeks are pink from the sun, and I wonder if her nipples are that color. Or are they darker? I get an image of her tits in my hands and my fingers playing with her hard nipples. *Fuck, even when I'm mad at her, I still want my hands all over her.* We haven't said another word to each other, by the time I come back with her keys. I drop them into her hand.

"There you go Miss Rose. Your car is parked out back." I turn away from her and head to my truck.

"I'm sorry Ethan. I was rude to you earlier and I shouldn't have been."

I turn to look at her. She looks worn down by something; there's a fragility to her that wasn't there earlier. I'm not sure what she wants me to say but fuck if she thinks I'm going to make it easy for her. I turn away again, fully intent on getting back to Old Blue.

"You don't get along with your brother." She's making small talk.

"You think?" I fold my arms across my chest and lean back against the truck. She's playing with her hands; picking at her fingers. I'm glad she's uncomfortable - she made me feel like a piece of shit earlier.

"That must be hard to work with."

"It's tolerable."

"Has it always been difficult between you?"

"Why the fuck do you care?" I feel like I'm being interrogated. I go and get a cloth to wipe my hands. Her cheeks are flushed now. I take her in again and notice the tight hug of her jeans on the curve of her hips. Her waist is pulled in and it makes her tits look even bigger. I'm obsessed with her tits and *I fucking hate myself for it.*

"I'm sorry, I've had a long day, *Miss Rose*. So, if you'll excuse me." I don't want to look at her anymore standing here in this garage. She doesn't belong here among all the memories and mess in this place. It's jarring and I don't know why.

"Will you stop calling me that for fuck's sake!"

"I thought that's what you wanted? Clearly your ladyship thinks I'm beneath her."

Her lips pinch together when I say that. "I don't think anything of the sort. I shouldn't have told you to call me that, it was rude of me."

She looks down at the ground like a shy little girl. I have an urge to go over there and put my arms around her. I put the cloth down.

"To answer your question, Rob and I used to get along, not so much now."

"Oh, did something happen then? Sorry. It's none of my business. Forget I asked. I'll just get my car and go."

Suddenly I don't want her to leave, and I don't know why. "Our mum died when I was fifteen. So yeah, that kind of fucked things up." I can tell by the look on her face that it was the wrong thing to say. It's not the sort of thing you just land on someone, and it's not something I usually want to talk about. I try to soften it. "She was sick, we knew it was coming." God even saying it now, the lie twists in my throat. I cough into my hand.

"I'm sorry you had to go through that." We study each other for a moment, and I swear the green in her eyes gets deeper. I feel like I'm being pulled into a forest that I could get lost in. I'm relieved when she looks away.

She crosses her arms and shivers. She must be cold. The temperature has dropped considerably since this afternoon, as it can by the coast, and this garage is full of ghosts; it never retains any heat from the sunlight.

"Do you want a tea?"

"I thought you Americans only drank coffee?"

"We do, but my sister-in-law is trying to gentrify us. Come into the office and choose what you want. There's a bunch of nasty looking herbal ones that you're bound to love." I grin at her.

She smiles back. "I'd love a nasty looking tea, thanks."

I hold her gaze for a moment and something inside me lights up. It's a feeling I haven't had in a *long* time and I'm not sure if I like it or not.

We sit together on Old Blue drinking our teas, steam rising, warming our faces. It's a welcome cool night.. Charlotte's swinging her legs like a child. I'm seeing a different side of her tonight. She's got a beautiful profile, a snub nose, and a pointed chin. She looks more delicate from this angle. Almost like she's made of something I could break if I'm not too careful. The thought scares me. I don't know anything about this woman, except she's my English Literature Professor.

"Do you have any siblings?"

"Now who's doing the interrogating?"

I put my mug down beside me and lean back, noting the different streaks of paint peeling off the hood. At one time this truck was orange. I rub my fingers over it and pick some of its history off. I imagine the tick and heat of the engine underneath me as I take those small roads in Vermont, back to visit my grandpa's old house. I realize that Charlotte's staring at me. I shrug my shoulders.

"I don't actually give a shit. I'm just making polite conversation; isn't that what you Brits do?"

She gives me a little smile; only half sure that I'm teasing her.

"I'm an only child. I'm surprised my mother even had me."

"Not a natural parent?"

She sighs and looks down, then tentatively takes a sip of her tea, and balances the cup on her knee. "My mother isn't *a natural anything*. Everything in her house is sterilized, including her. She couldn't possibly risk having another one of me."

"Wow."

"Sorry, I can be quite blunt."

"Really? I hadn't noticed." She slaps me on the leg, and I feel all my nerve impulses go off at once. I want to pull her down on top of me and kiss her. I want to know what that sexy mouth feels like. I need to keep talking to distract myself from my dirty fucking mind.

"Are you from London?"

"Why does every American think London is the only place in England?"

"Isn't it?" I'm fucking with her.

"No!"

"Where are you from then?"

She sighs, "London."

I nearly spit out my tea laughing.

"But my dad's from Dorset."

"So that proves what point?"

"That there are more places than just stupid London!"

Wow. I've hit some kind of nerve there. "Okay, I believe you. Why did you leave?"

She hesitates, then takes another sip of tea. "Lots of reasons, I just wanted a change of scenery, I guess. The weather here also helps."

"You never met an English man you wanted to marry?" I don't know why I'm asking her this, but curiosity gets the better of me.

She stares at her cup as if the answer is swirling around in there. "I did a long time ago; I was very young. It didn't work out."

I get the impression that she doesn't want to talk about it. We sit in silence for a while, listening to the muffled sound of traffic on the Pacific Coast Highway. I peel more paint off the hood with my fingers.

"Why are you taking English literature? It doesn't seem like the ideal choice for a mechanic."

I brush the paint flakes from my hands and sit up. "I don't wanna be a mechanic forever. It's just something I fell into after school. My brother had this business and I like cars. I needed to support myself somehow."

"That was nice of your brother to help you."

I shrug my shoulders. "He didn't really have a choice. I was living with him and his wife at the time and needed to make money to get my own place. There was a small amount of inheritance from my mum, but not enough." I don't want to talk about Rob.

"Do you want to get a degree?"

"I'm just taking some classes, figuring out what I want to do with my life." I'm not about to tell her that I got kicked out of high school and need these credits if I want to further my education. I don't want to get into why I got kicked out of school either.

"What other classes are you taking?"

"Math and astronomy."

"I hate math, but I *love* astronomy."

"Math isn't so bad when you understand that there's beauty in it. It's the building blocks of the universe. Astronomy helps me to understand my place in the world better. When I start worrying about stuff, it helps to remind me what a tiny speck I am in the grand scheme of things."

She looks at me quizzically. "I never had you down as being philosophical."

"What did you have me down as?" I can't resist teasing her. She presses her lips together and flashes her big green eyes up at me. I get a twitch in my pants. *For a goddamn minute, I think she might actually lean in and kiss me,* and I'll finally get to see what those full rosy lips taste like. Instead, she puts her cup down beside her and leans back onto her elbows.

"I've never thought about math like that before. For me, words do that. Words can create worlds; how else can you describe the beauty of a galaxy or moonlight? I also think that people can contain whole universes. One of my favorite poets was an astronomer."

"Oh yeah"

"Rebecca Elson, she wrote poems about how we're all made up of bits of the universe; of filaments of stars." Her face is tilted to the roof, to the little patch of grubby skylight, as if she's hoping some will fall through. My eyes trace the curve of her neck down to her breasts; they're rising and falling as she breathes. How the fuck am I supposed to keep my hands off her? I lean back next to her and look at the ceiling instead, watching the smeary night above us.

"Wait, I know where we can see falling stars tonight." I sit up again, kicking myself for not thinking about this earlier.

"Are you serious?" Her eyes light up.

"Yep, the Perseids meteor shower. It happens around this time every year. It falls near the constellation Perseus."

"Perseus?"

"Yeah, the Greek god who rescued his wife from a sea monster."

"You know about Greek mythology?"

"Do you think I was an idiot?"

"No, I just thought...Sorry that was again, rude of me."

She's just too easy to tease. "I'm just messing with you. Do you want to see it?" My heart's racing in my chest waiting for an answer.

"Where?"

"I know the best spot up the mountains in Malibu. I'd forgotten it's tonight, but I'm going to go anyway. You're welcome to join me." *Fuck. The last thing I want is for this woman to think I'm a nerd. But watching the stars sounds pretty damn awesome right now. And I'm not afraid to share what some girls might consider a less-than-cool past time with her, especially if it means that I might be able to make out with her.*

"Now?"

"Why not? It's past nine and by the time we get up there we should see them."

She runs her teeth over her bottom lip for a second. She's figuring out whether I'm still too much of an asshole to go and see a once in a lifetime lightshow with.

"Okay, sure, it sounds fun."

"Great. we'll take my car. I'll go get it and meet you out front." I hop off the truck and walk to the office to get my keys. Once I've got them and I'm out of sight, I break into a sprint. I don't want to give her time to change her mind.

Chapter Ten

Charlotte

What the freak am I doing? Why did I just agree to go and see a meteor shower with him? That's something you do on a date. This is the time that I need Lauren here to talk some fucking sense into me. I can't call her quickly - it's 5am there. I can't go and see stars falling out of the fucking sky with him, can I? He obviously knows what he's doing with women; you don't look like that and not be a super freakin Casanova. He said he knows, "Just the spot"- yeah, probably because he's taken hundreds of girls up there. Ugh - this must be his thing. I'm probably on the end of an extensive list of doe eyed women he's seduced up there on a Malibu Mountain top. Well not me!

I hug my arms around my body. A chill has lodged into my bones, and I shiver. How could it have been so bloody hot today and yet be so stupidly cold tonight. At least I'm not on the English coast with the north wind rattling me to my core. Just the thought of being there fills me with dread. The holidays we spent at my mother in laws - "*I don't believe in putting the heating on*" - drafty house. Her massaging her son's ego - whilst I did lots of staring out of the window at a vast wintry ocean; willing the waves to crash over the house and carry us all into the sea. Maybe it's not actually that cold tonight, and it's just the thought of Charles that's making my blood run icy. I emailed a copy of his letter to my lawyer. She's going to see if she can get a restraining order, but as I'm out of the country I doubt it'll hold much weight. I wanted to throw the letter away but knew I should keep it in case we needed it in court. So, I found a shoe box in the closet, pulled a pair of kitten heels out, tossed them aside, stuffed the letter in the empty box and shoved it to the back. I hate feeling this antsy all the time. I thought that moving countries would help; that somehow, I'd be the carefree Charlotte I once was all those years ago in Rio. Maybe tonight is just what I need. I can throw caution to the wind just this once, right? I may not be that young graduate again, but I can still have fun, can't I? I don't know why I didn't tell Ethan the truth; that I'm still married, that I have a husband intent on hunting me down. If I don't say it out loud then it isn't real, isn't that how it works? I don't want to go back to my apartment, it feels haunted by my past now. Who says I can't go and see stars tumbling out of the sky, with a man who looks like he stepped out of the pages of Italian Vogue. I laugh to myself at the absurdity of it. I mean, I did ask for Ethan at the garage tonight. I could've just got the keys off his disgusting brother - who talked only to my breasts when he addressed me. I told myself I asked for Ethan because

I wanted to apologize to him, but that's a lie. That's not all I wanted.

I can hear the rumble of his car's engine as he pulls up. The roof is down and he's sitting casually in the driver's seat with one hand on the wheel, and his elbow resting on the door. There's an ease about him that's *infuriatingly* sexy.

Calm down Charlotte, you're not a bloody teenager.

He reaches over and opens the passenger door. Time stands still for a moment. I have a feeling that as soon as I get in, I'll have crossed some kind of boundary. I can walk away now, get in my car, and go back to my lonely little apartment in Santa Monica. I can wait there, worrying about everything or...

"Are you getting in, or would you rather stand there and wait for a better offer? Not that you'd get a better one than this." He grins disarmingly at me.

Prick!

I scowl and slide into the seat. As much as I love the idea of a convertible and looking up at the night sky as we drive, I'm *freezing*.

"Can we put the heater on?"

"She's not warmed up enough for that yet. You cold?"

"A little." He takes off his seatbelt and pulls his hoodie up over his head. His t-shirt underneath rides up as he does, revealing his tanned, tight stomach. I turn away for a second; afraid that he might see me drooling.

"Here."

Wow, he's being chivalrous. I don't want to feel like a helpless little woman though.

I shift in my seat, "No, you'll be cold then."

"I'm a big boy, I can cope."

The way he looks at me sends my heart thumping into my mouth. I want to say, "*I bet you are.*" Instead, I just thank him. I can smell him as I slip it over my head. I inhale the earthy aroma as I pull it down over me. It's still warm from his body heat and for a minute I imagine it's his arms wrapped around me. It's huge; but I feel enveloped in it, safe. Ethan looks across at me before putting the car into gear.

"Better?"

"Better."

We pull out of the garage forecourt and merge onto the pacific coast highway. After five minutes he turns the heater on, and I stop shivering. I can't help but sneak a glance at him, his hair looks like it is part of the night sky. He turns briefly to meet my gaze, before fixing his eyes back on the road. His stubble is darker too tonight, it's hiding more of that scar on his chin that seems somehow to be the center of him. I want to put my finger on it again - as if it will reveal something to me about him. I realize I've been staring at him too long. I turn away as he takes a turn off to the right, up a small canyon road. The ground and the sky seem to merge into each other up here. It reminds me of the Grand Canyon, which I went to once with Charles on vacation. I'd peered down into the basin at night, and it had been like staring into a black hole; as if the sky had fallen in. It had scared me then, like some sort of mirror to my marriage. But as we climb through the mountains tonight, the darkness seems more poetic - like there are less things in it to frighten me. I lean my head back and close my eyes, feeling the motion of the car as it whips around the windy roads. The sensation is almost lulling me to sleep, and I surrender myself to the lullaby. I feel safe in the knowledge that Ethan knows his car well, and the road. I open my eyes to see the moonlight bouncing off the side of the mountain, illuminating it in such a way that I can just make out its old man's face. The sky up here is clear, and we're hovering above the pollution and light. We pass a small inlet on the left where cars have gathered. People are standing around with their binoculars and telescopes.

"This must be a good spot to see it."

"It is, but I know a better one." He carries on driving, taking the road that climbs higher, away from the gaggle of people making noise and star gazing. He pulls off into a spot that juts out over the edge of the mountain. I can see airplanes taking off from Santa Monica airport down below, they look like tiny paper airplanes from here. I wonder where they're going, and if any of their passengers are also running away from something. He turns the engine off and suddenly the silence swallows us. I can just make out lumps of rock and bits of dry brush. A coyote howls in the distance and I grip my seat. Ethan laughs, "Don't worry, they don't care about us." I breathe out in relief and now I just want to suck the quiet in. I want to pull it into my belly, like soft pieces of bread to savor later, when the thoughts that wake me in the middle of the night start haunting me.

"It feels like the top of the world up here. Do you come here much?"

"Sometimes, to think."

"Have you brought lots of girls up here?"

Shit, why did I ask him that? I know I was thinking it to myself earlier, but I hadn't meant to blurt it out! Sometimes I wish thoughts didn't just bypass my brain and trip out of my mouth without warning. I'm sure cool girls don't do that.

"Oh, wow, look at the view!" I exclaim, taking off my seatbelt and pushing open the car door before he can give me an answer about the girls. I'm sure I'm blushing red even in the dark. He gets out and opens the trunk. I can barely make him out; he's just a shadow moving around the car. My eyes haven't yet adjusted to the darkness. A chorus of frogs start to sing.

"Can you hold my phone and shine the light over here?"

"Sure" I take his phone from his hand and point the light in his direction. He's holding a blanket and lays it over the hood.

"Do you always keep a blanket in your car?"

"You never know when you might need it."

Right, he probably keeps it in the back of his car so he can get cozy with all the girls he brings up here. What a cliche.

He looks studious as he lays it out on the hood of the car. His jawline cuts sharp in the light from the phone, as if it's made from a piece of granite from these rocks. I give him back his phone. He turns around and pulls himself onto the blanket.

Am I supposed to do the same?

I stand awkwardly for a minute, pretending to still be taking in the view, then lift myself up beside him. I lay my head back against the windscreen. Ethan clicks off the light and I can sense the darkness humming around us. My eyes slowly adjust, but my other senses are heightened. I can feel the heat of the engine beneath me and hear its ticking and spitting as it cools down. The cacophony of frogs gets louder again. I look up and it's as if we're in our own observatory. The sky domes above us, pinpointed with starlight. We could be the only two people in the world up here. I can feel the heat coming off Ethan as well. I notice that I'm breathing faster, probably because I'm so close to him. It felt safer being next to him in the garage with the lights on, and we were on planet earth. Up here, it feels like we're floating through space. I'm not tethered to anything real, and I'm afraid I'll forget that I have edges and that he does too. I turn to him, but he's looking up at the sky and not at me. His Adam's apple is pale, and razor like in the moonlight as if it could cut me. His arms are folded behind his head and as his sleeve rides up, the scales on his fish tattoo shimmer. I have an overwhelming urge to kiss him. I want to sit on top of him, rip off his t-shirt and sink my face into his chest. I want my mouth on the zip of his jeans, to pull it down with my teeth and discover that part of him. I bite my lip. I was right, all edges up here are blurred. One minute in the darkness with him and I'm lost. I pull the sleeves of his hoodie down over my hands and stare at the sky to distract myself. I wonder what tiny specks we must look like from another planet's point of view. I hope we get to see the meteor shower.

"Do you think we'll see any?"

"We've got the best seats in the house, so I hope so."

The frogs stop their mating calls for a minute, and I can hear the wind rustling through the brush up here. I hope there's no embers to set it alight. Suddenly something bright shoots from the sky, diving towards us with it's tail on fire. It's so fast, that for a minute, I think I've imagined it.

"Oh my God!" I sit up. "Did you see that?" It was a star! A falling fucking star!" I've never seen anything quite so beautiful. I'm about to ask Ethan again if he saw it, when another one comes shooting out of the dark as if it's chasing the other one. Then another! I'm not sure if I want to laugh or cry.

"You're seeing this right!" I don't look at him, I don't want to see him lit up by ghostly lights trailing through the sky. His face is otherworldly enough, I can't help but reach out my hand to him though. I do it without thinking, instinctively. I need to be anchored to something, even him, because right now I feel like I'm in danger of wafting up and drifting away. He brings a hand down from behind his head and I swallow a gasp as he interlocks his fingers with mine. *It's just his hand Charlotte!* I lay back down on the Mustang to join him. His chest is rising and falling as if he's inhaling the stars.

"You know they're dying right? That the stars are falling to their death. I think their final burst of beauty is a way of saying goodbye."

"Wow, that's both depressing and beautiful." He turns to look at me, but I just keep looking up.

"Rebecca Elson, that poet I was telling you about, wrote a poem about eating the stars falling out of the night sky."

"Was she hungry?"

I slap him on the chest. It feels hard.

"It's actually a stunning poem; much more romantic and profound than the way I said it."

"I'd like to read some of them."

I look across at him to see if he's teasing me, but he gazes back at me seriously. I can see the reflection of a falling star in the corner of his dark eyes. I quickly focus above me again.

"I have her book. I can lend it to you if you like."

He shifts his head on the one hand behind him, the other is still holding mine.

"I'd like that." I can feel his eyes on me still, and I know he wants me to turn back to look at him. I can't. If I do, I won't be able to turn back.

"I haven't by the way."

"Haven't what?"

"I haven't brought other girls up here.

I don't know why but hearing him say that gives me a sudden rush of emotion. It takes me by surprise, and I swallow it.

Don't get carried away Charlotte, he's probably lying, isn't that what men do? Especially ones as hot as Ethan.

But something in the deepest part of me believes him. That this man whispering to me in the dark is more of an enigma than

I thought he was. We say nothing else to each other as another star falls to earth, extinguishing itself. Is that what I've been doing for the last ten years of my life? Putting out my own light? I've been numb to life for so long and I want to *feel* something again, I want to breathe life back into myself. I squeeze his hand harder and feel tough bits of his skin between my fingers.

"You have calluses."

"Yep, working on cars will do that."

My heart is racing in my chest as I trace those parts of his hand. I don't know what I'm doing, I just want to feel the roughness under my fingers. Charles has feminine hands; silky skin that he puts lotion on daily. I liked it at first, his pristineness. I thought it meant he took pride in himself. Then I realized it's because he's lazy and does nothing for himself. He wouldn't know manual labor if it smacked him in the face. I don't think he's so much as refilled the oil in his car. Ethan is everything Charles isn't. He's young and exciting and doesn't give a fuck. I feel like we're completely alone in the world up here, anything could happen. Would it be so terrible if I gave in just a little? If just for once I let myself go and said, "*Fuck everything.*"

I bring his hand to my mouth and kiss the calluses, then brush his fingers over my lips. It feels so good. I take one in my mouth and suck on it a little. He moans and I tilt my head back to suck on it more, but he pulls his hand away.

Shit, shit I've embarrassed myself. I read this whole situation totally wrong. Please, please let there be a spaceship nearby to beam me up and carry me away.

He rolls on his side to face me. I turn my head the other way. I'm mortified.

"Charlotte."

I ignore him.

"Will you look at me?"

"No." I know I'm being childish, but I can't bring myself to face him and have him *say what? That he's sorry, but he doesn't think of me that way.*

"God damn it, Charlotte." He puts his finger under my chin and turns my face towards his. His eyes are scanning mine and behind him the stars continue to die. "Are you sure this is what you want?"

I don't understand what he means. There are flecks of amber in his black pupils - so miniscule that I've never noticed them before.

"What I want?" I say it slowly as if trying to figure it out in my head.

"Because, if it isn't, then we need to stop now. Otherwise, I'm not sure I'll be able to keep my fucking hands off you." The flecks in his eyes glow a little in the starlight, and for a second, he reminds me of a wild animal.

I feel myself nodding and I hear a voice say, "Yes it's what I want." It comes out of my mouth on gossamer threads that I don't recognize. He tucks a piece of hair behind my ear, then moves his hand slowly down my shoulder to my waist. He grabs hold of my hips and pulls me closer. I close my eyes as he leans in, his warm lips graze gently against mine. Heat curses through my body and my head starts to spin. *What am I doing? I don't know if I can handle this.* We look at each other for a second and I know I have no choice; that my body has made the decision for me. I hear him whisper my name almost inaudibly, and my skin tingles as if all my nerve endings are responding at once. I part my lips and gasp as his mouth finds mine. He kisses me slowly, lingering, as if I'm something to be savored. I've never been kissed like this before. He tastes like the dark and it makes me *feel* like I'm *on freaking fire.* I arch my body into his and he groans as I press myself against his hardness. He grabs hold of my hair and kisses me faster now, hungrier, as if he wants to bruise me. His tongue searches for mine and as it does, I feel something metallic. I pull back.

"You've got a tongue piercing."

"Very observant, Professor." He grins at me, his face in shadow, but I can still make out the amusement in his eyes. Even now he wants to make fun of me.

"Shut the fuck up," I whisper back as I put two of my fingers in his mouth and find the small silver ball on his tongue. I press it between my fingers, and he sucks on them as I pull them slowly out, before giving him my mouth again. I wrap one of my legs over him and press myself into him. I can feel his hard dick straining against me. The wetness between my legs pools and I'm sure he must be able to feel the dampness through my jeans. I can't help but reach down to his groin and run my hand over the huge bulge there. My mouth waters, and before I know what I'm doing, *because this version of Charlotte just can't seem to help herself*, I start to unzip his fly. He groans and flips me onto my back, and pins one of my arms above my head.

"Not yet," he whispers. He brings his mouth to my neck and bites it; delicately at first. Teasing me with gentle little tugs at my skin. I put my hand on the back of his head, urging him to bite me harder, but instead he pins that one above my head too. He gives me that charming, knee quivering smile of his as I try to resist.

"Patience Charlotte, patience."

Motherfucker.

I struggle underneath him, but he just grips onto my arms tighter. His tongue flicks at my neck, then up to my mouth again to kiss me. I raise my hips up and bite his lip hard. He moans and loosens the grip of my arms. I wrap them around him and pull him close to me, inhaling his earth and pine scent, letting it flood my entire being as we devour each other with kisses. I have never desired someone so much in my life.

I'm afraid, afraid of losing myself to him right here on this mountain.

But again, my body takes control over my mind. I pull his hand down to my jeans, he slips it down inside the top of them and onto my inner thigh. His rugged hands stroke the soft skin there, before his fingers trace the lace of my panties with reverence; patiently searching for what they want. I arch my back a little, willing him to go further. I feel myself trembling as he gently slides his fingers underneath the lace, and into the wetness of me.

"Baby, you're so fucking wet," he says it with a voice so rough and raspy that I think I might explode. I moan into his mouth as he expertly swirls the tip of a finger around my clitoris; little butterfly movements that I had no idea a man of his age knew how to do. I close my eyes and let his beautiful hands play with my pussy.

"We need to take these off." He snaps the elastic on the side of my panties. "I want you naked on the hood of my car."

"Oh my God, yes," are the only words that come out. I don't care that we're outside, and that although we're alone; it's a public road. I hear that familiar voice in my head say *What the fuck are you thinking?* But I swat it away like a fly. I arch in anticipation as Ethan pulls the hoodie, and the T-shirt under it, over my head. He looks down at my body and I see that wild animal in his eyes again. This time it's wolf-like; as if I'm a thing to be hunted and feasted upon.

"Fuck, you're beautiful."

He brings his lips to my body and trails them down between my breasts. His hand reaches around my back and unclasps my bra in one snap. *Of course, he's a master at taking off bras.* He slowly pulls the straps down my shoulders, then completely off until my tits spill out; they're white and luminous against the dark. His hands cup one of them and he moans with the weight of it, before he brings his lips to my nipple and flicks at it with this tongue. My nipple hardens with each dart at it. He sucks on one nipple and then the other as if he has found a spring to drink from and is quenching his thirst. I hold the back of his head, and his ebony hair curls between my fingers.

"Anyone could see us." I gasp out, suddenly aware that I'm lying on top of a car with my tits out on display.

"Good." He replies, and my pussy drips again.

I push his head down, I want that tongue between my legs, but he takes his time kissing my stomach, spiraling his tongue around my belly button, before kissing the tiny star shaped birthmark to the left of it.

"This one took its last breath in you," he whispers, then kisses over the curve of my hips. My body responds like it's a river he's been kneeling beside for years. He undoes the button and zip on my jeans, and I lift my pelvis as he pulls them off, with my panties. He puts one finger back into the slit of me and follows with his tongue, rubbing the silver ball of his piercing against my clit. I gasp at the coldness of it and clutch onto his shoulders. He looks up at me and smiles, whilst pressing it to me again. He alternates between holding the tiny metal ball against my clit and darting his tongue quickly in and out of my pussy.

I feel like I might actually sink into the blanket and disappear. I, Charlotte Rose, cease to exist now. I am entirely his.

I grab the dark tangle of his hair and push his face further in and spread my legs. He groans my name and begins to lap at me, and everything seems to merge into the wildness of the landscape around us. I look down at myself, spreadeagled on his car, his gorgeous face between my legs. I feel as if I'm in a dream that I don't want to wake from. He brings his tongue back to the very edge of my clit and circles it in the same butterfly motion that he made with his finger. I move my legs further apart now. I want him to see all of me; be a witness to all that I have deprived myself of for years. He responds by delving in further with his tongue as I open for him. I try to say his name, but nothing comes out and all I can do is claw at his hair again. I can tell that nothing matters to him right now except eating me out. My pussy begins to pulse. He grabs my hips as I push them up to him, his tongue dipping in and out, his piercing tapping at the center of me. I grab hold of the blanket, and I hear a sound that I think must be coming from somewhere in the desert, but it's emerging from me. It's a low, urgent moan- like a creature howling in the darkness.

Oh my God, oh my God he's going to make me cum right here on top of this mountain.

My orgasm is deep and guttural and rips through my body in waves. He's there for all of it; eating me, licking me, until my body rests again on the blanket, He kisses the little spasms that keep coming for a few minutes afterwards as I slowly return to earth.

"Fuck, where did you learn to do that?" I manage to gasp out at him.

"I had a misspent youth."

"I can assure you there was *nothing misspent* about that."

He grins at me and makes his way back up my body, planting tiny kisses on the way.

"I aim to please, Charlotte."

"I bet you do and it's, *Professor* to you" I reply and sink my mouth onto his; not caring that I can taste my pussy all over it. I can feel his hard dick through his jeans pressing between my legs.

I want him inside me now! My God, I've never desired anything more.

I tug at his belt - scrambling to undo it as I bite him on the neck. *I want to mark him, claim him as my own.* I bite down harder, and he moans, his hair flopping down on my tits; his breath hot between them. His belt is off, and I start to undo his fly, but he pushes my hands away and props himself up on his elbows. He searches my face again, his pupils wide; night blooming irises staring back at me. I dig my nails into the metal of the hood.

"What?"

"Nothing, you're just so fucking breathtaking." He brushes a tiny hair out of my face.

I want to tell him that he's the hottest thing on freakin earth. That the moment I saw his face, it made me want to drop to my knees. But he can never know that. This is just sex, nothing more than that.

"You pulled my hands away from your dick, to tell me that?"

He looks confused for a minute, his forehead knots, but then he does that boyish smile of his.

"I was just buying time; getting you ready for my magnificent cock."

"Oh yeah, sounds just like a lot of talk to me."

He climbs down and stands in front of the car. My eyes adjust to the dark again as I prop myself up, surprisingly unabashed at my nakedness. My pussy is still throbbing from my orgasm, and I desperately want him inside me. He pops the button of his jeans and undoes his fly. I'm fixated as he slowly peels down his jeans and underwear. His dragon tattoo appears first. I can just make out its flicking tail, then its dark scaly body snaking down. The head of it tucked into his inner thigh, nestled next to the thatch of hair between his legs where his dick now springs up from. My mouth begins to water. *He was right, it's a magnificent fucking dick.* You don't have Ethan's kind of confidence unless your cock is total perfection. It's long and elegant, but with perfect width. He wraps his thick hand around the base, then slowly moves it up and down; looking down at my body as if he owns it. He looks like some kind of dark god silhouetted against the night sky. My pussy drips again at the sight of him playing with his cock.

"Is this what you want?"

I lick my lips and nod. I spread my legs for him, abandoning any tiny amount of modesty I might have had left. He reaches down to retrieve something from his jeans and slips something out of his wallet. The foil paper glints once in the moonlight as he tears the condom from its wrapper. By the time he's facing me again, he's slid it expertly down his shaft. He moves back towards the hood and climbs on top of me, and I raise my body to meet him. The last thing I imagined would happen tonight is that I would be begging for Ethan to be inside me. He cups my face in one of his hands, before entering me slowly. I gasp as his dick begins to fill me, he's so big; but perfectly so. Any other thoughts float out of my head, as I tilt my hips up and wrap my legs around him. He moans my name into my neck as I push him deeper. I want his naked skin on mine, so, I grab hold of his t-shirt and pull it over his head. His chest is tanned and smooth and I bury my face in it, smelling the sweat and musk of him. Suddenly, I hear a car in the distance, and can just make out the faint light of its headlamps as it comes round the bend. Any minute now its beam will hit us for one second. Ethan doesn't seem to care as he plunges further into me.

Shit, what if someone see us up here fucking? Are they going to stop or report us?

The car captures us in a flash, like a moment caught in a photograph and *I don't care either, I don't fucking care! I want them to see us. I want them to see us fucking, the two of us naked and tangled together.*

I dig my nails into Ethan's back and circle my hips underneath him. He grinds into me, groaning loudly. The car continues round the bend, then it's gone, leaving just the sound of its engine rumbling into the distance. Our fucking gets more urgent now, his lips are all over my face and my hands are pulling at his hair. I can feel him in the pit of my stomach. I know that we're both too aroused to hold this for long. I circle my hips beneath him again, and he grabs hold of my arms and pins them to the hood and licks the sweat from my breasts and my neck.

"I can't believe how fucking wet you are." He whispers to me, before pulling at my ear with his teeth and biting it as he thrusts himself inside me harder. I want him to rip me apart, I want him to ruin me. I grab hold of his face and make him look at me. His pupils are black and dilated, he has part of the night inside him. My thighs grip him as my pussy molds itself around his cock. He lets go of my arms and I wrap them around him, we're like one being now rocking back and forth together. Our bodies are slick with sweat against each other, my tits smeared against his hard chest, "Oh baby, oh my God!" he gasps, then he's coming. His whole body begins to shudder as his cum shoots into me. My body responds by orgasming for the second time tonight, surprising me with its intensity as it ricochets through me. I've *never* orgasmed twice like this before. We lay still for a minute. I look up at the milky way and listen to the rise and fall of our breath, his head resting just above my breasts. I unwrap my legs but keep my arms around him. I run my fingers down his back in small, delicate movements. He's still inside me and I don't want him to move. Finally, he raises his head and props himself up on his elbows.

"Hi."

"Hi," I respond, a little sheepishly now.

He kisses me on the nose, then puts the tip of his finger on it. "You've got tiny freckles. I've never noticed them before."

I suddenly feel self-conscious. *Now you feel self-conscious Charlotte?*

"Yeah, I don't like them."

"Why not? They're sexy."

I laugh, "Freckles aren't sexy."

"I disagree." He plants a little kiss on them, and then on my cheeks and my eyelids. He tucks another one of my errant hairs behind my ear.

"You're a surprise."

"What do you mean?"

"I mean you're not quite as innocent as you make out, are you Professor?"

I'm not sure what to say to that. I'm certainly not going to tell him it's the first sex I've had in two years and that it totally just blew my mind.

"There's a lot of things you don't know about me." I can feel the anxiety start to creep back a little.

"I damn well bet there are." He winks at me. He kisses me again. His lips are cool now as the desert night wraps itself around us. He rolls onto his back and looks up at the sky. There are no stars falling from it now.

"I think we missed half of the light show."

"We did."

"I preferred our own show, anyway." He looks over and smiles at me. He's impossibly good looking and my heart melts for the hundredth time tonight.

"Me too."

"You're shivering." He reaches around and folds the side of the blanket over me.

"Thanks."

"I could look at your naked body all night long, but I guess we should be getting out of here. It's pretty late."

I want to tell him that I don't want to leave. I want to stay up here with him, and pretend that everything is okay; everything is horrible down there.

I shrug my shoulders, "I guess so."

"Okay, I'll grab our clothes." He leans in and kisses me one more time. "You're quite the mystery, Charlotte Rose." He jumps off the hood, the muscles in his arms and legs toned and strong. I sit up and hug my knees and watch him. I don't want him to know yet that I'm not a mystery. I'm just a person made from secrets and lies and flesh and bones, and I just want to stay here, like this with him, forever.

Chapter Eleven

Charlotte

"Wait, what? You had sex under shooting stars with a hot student? Hold on, I need to get more wine for this. Back in two secs."

I can see Lauren go into the kitchen on my screen, whilst I pour myself another glass of wine. She's the only person I can talk to about this. We've been friends since college, she was the one to encourage me to leave my unhappy marriage, to apply for this job. Without her help with everything, I doubt I'd have made it out.

"It's not running away," she'd said. *"It's starting again. He's never going to let you go, so you have to be the one to leave."* I should've tied up all the loose ends before I left; not just assumed that it could all be sorted out from the other side of the world. Lauren had been in Rio de Janeiro with me when I went. We did our master's and PhDs together. We lost touch for a few years after I married Charles. She'd warned me about him, but

I was too star struck by him and his career. He was a bestselling author, head of English at one of the top Universities in England, and he'd singled out *me* as his prodigy. *"It's not your brain he's interested in."* Lauren had told me. I didn't care though; he could have had anything he wanted from me. He was handsome and brilliant, with piercing blue eyes and white, blonde hair. He spoke five languages and was utterly charming. Women loved him. They still do, even though he's fatter around the middle and the blonde hair is more of a nicotine yellow now. He was mine and Lauren's tutor on the Master's Literature Program. I interned for him. He even got me on the expense account as his assistant to travel with him for international conferences. He put me down as, *'Briefcase carrier'* which was code for, *"I'm fucking my student."* I thought I was being daring and wild. Every girl in class wanted him and *I had him*. I didn't realize though that I wasn't the only one carrying his briefcase. I found that out too late, after I married him. I couldn't face Lauren; to admit she was right about him. So, I just avoided her. I couldn't tell her that I'd married a narcissist who wanted total control of me. I'd ruined my life. Everyone told me it was an ugly thing—a professor sleeping with his student—but I'd been blind to it back then. Now, I've just slept with one of my students. *My wine turns to battery acid in my mouth as a horrific thought occurs to me: Am I just like Charles? Am I some disgusting* sort of *predator, taking advantage of my position of power, to take something that doesn't belong to me?*

"Okay, I'm ready, continue!" Lauren's back, with a whole bottle of Chardonnay.

"What else do you want me to say?" Suddenly, I'm not sure if this is something I should be talking about.

She blinks, then makes a face.

"Details, Char, details! Thirsty married woman and mother of three here!" She fills her large wine glass.

I shift on the sofa, pull the cushion out from behind me, and bring it in front of my chest. "I don't know, it feels weird talking about it."

Lauren sighs, then takes a big gulp of wine, "For fuck's sake, it's *me* you're talking to, not your judgmental mother."

I can't help smiling and try to shake thoughts of any comparison to Charles out of my head.

"Okay, well it's like nothing I've ever experienced. It's the kind of thing you think only happens in movies."

She squeals, "I'm not surprised! You had sex on the top of a fucking mountain in Malibu, under a meteor shower with a guy so hot, or so you tell me, I'm amazed you didn't spontaneously combust!"

"I think I might have done." We both burst out laughing. It actually feels good talking about this to her.

"I still can't believe that you've only been in California a couple of weeks, and you've already *had sex* with a hottie!"

"More like three weeks, now."

"Not the point Charlotte!"

"I know, it's just that I feel that I've known him forever, does that make sense?"

"*Hellooo*, am I talking to your *vagina* now?"

"Ha ha, no!" I *laugh, hiding my blush in my wine glass as I take another sip, waiting for the color in my cheeks to go down. Only, it doesn't. The memory of Ethan's wet tongue expertly lapping at my peaked nipple crashes into me out of nowhere, and my whole body lights up. Fuck!*

"It's just that I got this feeling when I first saw him, it was strange. It sort of hit me in the gut. I mean, my God we saw *about t*welve shooting stars together. If that's not a sign, what is?"

Lauren leans back on her sofa. "A sign of what? You were lonely and horny. You went to see a meteor shower and you haven't had good sex in years. Then you go and have it with, apparently, the hottest thing on God's green earth! Of course, you feel there's a connection."

I bite my fingernails. Maybe she's right. Maybe I'm just making connections where there aren't any. I've been vulnerable after getting that letter, and I've been reckless by having sex with a student. The worry that I'm just like my husband rises in me again, like bile, and I clutch at my throat. Lauren must have caught the look on my face as her tone softens.

"I'm sorry, I don't mean to make you feel bad. I can't imagine how it must feel to have that kind of connection after all this time. Christ knows Charles hasn't paid you any attention in years, not that you'd want him to, ugh." She shudders and downs the rest of the wine in her glass, before pouring another. Clearly her day has been as long as mine.

"Omg, didn't he used to call you Charlie and introduce you as that sometimes? Like you were just an extension of him?"

"Yep."

Lauren mouths into her glass, "Prick."

"Speaking of Charles." I move the cushion to the side. "He wrote to me."

"What? How the fuck did he find you? I thought you locked that shit down?"

"I did! I thought everything through so carefully. The only thing I couldn't do was wait there for him to sign the divorce papers. It was too risky."

"Does he have your home address?"

"No, but he has my PO Box number, and if he found that; the next thing he's going to do is try to find me."

Lauren's face turns pale, and she leans forward. "Are you afraid that he'll come looking for you?"

I bite my nails again, "I hope not." Had I really thought I could escape him that easily? Charles Armstrong isn't a man you can simply walk away from. It's a game of cat and mouse for him, and I'm always his prey. I instinctively never took his last name, I wanted people to see me as Professor Rose, not just an appendage of him. He got round it by using that little pet name of Charlie for me, which ended up being worse. He wanted to take credit for my career. He didn't like it either when students asked to switch classes to mine. It sent him into a rage, accusing me of deliberately sabotaging his career. The truth was that he was just too damn up himself to see the reality. The truth was that he believed himself bigger than the job, and any brilliance he had was increasingly tainted by his ego. He still had his sycophants and students he groomed as his 'proteges' but, really, at this point it's nothing more than his celebrity that draws people to him. When he encouraged me to take time off to write the book I'd always wanted to, I had become so weak that I believed him. It was really his *next two books* that he wanted me to write, and to get me away from the university, out of his limelight.

"What does the letter say?"

He waffles on about himself for a bit, then it says, "*You're nothing without me,*" and *"I've invested in you, and this isn't how I expect to be compensated."* I do my best impression of him, and my voice sticks in my throat.

"What an asshole! No wonder you reacted by fucking someone else."

"He says if I don't return home immediately, he will make sure I never work in any British university again."

"He can't do that!"

"Oh, c'mon Lauren, you know the influence he has. You lived in that world once."

She takes another sip of her wine and flops back on the sofa again. "Yes, but that was before I had three kids and a senile mother-in-law to look after. Sometimes I don't even think she's senile, she just does it to piss me off."

I smile at my friend; she still looks the same under her tired demeanor. I can still see the Lauren I partied till dawn with, in Brazil, but right now she has a lot to deal with. I feel like a whiny, selfish friend.

"I'm sorry, you probably don't need any of this."

"Are you joking? I'm living vicariously through you right now, the closest I get to sex these days is having Paul rub my feet in bed."

"That actually sounds nice."

"Maybe Charles was just letting off a little steam with that letter. Perhaps he'll sign the divorce papers and in six months you'll be free."

I shake my head; I know she's only trying to make me feel better. "He says the consequences will be severe if I don't go back."

"God, I *hate* that man, who does he think he is? *The fucking Godfather?*"

"I wouldn't put anything past him."

Lauren puts her glass down. "You've got to put that man out of your head, Charlotte. The whole point of you leaving, *of us* planning all that, was to escape him. He's all talk and he's *lazy*. He's probably moving your replacement in right now."

I hope she's right. I can't shake this feeling, though, that he's going to tear the whole world apart searching for me.

"Let's get back to talking about *hot boy,* which was a much better conversation. Now tell me more about what he looks like."

I smile, talking about Ethan is a good distraction. I lean forward. "He looks like he walked out of the pages of a poem."

"A good poem? Or the kind of poems we used to write in undergrad?"

"A *very, very good* poem."

"Mmm...yum"

We both laugh again, and I feel lighter.

"I've been ignoring him since it happened though."

Lauren nearly spits out her wine. "For fuck's sake why?"

"I don't know how I'm supposed to act! This is all new for me. I clearly can't let it happen again and at the same time it's all I can bloody think about." The image of Ethan's gorgeous face looking up at me from between my legs, flashes at me. I feel my cheeks color. "I just wish he wasn't in my class. It'd be *so* much easier."

"Do you spend the whole time mentally undressing him?"

"More than that." Hearing myself say it, I feel guilty again. I want to ask Lauren if she thinks that I'm just like Charles.

"Shit! I can hear Elliott up and about and it's a school night. As much as I want to hear more, I've got to go be a parent. Love you."

"Love you too." The screen goes blank and I'm alone. It's great being able to talk to people over skype or on the phone, but it's not the same as seeing them. It's been a couple of weeks since I slept with Ethan. Now every time I see him, I'm embarrassed. The man had me naked and spreadeagled on his hood for Christ's sake. I can't look at him sitting at the back of the class without remembering how it felt kissing him, or how it felt to have his hands all over my body. I relive it every night in bed, giving myself orgasm after orgasm, mentally picturing every little detail. I'm still shocked at my behavior; it's as if something primal took over up there. As soon as I was back at sea level, my senses came back to me. I just got in my car at the garage, said goodbye to him and drove home. He must think I'm nuts, I've totally shut down on him. I scramble out of the classroom as soon as I can before he gets a chance to say anything. The only way I can cope is not to be around him. I do my best to not make eye contact in class. I have a feeling though, that this ingenious tactic won't hold up much longer.

Chapter Twelve

Ethan

Charlotte's been avoiding me. Not to sound like a total douche bag, but this isn't how girls usually behave after we have sex. Normally they're up for a replay. I see them once or twice more, and that's it. Occasionally I get called out for the piece of shit that I am, but I would happily fuck Charlotte senseless again many times over. *I mean, wow, that body of hers is really something.* She's my professor though and when I inevitably end it, things could get weird. I need to talk to her today, if for nothing else but to clear the air between us.

"Are you coming to Carl's party tonight?"

The girl in front of me has swung around on her chair. Her chin is in her hands and she's fluttering her eyelashes at me. She's pretty with red hair and freckles smattered across her nose. I'm surprised I haven't noticed her before. Cute though she is, I have Charlotte on my mind as I stand and begin to pack my bag.

"Carl?"

"Yes Carl, I thought Gina had invited you?"

Oh, so this is one of Gina's spies.

"No, she hasn't mentioned it."

She twirls a piece of hair in her fingers. Normally I would flirt back, just for the hell of it, but right now I want to get rid of her. I need to catch Charlotte before she leaves. I can see that she's already packing her stuff. She's still trying to avoid me, but I've had enough.

"Well, I'm going to text her to make sure you come." The girl leans forward as she says it and puts a finger on my chest, then runs it down my t-shirt.

Subtle.

"Okay." I'm glad when she stops touching me. I flash a look up at Charlotte, but she's looking down at her desk. I don't know why it bothers me that she might've seen that.

"Great!" The girl squeals as she says it. "I'm Debbie, by the way, but you can call me Deb."

I give her one of my best smiles, "Okay Deb. Maybe I'll see you later."

"Hope so." She blushes, then squeezes herself out of her seat, deliberately showing off her legs, and winks at me as she leaves. I've no intention of going to some college party, but Deb here doesn't need to know that.

"Got yourself another fan?" Charlotte raises her eyebrows at me as I approach her desk. She puts her hair behind her ears as she looks down to put the last of the papers in her bag.

"Jealous?" I can't help myself. I kind of want her to be.

She looks up at me through her glasses that are perched on the end of her nose. "No."

God*damn*, she's so sexy wearing those glasses. They just do something to me. And by something, I mean that the sight of her wearing them *makes my fucking dick hard.* I sit on the desk in front of hers and watch as she tries to gather her papers together, clearly flustered.

"I can't help but notice that you can't seem to get away from me fast enough these days, Charlotte."

She looks up at me, "You mean, Professor Rose."

"This again? I noticed you were quite happy to drop your title when you wanted my tongue in your pussy."

"Stop that!" She takes a break from fussing with her papers and looks around to see if anyone overheard.

"Well finally, I've got your attention." I can't deny that I'm enjoying this, watching her get all hot and bothered. That's exactly how I like her. She ignores me and picks up a book from her desk. She flicks through it until the last student is out of the door. She throws it on the desk as soon as they're out of sight.

"What do you want?" She's wearing a lemon dress today, one that pulls in at the waist and shows off the curves of her hips. I want to rip open the top of it and watch her beautiful tits fall out. *Fuck, I'm obsessed with them.* Maybe I do want to risk taking her out again, just for another look at that gorgeous body of hers. I still haven't had her sweet mouth round my cock.

"I just thought we could go out for a drink tonight, or another drive." I emphasize, *"another drive,"* and I don't think she appreciates it. She pushes her glasses back up her nose and comes to stand by the side of her desk. She taps her fingers on it absentmindedly.

"It wouldn't be appropriate for us to go out in public together."

I get up off the desk and stand in front of her. She's shorter than me, even in her heels, and I notice again the delicate curve of her breasts pushed into that tiny dress. I move closer, towering over her. Her perfume smells like figs. How easy it would be now to lift her onto that desk of hers and slide myself inside her, and to hell with anybody who saw us.

"So going out together isn't appropriate, but *fucking on the hood of my car in public is?*" She's going to *hate me* for saying that. Her face turns bright pink.

"Neither is appropriate. I don't know what came over me that night. I was feeling vulnerable, and I was taken over by the moment. I didn't know what I was doing."

"I think you knew exactly what you were doing, Professor Rose."

She looks at me for a moment and I can see her pupils dilate a little. *I'm right, she knew exactly what she was doing.* She turns and takes off her glasses, rubbing her nose, before placing them on the desk. Her green eyes wash over me. "Ethan, I don't know what you want from me, but it's an impossible situation. We should never have done that. Not just because I'm your teacher, but other stuff that you don't even know about."

"You could tell me."

"I can't."

"Can't or won't?"

"Both" She looks up at me. "I'm your teacher for fucks sake! Don't you think that's wrong?"

"I'm not in high school!"

"You're still twelve years younger than me! How the hell would this ever work?"

"I'm not asking to marry you, just to see you again."

"Why? So that you can boast how you fucked your professor?"

"Jesus Charlotte." I slam my hand on the desk and walk away. "Do you think I'm that much of a dick?"

"I don't know Ethan. I don't know you at all and you don't know me. So, let's just leave it at that." She closes her laptop.

I hate that she thinks that way about me. But why shouldn't she? It's what I am. I would never boast about being with her though, that's not my thing. I do want to see her again, it's not a feeling I usually have. But this woman *does something t*o me, and I *can't fucking control it.*

"I like you, Charlotte. Even though you can be a stuck-up bitch, I like you, God damn it." I take a breath and walk back towards her. "You're the hottest woman I've ever met."

"Ha! That's a line." She goes to pick up her bag, but I put my hand out and stop her.

"Will you just for a minute, consider that I might actually be telling the truth."

She goes to say something, then obviously thinks better of it, and closes her mouth. I move in towards her, and she doesn't turn away. We're so close now that I can hear the rise and fall of her breath. What is that scent she's wearing? *It's fucking intoxicating.* I lean in and bring my hand to her face and bring it down to her chin, keeping my finger underneath. Slowly, I tilt her face up to mine. Her lip's part and I know she wants this as much as me. I kiss her gently, but it takes every ounce of willpower in me not to devour her right there. Her mouth is yielding to me for more. *Fuck, I want to take her right here.* I kiss her again; harder this time and she moans a little. The sound of it makes my cock almost burst out of my pants. I pick her up and she wraps her legs around me. Her dress is up around her thighs, and I squeeze the sweet milkiness of her skin under my hands. *I want my mouth all over her.* I place her on the edge of her desk, and she looks back at me. Her pupils are blown, and her blonde hair is messed up. She's the most beautiful thing I've ever seen. I start to slowly peel down the straps on her dress, I want to savor this moment, *fuck anyone coming in*. I'm too far gone to care. She reaches down to my jeans and runs her hand over the outline of my dick, before searching for the zipper. I'm so fucking hard it hurts. She bites me on the lip, and I yank the top of her dress down until her breasts spill out. I've missed them. Two gorgeous white mounds with pink nipples standing on end, I cup one in my hand. The weight of it makes me push myself into her hand harder as she reaches inside my pants. I take one of her tits in my mouth and suck on it, flicking and licking her nipple. Nothing else matters except us right here. I'm going to have to fuck her on her desk and to hell if anyone comes in. I reach under her dress and start to pull her panties down. but suddenly she pulls away. I'm left standing with my fly undone and my cock rigid beneath it.

"No, we can't, I'm sorry, I don't know what came over me, again. We mustn't!" She's pulling up the straps on her dress and moving away from me. *Fuck.* I put my hands on the desk to steady myself and catch my breath.

"Ethan, it's not a good idea. There's too much at stake. I let my guard down once but I won't make that mistake again."

"Mistake?" I'm still recovering, and my dick is still hard, I can't think straight. There's a knock at the door. Charlotte looks like she's about to say something else, but instead smooths her dress down and tries to straighten her hair.

"Come in."

"Ready Charlotte?" It's fucking Frank, *again.* My hard on instantly disappears.

"Ah Delaney, playing catch up again?" I don't even bother to turn around.

"I'll be there in a minute, Frank. Just finishing up here."

"Right ho, as they say where you're from. I'll meet you by the entrance."

She flashes him a smile as he leaves. I feel like I've just been punched in the stomach. "You're going on a date with *him*?"

"It's not a date. I need to keep on the right side of him if I want to extend my work visa."

"Is he the reason you took your hands out of my pants?"

"No, absolutely not! But just imagine if he'd come in just a couple of minutes earlier -what would've happened?"

"I would've enjoyed the look on his face." Okay, not the right thing to say, but I hate Fletcher and would've liked nothing better than to wipe that smirk off his fat face.

"That's very mature of you Ethan."

"What can I say? I'm just a student after all." I know I'm not dealing with this well, but I can't stop myself. I could still salvage this, say that I'm sorry. I could be a gentleman - except I've forgotten how to be one.

"This was a mistake, *again*. Just go, will you."

"My pleasure, *Ma'am*." I pick up my bag and don't look back, slamming the door behind me. Yeah, she's right - *real mature Ethan*. I pull out my phone as I walk down the corridor and text Gina. "*So, am I taking you to Carl's party tonight?*" Debbie looks like fun; it's time to forget about Charlotte.

Chapter Thirteen

Charlotte

I'm in the bathroom at the restaurant. I've been here for nearly ten minutes, sitting in one of the stalls, scrolling through my phone. It's not like I can call anyone to pass the time; everyone in England's asleep. I wonder how much longer I can reasonably stay here without Frank getting suspicious. I'm sure I've passed that point already, but I honestly felt like I was going to faint out there. We're in a fancy seafood restaurant perched on the edge of a cliff in Malibu. It's seven thirty on a Friday night and it's crowded. The sunset is visible from the windows that stretch across the back wall. It's like looking out at a watercolor painting. It could be romantic, if I wasn't here with Frank and everyone wasn't squashed together at the bar waiting for a table. There's about *zero chance* we're going to get a table on the patio with a sea breeze on our faces, and the waves lapping beneath us. There are black and white pictures on the wall of celebrities dining here. There's a man in all of the pictures wearing a gold chain and smoking a cigar, he must be the owner. His arms are looped around Hollywood stars as they sit and pose in one of the booths. I hope the guy isn't around - he looks like a creep. The heat at the bar was suffocating and we could barely move for people. It gave Frank a good excuse to press himself a little too close to me. He stank of stale sweat and antiseptic, and I thought I might wretch. I excused myself and pretended I needed the bathroom.

I sigh and put my phone away, I flush the toilet to make it look like I wasn't just sitting in there contemplating *what a shit night I was having.* There's a couple of women waiting in line. The first one tuts before brushing past me, into the stall, whilst the other one folds her arms and scowls. I wash my hands and look at myself in the mirror. I wish I wasn't wearing a dress that showed this much cleavage. It was all Frank could do to remember that I have a face. I should have probably worn something baggy; like a potato sack. My dress certainly hadn't discouraged Ethan earlier.

Shit, what had I been thinking? My head starts to spin as I remember his hands riding up my skirt, his fingers digging into my thighs, his mouth all over my tits. I run the tap and splash my face with cold water. *Get it together Charlotte, you've still got to get through this dinner.*

The last place I want to be right now is out with Frank. I've turned him down twice already though, and I really do need to stay on his good side if I want to keep hold of my work visa. The tricky bit is navigating a night out with him, without him getting the wrong impression. I figured that a little dinner wouldn't be too hard. He's married after all. I was hoping that his wife would be back by now, but as rumor has it, she isn't.

"Professor...Charlotte, over here!" Frank's half standing up, waving at me from across the room as I come out of the bathroom. He's wedged between the chair and the table he finally got us. I navigate the best I can through the sea of faces. The policy of this place is clearly just to shove in as many people as possible before the fire department shuts them down. As I pull my chair out, I accidentally knock into the man seated at the table next door. I apologize, and he winks at me. His female companion pretends not to notice and stuffs another piece of buttery salmon into her mouth. I'm not a huge fan of fish, but looking at the menu, there's nothing else on offer.

"I thought you'd got lost. I was about to send out a search party." Frank says it with disguised irritation in his voice.

"Sorry, there was a queue."

"A queue? Oh you silly Brits and your funny little words for things. We say *line* here."

"Yes, us silly Brits." I take a sip of water. *Patronizing prick*.

I look up as the waiter comes over with a bottle of champagne. "Are we celebrating something?" I look at Frank, and he nods for the waiter to fill our glasses, before placing the bottle into a small, silver bucket of ice.

"Yes, my dear, we're celebrating *you.*"

"I don't understand."

"Well, actually we're celebrating both of us. *Me*, for having been clever enough to hire you, and *you* for being so damned well..." He stares at my tits for a moment, "Damned well wonderful. Here's to you, Professor Charlotte Rose."

He raises his glass and I follow, clinking his, and taking a sip. I felt uncomfortable before, but now I'm in downright *hell*. I can feel the sweat start to form on the backs of my legs. Before the night is out, I'll be permanently stuck to this chair. Perhaps I can use this opportunity to talk about my career prospects, given that is the reason I agreed to this dinner after all. I flash a smile at him.

"Thank you, Frank. I'm so looking forward to working with you, for many more months to come."

"Now hold your horses there, young lady." He puts his glass down and waggles a finger at me.

The man might be Californian born and raised, but he sounds like he just walked off the set of Downton Abbey.

"Just because you're doing well so far, doesn't mean I'm going to automatically extend your work contract. You still have a way to go to prove yourself to me."

I don't like the way he says, *"Prove yourself to me."*

A knot forms in my stomach and I feel queasy. I don't want to show it though, so I smile, and take another sip of champagne.

"Of course not Frank, I wouldn't *dream* of being so presumptuous." I curl a piece of hair between my fingers and look up at him through my lashes. *Two can play at this game, asshole.*

He looks pleased with himself and tips back his glass. "More champagne?"

I hold out my glass and giggle, "Love some." I can play the dumb blonde all he wants as long as it gets me what I want. I've had practice at this for years.

We order and I continue to make polite conversation. Mostly, he just talks about himself, and I pretend to be interested. He tells me about his collection of model airplanes, his one trip to Paris, which he enjoyed, but was disappointed that the French didn't make more of an effort to speak more English. I keep a fixed smile on my face and nod occasionally, pushing the overpriced tuna around my plate. He says all this between great gulps of food. I gaze out of the window when he picks up a piece of bread and chews it with his mouth open. There's a man sitting on the patio looking out towards the ocean. His back is to me, and he has jet black hair that curls at the nape of his neck. For a second, I'm transported to this afternoon with my hands in Ethan's hair as he lifts me on the desk, and my hand searches for that dragon.

"Did you hear what I said Charlotte?"

"Hmm?" I turn back to Frank; his mouth is glistening from finishing the last of his mussels. I can't bear mussels. I imagine they're still alive when they slide down your throat, the sliminess of them grosses me out. He mops his brow and slouches back in his chair.

"I said what was Delaney doing in your classroom after hours again?" He raises his eyebrows at me as he says it.

Shit, why is he bringing this up now? Did he see something? He'd have said something earlier, surely.

I take a sip of champagne to buy some time and avert my eyes from his mouth. I wish to God, he'd wipe it. I'm tired and I really don't want to be doing this now.

"I was just giving him back his homework, going over a few things."

"I really wouldn't waste my time on that one."

I look up at him, *what is this animosity between them?* "Why do you say that?"

Finally, he dabs at his mouth with his napkin - *thank God*. He strums his fingers on the table, "He's trouble that's all, you'd be wise not to spend too much time on him. There are others who are much more worthy of your attention."

You mean, like you? I want to question him about it more, but I sense he won't like that. No, it's better if I just agree. "Whatever you think is best."

"Good, good." He gives the table a happy little slap, and his eyes glance down to my tits again. He wipes more perspiration from his brow with his napkin. I make a mental note to only wear turtlenecks around him in the future.

"So Frank, tell me about your wife." Perhaps this will get us on solid ground.

"My wife?"

"Yes, Elaine, isn't it?" I pretend that I'm not sure of her name, when in fact, the whole staff room is gossiping about her. He looks down and twists the gold wedding band on his finger. I left mine in the glass bowl by the front door when I left Charles. I stuck it in amongst the keys and random business cards. Frank picks up the bottle of champagne and pours the last of it into his glass - not bothering to ask me if I'd like some first.

"What do you want to know? "He seems uncomfortable that I've brought her up. I'm happy to make him squirm a bit.

"What does she do for a living?"

"She's on the city council- worked there for thirty-five years."

"How long have you been married?"

"Thirty years last month. We were supposed to be going to Hawaii for our anniversary, but she..." He waves his hands about a bit, "She had other plans."

I nod. I know what her other plans were - they involved a certain yoga teacher and his yurt in New Mexico. I act dumb. "I'm sorry. Is she still away?"

"Yes, on a course...for the city, a planning course." He loosens his tie; he's really starting to sweat now, and I've suddenly started to enjoy myself. I look at the time on the clock behind the bar. It's nearly ten. Surely, we've been here long enough now, and I can count this as one step closer to getting my contract extended. Without it, I have no visa and won't be able to stay in the country.

"Well Frank, it's been lovely but it's getting late and..." I start to stand.

"My wife's in New Mexico. She's gone away to find herself, or so she says. I...I, don't know when she's coming back." He blurts it out then looks down at his lap and for a moment I feel sorry for him. I can see his bald patch. It's presented to me like a pale egg, with a few wisps of hair plastered across it. His clothes are crumpled, and his fingernails are lined with dirt. I sit back down.

"I used to bring her here. She loves this restaurant. The owner's a good friend of mine."

What a surprise. I reach out to his hand on the table and squeeze it. It's pudgy and soft like a lump of clay, not like Ethan's worn masculine hands.

"I'm lonely Charlotte." He looks up at me, the whites of his eyes yellow. "You must be lonely here too. All on your own in a strange land."

"Oh, I'm used to being on my own. I'm quite enjoying living in a new country." I go to take my hand away, but he clamps down on it.

"It's funny isn't it."

"What is?" My heart is beginning to race. Instinctively, I look around for an escape route. *Old habits die hard.*

"It's funny, that I'm the person that gets to say whether you stay here or not." He's starting to slur his words. Two whiskeys at the bar and most of the champagne and he's drunk. He turns my hand over and starts running his fingers over my palm. Every fiber in my being is crawling with disgust.

"What do you mean?"

"Oh, you know what I mean, *Professor.* He spits the word at me. "I could choose not to continue to sponsor your work visa and *it's…bye, bye America.*"

I hate him.

His hand goes limp, and I snatch mine away. I indicate to the waiter to bring us the bill and pour Frank a large glass of water. "Here, drink this. You'll feel better." I slide him the glass and he gulps from it, dribbling half of it down his shirt. I get the feeling he started early today and has been knocking it back from that bottle in his desk. I'm trembling, but I don't want him to see it. I want to maintain my composure until I'm as far away from him as possible. I stand and help him up. "Come on, I'll call you a cab. You can't drive like that. What's your address?"

"I don't want to go home, *please* don't make me go home. It's lonely there. Can I come home with you?" *My God, he's pathetic.* He stumbles and one of the bus boys helps me get him upright again.

"No Frank, you can't. Is there anyone else you can stay with? A friend or a relative?"

"Take me to my sister's, she lives close by." Finally, some sense comes out of him. I'll drop him off there and then continue to my place.

Once outside, the fresh air seems to sober him up a bit. We wait in silence; I hope he feels *like total shit* tomorrow. When the cab arrives, I sit in the front. There's no way I'm getting in the back seat with him. My plan is to stay in the car whilst he gets out, I have no intention of letting his hands near me again. However, as soon as we pull up to his sister's house, it's obvious that there's some kind of party going on. Loud music is streaming through the open windows. The front door is open and there is a couple leaning against the frame. Frank opens the back door of the car and clambers out; it takes a few tries to get himself up to standing. I can see him in the wing mirror staring up at the house, his eyes glazed. He's swaying a little. He knocks on the passenger window. I want to ignore him, but his knocking just gets more frenzied. I let the window down.

"What is it, Frank?"

"I forgot that my sister's away this weekend. My nephew must be having a party."

"Well, enjoy yourself." I go to put the window back up, but he puts his hand on it, the fleshiness of it spills over the top. I'm tempted to just keep my finger on the button. "What now?" I'm over being polite to this guy tonight; I just want to go home and take a shower.

"Would you mind coming in with me? Give me some moral support. I'm afraid some of my students might baulk if they see me walk in. You might soften them a little, they like you. I really would owe you."

Yeah, you fucking would.

The last thing I want to do is go to some teenagers' house party- *especially with my boss.* Maybe though, this favor will be enough to add another six months to my contract. I sigh and reluctantly undo my seatbelt. The air is heavy with the smell of weed and I inhale. It's been a long time since I've smoked a joint. It was probably when I was in college with Lauren. We used to sneak out of the dorms at night and sit on the fire escape, huddled with a blanket around us, blowing smoke up to the stars, trying to find the big dipper. Maybe I could bum a joint off someone. Most of LA is high on any given night, though I'm sure Frank won't be up for it. I can smoke it on the balcony when I get home and tonight won't have been a complete waste of time. Frank straightens his tie and rubs his face. He's sobered up just enough to give the impression he's in control of himself.

The kissing couple don't bother to move as we pass through the front door. Frank averts his eyes and mutters, *excuse me*. I catch the eye of the girl, and she smiles at me, before turning back to the boy and sticking her lips on his. His hands are holding her hips and he pulls her towards him.

In my head they're Ethan's hands on my hips and he's about to pull off my panties. I shake my head, *enough Charlotte. It's over, you need to stop thinking about him. How wonderful it would be to be so young and carefree again though.*

The music's loud inside and there are more couples lounging around, some kids dancing. Frank rubs the collar of his shirt and clears his throat. I hope he isn't about to make an announcement. I look around, wondering who I can get a joint from, maybe the girl in the doorway will know.

"Oh dear, this won't do at all. I must find my nephew." He's in a panic. I don't want to run about the house looking for some errant teenager.

"Okay why don't you go and do that; I'll get myself a drink." He grunts in reply. I turn in the direction of the kitchen, intent on getting a glass of hard liquor when something across the room catches my attention. There are three people standing at the end of a pool table. I recognize one of the girls as Debbie, from class. The other girl I haven't seen before. She's petite and tanned with dark hair in a bob. She's wearing a crop top, showing off her toned body. They're pulling the t-shirt off someone and as it comes up, I see the black tail of a dragon. Ethan. He's here, shirtless! That hard body was under my hands this afternoon. Now he is here with two girls, and he's letting them undress him. He looks breathtaking, his shoulders broad, his stomach tight. His head is bowed and he's laughing, his black hair falling on his face. He hasn't noticed me yet. Time seems to stand still, what's he doing? Debbie sees me and waves, then Ethan turns and sees me. His face drops. He really is just a fuck boy isn't he. I feel like such an idiot.

"I see Delaney is the star of the show again." Frank's back, clearly unable to find his nephew.

"What does that mean?"

"Oh, you know, always has a little harem following him. He was the same in high school."

"In high school?"

"Yes, I had the displeasure of being his principal then. As I said to you earlier *-nothing but trouble that one.*" He leans into me as he says it, his breath stinking of booze. At least he's standing upright now though.

"I don't know what Gina sees in him. They've been on and off for as long as I can remember."

"Gina?"

"The girl with the bob, pretty little thing." Frank indicates to the other girl and waves at her. She heads towards us as Ethan pulls his t-shirt back over his head, and fusses with his hair.

"Principal Fletcher! OMG I forgot you were Carl's uncle! I haven't seen you *for years*." Gina exaggerates the years in a high-pitched girly voice, before turning her attention to me and giving me the once over. I can see Ethan from the corner of my eye talking to Debbie.

I just want to get the fuck out of here.

"I thought you were married, are you being *naughty?*" Ugh. She's talking to Frank in a baby voice as if she's flirting with him. Frank looks pleased that she thinks I'm his date.

"No, Gina, this is Professor Rose. We were out on a…work meeting and before dropping her home I thought I'd come and check on Carl."

Yeah right, that's exactly what happened.

Gina smirks, then looks at me from under her thick eyelashes. "So, *you're* the new professor. I've heard all about you." She points her finger at me on the *"you,"* and I wonder if Ethan's told her something about us. I swallow my nervousness and hold out my hand.

"It's very nice to meet you, Gina." She limply shakes it, not taking her eyes off me. Ethan comes over then, and everything becomes a blur. He might have said hello, but all I can see is Gina flinging her arms around him and saying, *"Baby cakes"* as if she's squeezing him with her voice as well as her tiny body. He shifts on his feet and keeps his arms by his side. He looks nervous as shit, *probably because I've shown up and his girlfriend is here.* I suddenly feel ridiculously warm.

"To be honest Frank, I'm feeling a little nauseous. I'm just going to pop outside to get some air."

"Oh dear, well let me come with you."

I put my hand on his chest to stop him. "No don't, I'll be fine. You need to find your nephew." I have to get outside; I can't breathe in here. I stumble out into the front yard and put my hand over my mouth. The champagne hasn't helped, and I feel like I'm going to vomit. I lean on a car in the driveway and take some deep breaths.

Okay. Okay. Fine. Ethan's inside and there are hot, twenty-one-year-olds flirting with him. Stripping him out of his clothes. At a party. And they're drunk. I'm not mad. I don't care. Whatever. It's not like it matters anyway.

Even the voice in my head sounds a little hysterical. I pace back and forth across the driveway, stabbing my fingers into my hair, huffing out breath after labored breath.

I mean, why the fuck should I care? He was all over me this afternoon and I was the one who told him to get the hell off me. I was the one who—

"Charlotte."

I freeze at the sound of Ethan's voice. *I just fucking can't with that voice right now.* I don't turn around, even though I can hear his footsteps coming closer. He puts his hand on my shoulder. "Fuck off!" I push him off me and he takes a couple of steps back. I know I'm acting *insane,* but I just can't stop myself.

"What's wrong?"

What's wrong? He had to be fucking joking, right?

"You're a *fuckboy* Ethan Delaney! I knew you were and yet I still let you...*twice!*" I start pacing again. I'm sure I look like a complete lunatic at this point. He comes closer to me, and I back myself up against the car.

"You're right, I'm an asshole."

I slap his face. He stares back at me in disbelief, but he doesn't move. "*I hate you.*" I go to push him away, but he pins my arms against the car. His face is in mine now, *his beautiful, goddamn Botticelli face.*

"Why do you care what I do? You told me you weren't interested. Did you expect me to wait around for you to change your mind?"

His arrogance is maddening! I try to get away, but he holds me firm against the car.

"Do you care about me, Charlotte? Because you're sure as fuck acting like you do." His dark eyes are searching my face.

How can I tell him that he's all I think about, that pushing him away today was the hardest thing I've had to do. That every time I look in his eyes -I see God or something, or the starry belt of the universe - or all the way back to the beginning of time. That my mouth waters every time I get the image in my head of where that dragon leads.

"No."

He lets go of me and takes a step back, "So what's the problem then?"

I put my arms behind my back and stare down at my feet. It's easier if I don't look at his face. "I just didn't expect to see you here, that's all. Especially with your...*It sticks in my throat to say it*...your girlfriend."

He folds his arms, "What are you talking about, *my girlfriend?*"

"Gina. Frank told me all about her."

"She's not my girlfriend. We used to date. She's staying with me right now until she finds her own place. I wish to God, she wasn't. There's nothing going on between us."

"Why should I believe you? Why would Frank lie?"

"Because he's a piece of shit! Haven't you worked that out?"

"Of course, I have. I just had the most hideous night of my life with him. He, he..."

"He what?" I can hear a hint of anger in his voice.

I shake my head, "No. no its nothing. I can handle it. I'm just tired and..." I can feel the tears well up though, and I can't stop them. All the emotion about Charles and the letter, Frank's behavior tonight and seeing Ethan with those girls...it all floods out. I'm standing in a driveway at a teenager's party and I'm crying... it's like I'm fifteen all over again.

"Hey, it's okay." Suddenly Ethan's arms are around me and I don't push him away. I press my face into his t-shirt - it smells so unmistakably of him. He pulls me closer. I try to catch my breath and instead begin to hiccup, just when I thought tonight couldn't be any more humiliating.

He looks down at me and grins impishly. "Have you got the hiccups?"

"No." I hiccup again. "Yes, I get them sometimes when I'm upset."

He puts his hand up to my face and wipes my wet cheeks. He does it so delicately that my heart skips a bit. It feels too intimate. So, I pull myself out from his arms and run my hand under my nose, *that must look attractive.*

"What are you doing here?"

"Debbie invited me." He says it nonchalantly.

"On a date?"

He shrugs his shoulders, "No, just a bit of fun. To be honest. I needed the distraction." He runs his hands through his hair.

"From what?"

"From thinking about you every damn minute."

His comment catches me off guard and I put my hand on the car to steady myself. His lopsided smile is making my heart do butterflies in my mouth. I think I'm going to hiccup again, but thank God it doesn't come.

"You seemed to be doing a fairly good job at distracting yourself. You were half naked in there."

He raises his eyebrows at me and tilts his head to the side. "Yeah. We were playing pool and I bet my t-shirt that Debbie couldn't sink the eight ball." He shrugs his shoulders, "I lost."

"Ethan, it's your turn to play pool. Are you coming back inside?" It's Gina, her small scowly figure, appearing in the doorway. There's a rambling red rose climbing over the porch, some of its petals have fallen to the ground by her feet.

"In a minute." Ethan doesn't turn to look at her; he keeps his eyes fixed on me.

"But we're waiting for you."

"Don't."

"Well don't forget I'm coming home with you." She gives me the once over again, before going back inside.

"She seems friendly..."

"She's a lot, but she's harmless." I'm not sure if I believe him. I saw the look Gina gave me and it didn't seem harmless.

"You'd better go back inside; I'll call myself a cab."

"I'm not leaving you here. I'll take you home, Gina can get a ride with Debbie."

"No thanks. I'm a big girl, I can take care of myself. Besides, I'm sure they'll want to play more *strip pool.*" I sound like a jealous teenager, but my mouth has a mind of its own as usual.

"I'd rather play strip pool with you."

I feel my cheeks flush pink. "That's not going to happen."

"Isn't it?"

"No, we already had this conversation today, remember?"

"I don't believe you."

I've never met anyone so cock sure of themselves. But I'm not surprised, having seen just exactly the perfection hiding in his pants. I bite my lip.

Should I tell him the truth? That I'm afraid I'm just like my husband? That I've taken advantage of my position? He doesn't even know I have a husband! I lied to him and said that that was all over a long time ago.

"You're my student, it's not right."

"I'll switch classes."

"No, I don't want you to do that. It's not fair. We just...We just..."

"Just what?"

"We just...can't."

He takes a few steps towards me. The moon is full and fat above us, its light illuminating his face. He must have inherited his bone structure from a lineage of a thousand beautiful men. If I reach out, I can touch him, run my fingers along the cut of his jaw. He looks like a fallen angel standing over me and, despite everything I just said, I'm not sure I can resist him anymore. I can just make out the jagged line of his scar under his stubble. I place my finger on it and trace it. For some reason, I'm mesmerized by it.

"Are you going to tell me how you got that?"

"I already told you; I can't remember."

He's lying. I'm not the only one with secrets.

He takes hold of my finger and gently kisses the tip of it. "We're not doing anything wrong Charlotte. We're both adults. Why don't we just see where this takes us?"

"What if it takes us somewhere terrible?"

"What if it takes us somewhere fucking amazing?"

My mind wants to say no, but my heart won't let it. I've spent too many years doing what my mind told me to and where has that got me? Wasn't the whole point of this move, to start again? To try something new? I want to kiss him so badly right now. I glance over at the house, but I can't risk Frank or Gina seeing us. Ethan must have read my mind.

"Come on, I'm parked out on the street." He holds out his hand, and I slip mine into it as he leads me away from the house.

We take a slow drive back to my place. He puts his right hand on my leg at the hem of my dress, then slides it underneath. My whole-body tingles as it travels up my thigh. I part my legs and tense in anticipation of what he's going to do next. But his fingers just stay there, skimming and tracing the lace of my panties, teasing me. I keep glancing at him, but he keeps his eyes locked on the road. Eventually I lay my head back against the seat, enjoying his hands grazing my thighs. We pull up to a red light and his fingers slip under the lace and start stroking me. I want them inside of me and I raise my hips a little. He obliges and slides one finger into my wetness. He still doesn't look at me, his face is concentrated on the road ahead and his sharp jaw is set. He's not acknowledging that he's got one hand on the wheel and the other one is *finger fucking me.* In between changing gears, he keeps dipping his finger it in and out of me, rubbing up against my clit then fucking me with it. I want to scream with the pleasure of it, but instead I bite down hard on my lip.

"Take them off." It's the only thing he says to me as he pulls away from the light. I take my panties off and throw them in the center console. I spread my legs and I can see his dick swell beneath his jeans. I reach my hand over to undo the fly, but he pushes it away.

"Do you want us to crash, Charlotte?"

"I want to see your hard cock, Ethan; I want to see it sticking out of your jeans." My mouth is watering at the thought of it. "I promise I'll only look, not touch." *That's a bare faced lie.* He glances at me, his pupils wide, his wild hair falling in them. *Fuck, I want to sit on his face.* I reach my hand over to his jeans again and, this time, he lets me pop the button and pull down his zipper. His dick springs up in all its perfection and it takes every inch of will power not to undo my seatbelt, lean over, and suck the cum out of him. Instead, I wrap my hand around his thick shaft and glide it up and down.

"Fuck, Charlotte. I said no." His voice is raspy, and both his hands are on the wheel now.

"Don't tell me what to do." I whisper it into his ear before flicking it with my tongue. The car veers to the left and I fall back in my seat as Ethan steadies it.

"I thought you were a good driver."

"I'm a great fucking driver, but your hand on my dick is a fucking liability. Now, sit back, open your legs, and touch yourself. I wanna hear your moan."

I do as he asks. I find my clit and start to rub it, circling it with my finger, then pushing my hips up. Every so often he glances over, his cock still sticking out of his pants, straining upwards.

"Let me taste you."

I take my finger from my pussy and put it in his mouth, he sucks on it then licks it clean. "You taste so good; you have the best tasting little cunt." I put my wet finger back inside me. I'm so turned on, I could cum right now, but I will really want his tongue inside me for that.

We pull up into the carport outside my apartment and he switches off the engine. He lets the car tick over for a minute, before he turns to me wolf like. He knows what I want and leans his seat back. I snap open my seat belt, climb over to his side and straddle him. His hands are in my hair, and I kiss him hard on the mouth. Our tongue's search each other's out. He pushes my dress up around my waist, then slides himself down. He puts his hands under my ass, and I hold onto the back of his seat and push his face between my legs. The only light is coming from the moon outside and its shining on him again, highlighting every inch of his beauty. I hold my breath as he grins up at me then slowly licks my pussy up and down, his whole tongue lapping at me. I'm so horny from the car drive, it's not going to take long for me to cum. He digs his tongue into me, finding my clit and I move up and down on it. He delves in further, his hands gripping my ass, my hands clawing at his hair. My body shudders as I grind into his face, he moans, "*Good girl, Charlotte*" and eats me out like he's *fucking starving*. I explode quickly, the sound of my orgasm ripping through my chest and out of my mouth. The car windows are open and the night swallows my orgasm, whole. He kisses each one of my thighs as I pull back, but I'm not done with him yet.

"Take off your jeans." I order him and he groans as he slides them off his ass. He sits back upright, and I push straight down on his hard cock.

"My God, Charlotte." His eyes roll back as he enters me, and I wrap my legs around him. I knock my left knee into the gear stick. There's not a lot of room in the Mustang, but I don't care, I plan to fuck his brains out in here. His mouth is on mine again and I'm riding him, hard. I want him so far up me; I want him to split me in two. I've missed his dick so much, I've never been obsessed with that part of a man before, but it's like Ethan's has possessed me.

"I haven't got a condom, have you?" He's gasping it out at me, as I circle my hips on his cock each time I push down.

"No, just pull out."

"You think I have that kind of will power?"

I bite him on the neck, and he plunges further into me. "No." I whisper. I want his cum inside me. I want to be full of it, to carry that part inside me all night. I'm on the pill, but I've been a bit hap hazard with it lately, so rationally I know it's not a good idea. Rational Charlotte isn't in control, though. I pull my dress off over my head and my tits fall out into his face, he groans, and his cock pushes into me so deep that I clutch onto him. He sucks and tugs on my nipples whilst I gyrate up and down on him. I love knowing that I'm driving him wild, that this gorgeous beast is deep inside me and has lost all control.

"Charlotte, I..." His legs start to shake, and I know he's close. I move faster. I want to fuck him dry. "Christ, I can't hold it..." He puts his hands under my ass and pulls me off him, I reach my hand down and stroke him as his body jerks and cum spurts out all over my stomach. The reality of what just happened hits me *and thank fuck* one of us had some sense. I will be more careful with taking my pill from now on. I put my hands on the side of his face and kiss it all over. "Thank you for pulling out."

He takes a minute to catch his breath. "You didn't make it easy."

"I don't make anything easy, Ethan." I look directly into his eyes and wonder if he knows what he's getting into. *Do I even know?* I just fucked a student in his car and now I plan to take him inside and fuck him all night. I'm too far gone to think about consequences though. I want this man, and to hell with whatever heartbreak comes with it.

Chapter Fourteen

Charlotte

I open my eyes and squint at the bedside clock; it's already ten am. I close my eyes again and stretch. I've woken up late today. The students have a free study period ahead of our test this week, so I don't have to go in until one. It's nice to have a Monday morning in bed for a change, and I plan to make the most of the next hour in bed. I roll over, expecting to find Ethan's warm body next to me but when I reach out, he's not there. The sheets on his side are crumpled and cold. I sit upright, a hard knot in my chest. I'm normally a light sleeper, I must've passed out; because I didn't hear him leave. I reach for my phone, there aren't any texts from him. I pull the duvet up around me and hug my knees. I can still smell him on it and pull it closer under my chin. *Where is he?* The last two mornings he's roused me early: his body spooning into mine. His hardness pressed against me as I pushed my ass against him. He'd moan into my neck as I parted my legs, and he'd slip his cock deep into my pussy, fucking me for the hundredth time in two days. His hands reaching round to my tits, pinching my nipples between those expert fingers of his. Then down between my legs, searching for my clit - teasing it and circling it- whilst he fucked me slowly until one of us came, then the other. We hardly left my apartment, except to get a little dinner on Saturday night. We went to a tiny bistro on the corner of Montana Avenue, with fairy lights strung up outside. Summer jasmine and papery bougainvillea vines twisted around the patio. The waiters brought us red wine and homemade bread with rosemary butter, rigatoni thick with a sage and mascarpone sauce, and then tiramisu laced with a rich coffee liquor. Couples talked softly to each other under the twinkly lights. We walked home along the beach promenade, Ethan's arms around my shoulders, giggling and kissing each other. It's been the most wonderful weekend of my life - and now he's not here. *Did I dream it?* No, his hoodie is still on the chair. I swing my legs out of the bed onto the cold wood floor and pad over to it, pulling it over my head and down my naked body, bringing the sleeves over my hands. I feel like a little girl in it. I walk back over to the bed to get my phone, and I almost skid on something. It's a piece of folded paper, I open it.

C

Gone home to get clean clothes. Going into work for a couple hours.

See you in class. I'll be the one at the back, looking bored.

E x

PS. Try not to miss me too much. Difficult, I know.

I sit back down on the edge of the bed. Relief curses through me. The breeze through the open window must've knocked his note onto the floor. I *love* his handwriting, the way he carves the C of my name; the looseness of it. It's nothing like the tight handwriting on the letter from England hidden in the closet. I realize that this is the first time I've thought about that letter since Friday. I lean back on a pillow and close my eyes. On Saturday night after dinner, we stopped at the liquor store and got more wine. We drank it outside on my private little deck overlooking the ocean. The moon was silver and bright and there wasn't a cloud in the sky. The only sounds were a few late seagulls and the waves rushing over the pebbles on the shore. I sat on the ground with my head in his lap, whilst he stroked my hair and whispered all the things he planned to do to me later. Hot, filthy things that made me so horny I unzipped his fly, took out his cock and knelt in front of him.

I sucked him off right there, with the sound of his moans drifting out towards the horizon. I lick my lips, remembering the taste of his pre cum, and how excited he got as I tipped my head back and took all of him in, letting the tip of his dick hit the back of my throat. I've never wanted a man's cock as badly as I want Ethan's. I want it to fill every part of me. I trail my hand down between my legs and slide my fingers inside my panties. I'm wet from thinking about him. We took some photos of each other over the weekend. I want to touch myself and look at a picture of his naked body standing over me, his hair messy in his face; the intense look of desire in his eyes right before he fucks me. I go for my phone to find the photograph I want. It's been on silent, and there's a missed call and a voicemail. I put the phone to my ear and listen to the message.

"Charlotte, please call me as soon as you get this." It's from Penny, Charles's secretary. She was a good friend of mine once, but I haven't spoken to her since I left my job at the University. There's an urgency to her voice that knocks any thoughts of a lazy morning orgasm out of my head. My heart is in my mouth, my hands tremble as I press the redial button.

"Charlotte!"

"Hi Penny, Is everything okay?" The words choke in my mouth. I'm greeted with silence, then there's another voice in my ear.

"I miss you. I'm lost without you darling. When are you coming home?"

The sound of my husband's voice stabs me in the stomach, and I almost double over. The room pitches like a fair ground ride. My mind goes back to a particular night a few months ago. He'd been away for two weeks at a conference, or at least that's what he told me. It had been so lovely, having the place to myself. It was easier to breathe when he wasn't there. He came home a night early though, crept into the house and snuck up behind me. By the time I realized I wasn't alone, his hand was covering my mouth stifling my scream.

"That's no way to greet your husband." My body froze. I thought about biting down on his hand but knew that it would only excite him. He sniffed and licked my neck like I was a piece

of meat, and I had to swallow my disgust. I made myself go limp so that he'd move his hand from my mouth. I took a step forward, but he pulled me back, his arms reached round my waist. "I've missed you, Charlotte." I tried to bat his hand away as he fumbled under my shirt, but he grabbed hold of my wrists.

"You're hurting me." I told him, but that only made him hold them tighter.

"Why are you always so difficult?"

"Let me go Charles."

"Why should I? You're my wife."

"That doesn't mean I'm your property." I pushed against him and managed to free myself, but he still had a grip of one of my arms.

"Get the fuck off me!" I screamed at him as he pulled me back towards him.

"Don't you ever raise your voice again to me, you bitch." His lip curled and a vein on his neck bulged with rage. I didn't see his other hand come up to hit me until it was too late.

That was the night I knew I had to plan my escape.

"Charlotte, Charlotte are you still there?" Penny's voice startles me back into the present. Sorry he just snatched the phone off me. I ..."

I hang up on her and throw the phone across the bed. The taste of acid is back in my mouth. I go to the bathroom and squeeze some toothpaste on the brush, but my hands are shaking so much that I can't hold it. I toss it in the sink and lean over the basin. I can feel the beginnings of a panic attack. I'd stuffed the memory of that night deep down somewhere. I can still smell the alcohol on his breath, and the candle I had burning on the kitchen table. I haven't been able to bear the smell of sandalwood since. I sit on the toilet as the room starts to spin again.

Breathe Charlotte, breathe. He's not here, he's thousands of miles away, He can't hurt you here.

I put my head between my legs and focus on my breath going down into my stomach. Why did I even call her back? *Penny's a total cow*, I should have known it was a set up. She's like my husband's little lap dog. The last time I saw her was the night I left my job at the university. We all went out to celebrate my fresh start; *what a joke that was.* There was a cute blonde waitress serving us, Charles was drooling over her all night. I saw Penny talking to her in the corner for a bit but thought nothing of it. In the taxi on the way home Charles pulled a piece of paper from his pocket, it had the waitress's number on it. Penny had got her number for him. He told me as much, laughing at the look on my face, before folding it up and throwing it at me. He wanted to screw her; it was just that he enjoyed the power play over me more. He needed me to know that he could get whoever he wanted.

I lean to the side, and rest my head against the cool tiles. I can't be alone with my thoughts right now. I need to call Lauren. I get up and go back into the bedroom and retrieve my phone from the duvet. I pick it up like it's been poisoned. My hands tremble as I call her.

"Lauren."

"Hey, what's up? You sound out of breath."

"Did you tell Charles where I am?"

"What?"

"Charles. I need to know if you told him that I'm in LA."

"No! Fuck, why would you even ask me that?"

I sit down on the bed and try to calm down. I know that Lauren would never betray me like that, I just had to hear her say it.

"I'm sorry, he just called me and I'm freaking the fuck out."

"How did he call you? I thought you had him blocked on everything."

"I do, but Penny, his secretary, rang me saying it was urgent. Then his voice came on the phone."

"*Motherfucker!* What the hell is he playing at? What the fuck is Penny playing at? I always thought she was a two-faced bitch."

I love that Lauren doesn't mix her words. I start to feel a little better, knowing she's on my side. "I'm sorry, I didn't even ask if you could talk, I just landed stuff on you."

"I'm just balancing a child on my hip and stirring the spaghetti sauce for dinner that no one is going to appreciate, so yeah, I can talk. What did he say?"

"That he misses me, and he's lost without me. I mean that's just bullshit."

"Not necessarily."

"Oh, don't tell me you believe him!"

"Of course not! I do believe that his giant ego is lost without you though. His beautiful, clever wife has up and left him. Do I think he *genuinely* gives a shit? No."

"True." I sit back on the bed and pull Ethan's hoodie over my knees. "He's broken the no contact rule twice now though."

Lauren laughs. "As If Charles gives a shit about rules, he thinks he's above them. Hold on, I have to take Molly off before my side seizes up."

I hear her move away from the phone and talk in a soft baby voice to her daughter. I always knew she would make a great mother.

"Okay, I'm back. I wish I had wine for this conversation, but I just put the last of it in the sauce."

I smile. "How are you going to cope?"

"I'm not sure. I might have to get Paul to pick some up on the way home - when he eventually leaves the office. He was in charge of the booze when we went grocery shopping, but he forgot. Too busy on a work call."

I can hear the frustration in her voice. I remember years ago when her husband first got that job, she was so excited *"We can finally afford to rent a place that doesn't shake every time a bus goes past."* Now, whenever she talks about him, she seems irritated.

"Is everything okay with, Paul?"

"Yeah, he's just working late, again." She sighs, "It seems we have no time together these days."

"I'm sorry."

"Don't be, he's working his ass off so we can afford a mortgage on a house in the country." She pauses, "At least that's what I keep telling myself. I want my kids to know what the outdoors is before it's too late. I swear Elliott was born with an iPad clutched in his hands. Anyway, any updates with hottie mechanic man?"

"You mean Ethan."

"If he's the *'Under the stars, one night stand'* guy, then yes."

I laugh and pick up his note before it gets lost in the covers. I rub my finger over it. "Actually, we've had more than a one-night stand."

"You slept with him again?"

"From Friday to Sunday." I can't help smiling when I say it.

"*OMG you had a sexathon!* Paul and I haven't had a sexathon for years. I need more information this time. Does he have a big cock?"

"I hope Molly can't hear you!"

"Molly is barely a year old, the only two words she understands are 'dog' and 'biscuit'...we're so proud."

"Ha ha! His cock is big, yes, and it's *purrfect* and he's given me more orgasms since I met him, than my husband managed in ten years."

"Okay, you need to make that the first line of your next book and you need to dedicate it to Charles!"

I laugh, "Can you imagine?"

'Give me a sec.' I hear Lauren moving around in the kitchen, opening cupboards, and getting dinner plates out. She hums as she does it. For all her complaining about it, I know she loves being at home with her family.

"So, when are you seeing him again?"

"This afternoon, in class."

"How on earth are you managing to focus with him in it?"

"I just avoid looking at him."

Lauren snorts, "Didn't you try that tactic before *and fail*?"

"Yes, but it's different now, I'm no longer actively trying to resist him."

"Yeah, but sex flashbacks Char! You might get one halfway through. Do you remember that time in Rio, when I was doing the history teacher and we had to teach a class together?"

"Yes, and *I* had to take over because it was so obvious! But it's alright, I'm hoping that my years of teaching experience will pay off."

"I bet he loves that you're his professor."

"He probably gets a kick out of it."

"What does he think about you being married?"

"I haven't told him. Well, I told him I've been married in the past." There's silence on the other end of the phone. "Lauren?"

"Sorry, I'm just a bit confused as to why you would lie to him?"

My hands feel clammy in my lap, "I don't know why, it just sort of came out like that. I didn't want to talk about Charles. I felt like just saying his name would ruin things." I sit higher up against the headboard and put my knees down, Ethan's hoodie rides up to my thighs.

"Just saying his name won't conjure him up! He's not a fucking genie, Charlotte." I hear her opening and closing the fridge.

"I know it was stupid, but it would be weird to tell him now, wouldn't it?"

"No, you could just be honest with him. I'm sure he won't care, it's just a summer fling after all."

"I think it might be more than just a fling, Lauren." I bite my lip as I say it, it's the first time I've considered this out loud.

"He's *twenty-three years old* Charlotte, it's never going to be anything more than a fling."

"You don't know that."

"*Elliott, can you tell your brother and your grandma that dinner's ready? Also make sure she remembers to put her skirt on this time and leave your iPad upstairs!* Sorry, Mary's going through a stage where she either forgets to get dressed or puts on all her clothes at once. What were you saying?"

"I was saying you don't know him. He's not like any guy in his twenties I've ever met. He's mature, for a start. We have a connection I can't describe."

"Oh lord, not that again. You have a connection to his cock! For god's sake you're high on oxytocin right now from all that sex, you're not thinking straight."

She's pissing me off now, I called her for reassurance - not this.

"I am thinking straight. It's as if I knew him in another life or something."

Silence on the other end of the line again, and I know a lecture is coming.

"Now I understand why you haven't told him you're married. You think this is the new love of your life. You're going to get hurt, you haven't been with anyone but Charles since your twenties. It's like you're a teenager all over again. By all means fuck his brains out, but don't make out it's something it's not."

"I thought I'd have your support."

"You *always* have my support, but I wouldn't be a friend if I didn't call you out on this bullshit fantasy that you're going to end up with this guy! From what you've told me- he's the hottest thing on two legs. Guys like that don't hang about, especially not with a married woman twelve years older than them. I don't want you to get hurt. You're just pulling yourself out of an awful, mind fuck of a marriage, and you need to figure shit out. Don't get distracted, you have to keep this job if you want to stay in America. Having a full-blown love affair with a student isn't going to help that."

I don't say anything for a minute. I can hear Lauren's family clattering into the kitchen. *Am I living in a fantasy world? It was only on Friday that I called Ethan a fuck boy*

"Also, what happens if this does end up being more than just fun like you think it is, and then he finds out you're still married! What happens then? You haven't thought this through. You know I'm only saying this because I love you."

I know she is, I'm just not in the right state of mind to hear any hard truths just yet. "I love you too."

"Okay, gotta go. My mother in law's come downstairs with just her tights on again."

I hang up the phone feeling deflated. I put Ethan's note in the drawer beside the bed. I'm having the best time of my life right now and I don't want Charles or Lauren to pull me away from that.

Chapter Fifteen

Ethan

I open the front door as quietly as I can, not wanting to disturb Gina. I want to grab some clean clothes for today and get out of here. It's 7am and she's not an early riser, so hopefully I can get in and out without waking her up. She texted me early Saturday morning asking where I was. I told her I was staying with a friend, and she texted back, "Who?" I didn't bother to reply to that, or to any of her subsequent texts. I should never have let her stay here after we broke up; it's as if she thinks I need her permission to do anything. We shouldn't have got back together in the first place. I thought it would ease the guilt, it didn't. As much as I've enjoyed spending the last few days in Charlotte's bed, let me rephrase that, as much as I've *fucking loved t*he last few days, I've got to sort this Gina situation out. However, right now I'm too tired, and it's too early to have that conversation. Besides, I don't want anything to break my mood, I'm high from such a great weekend. I collect some toiletries from the upstairs bathroom and the mirror reveals how exhausted I am. I need a shave and dark circles have formed under my eyes. I guess a weekend of nonstop fucking will do that. Now to just pick up some clean clothes and get the hell out of here, but as I open my door, I see there is someone on my bed. I turn on the light.

"What the fuck are you doing Gina?" Shielding her eyes from the light, she sits up and I see now that she's wearing one of my t-shirts, my *favorite t*-shirt.

"You're back."

"What are you doing in my room, in my bed, in my t-shirt?"

"You make me sound like Goldilocks."

I instinctively bring my hand to my face and rub my chin. I'm not going to let her joke her way out of this one.

"I missed you baby." She also looks like she hasn't slept all weekend. She has mascara smudges under her eyes and her hair looks unwashed. She grabs a pillow and hugs it. This is going to be difficult. As angry as I am with her, I don't want to hurt her. She was, after all, there during the hardest time of my life and I didn't exactly treat her well. Maybe this is my karma; her having a *total mental fucking breakdown* in my bed. I walk over and sit at the end of the bed. She hides her face behind the pillow.

"What's going on Gina?" She brings the pillow down and begins to pick at the edges. For a second, she looks like the eight-year-old Gina I knew - my best friend. I take a breath in and remind myself to go easier on her.

"Nothing."

"It doesn't look like nothing. I go away for three days and when I come home it's like *'Single White Female'* in here."

"I was just worried about you. I didn't know where you were, and I missed you. I wanted to feel close to you."

Shit, I'm not sure how I'm supposed to handle this.

"I thought I made it very clear when I let you stay here - that I was just helping you out as a friend. We're not fifteen anymore. We both knew it wasn't working out the second time around. We've moved on - I've moved on- I thought you had too?"

She doesn't respond and instead brings the pillow up again.

"I'm sorry if you thought otherwise, the last person in the world I want to hurt is you." She doesn't say anything, just keeps staring into space. She looks so lost, and I remember her as a little girl again. Both of us eight years old when life was still innocent.

"I think it's best if I just give you some time alone." I get up and start throwing some clean clothes into my gym bag. I can stay with Charlotte for the next few days.

"Are you going to stay with your *friend* again?"

"No, I'm probably going to stay with Rob & Mo."

"You can't stand your brother."

"If I can stomach working with him, I can stay with him for a few days whilst you find somewhere else."

"So, you're kicking me out now?"

"No, stay as long as you need to. I've packed enough here to last me a while."

I pick my bag up and look at her. She looks like she's about to cry. I'm obviously not dealing with this well.

"Look, why don't I give your mom a call, and see if she can come and spend a few days with you."

"I'm not a sick child." She throws the pillow at me, and I catch it.

"Well, you're sure as hell behaving like one!"

"Can you get out please?"

"I'm trying to!" I turn to go, but I'm still not sure if she's okay. I'll text her mom as soon as I leave. Even though I'm not her favorite person in the world these days, she needs to come and take care of her daughter.

"Why didn't you choose me? You never choose me!"

"I don't know what you're talking about." I know exactly what she's talking about, but I'm not going to let her know that.

"Liar!" She's kneeling on the bed now, looking like she's going to throw another pillow at me.

"You're fucking that Professor! I'm not stupid, I saw you both standing by the car. I saw the way you looked at her. That's where you've been, isn't it!" She's screaming at me. There's no use talking to her when she is like this.

"I'm going to go now, but we can talk later. You can stay here while you figure things out; I'll move out for a bit."

"You're going to her aren't you! I hate you!" I hear the pillow hit the door as I close it. I go down the stairs and text Gina's mother. I hope she can calm her daughter down. I'm going to have to deny anything is happening with Charlotte. I can't risk her losing her career over me. I get into my car as quickly as I can, shift it into reverse, and back off the driveway. I look up, half expecting to see Gina throw something down at me from the bedroom window.

"You look like shit."

"Thanks bro."

"You get any sleep lately?"

"Enough." I know he's trying to needle me. I haven't come into work since Friday morning, and he's pissed that I took Saturday off. It's been the same since I was a kid, trying to get under my skin to provoke a reaction. He probably lost at poker again last night and needs someone to take it out on. The best way to deal with Rob when he's like this, is to ignore him.

"You got my schedule in the office?"

"No need to check that, you can wax the two cars that are being signed out today."

We normally save that job for the apprentices. He's punishing me, but I don't want to get into it with him this morning. He's looking for a fight and I'm not going to give him one. I put down my keys and go fetch the supplies I need from the cupboard. I need a distraction from what happened this morning. I see that Rob has got himself a coffee and hasn't bothered to ask if I want one. He pulls up a stool, intent on watching me by the looks of it. I ignore him and just start to get on with the job at hand.

"Gina came over last night."

I hesitate for a moment, what am I supposed to say? The car isn't dry yet from its wash, so I grab a small towel from the shelf. "Oh yeah."

"Yeah. She thinks you've been sleeping with that English Professor."

My stomach knots. I don't want to give my brother any more information than I have to. I shrug my shoulders, "Does she?"

"Yeah, she does. Said last time she saw you; you were talking to her outside a party, and you haven't been home since."

I put the towel down. "I'm a grown-up Rob, last time I checked I can see who I want."

Coffee comes out of his nose. "God damn it, you're fucking your professor. You've only been in that class a few weeks, and you fuck it up by fucking your professor. You just can't help yourself, can you, my God you're a piece of work."

I don't recognize my brother these days. He looks as if he asked the world for a fight and lost. *Who has he become?* The drinking and the gambling have taken its toll on him. He's even cheated on his wife a few times. He spent the night afterwards, either on the sofa in the office, or in my spare room - feeling too guilty to go home. I don't know why I let him, I felt like shit betraying Mo like that. I've watched my brother lie to his wife time after time. I turn and look at my brother squarely in the face.

"If we're going to talk about choices Rob, why don't we talk about the last time you cheated on your wife?"

He flexes his knuckles, and his face keeps getting redder, but he doesn't say anything. I doubt he wants a rerun of my fist slamming into his jaw.

"You go about your business brother, and I'll go about mine. Now I'm going into the office to get the schedule your wife has printed out for me. If you want those cars polished, do them yourself." I throw the towel at him and walk away, unclenching my fist as I do.

Chapter Sixteen

Charlotte

Frank's waiting for me on the college steps. As soon as he sees me arrive, he takes a comb out of his pocket, and runs it through the last few strands of hair on his head. I wave to him, and he raises his hand quickly before looking around sheepishly. He probably doesn't want to draw attention to the fact that he's out here waiting for me. I hope he isn't going to give me any trouble. He texted me on Friday night, asking where I was. I didn't see the message until Saturday afternoon, as I was too busy getting naked with Ethan. I texted him back that I'd felt sick, so I got a cab home and still wasn't fully recovered. He asked if he could bring me anything. It seems like a nice gesture on the surface, but I know what Frank really wants, especially after his behavior at dinner. I wonder if Gina has said anything to him, she must have her suspicions after seeing me outside talking to Ethan.

I reach into the back seat of my car for my textbooks, taking the opportunity to smooth down my own hair. I want to make sure it still looks perfectly severe. I've deliberately dressed conservatively today; I'm not taking any more chances with Frank. I'm wearing a navy linen trouser suit with a cream shirt buttoned up to the neck. My hair is in a tight bun. Studying myself side on in the mirror before I left, I look quite the school mistress, particularly when I put my glasses on. I don't want Frank to get any ideas and I knew he would want to see me today. I head across the parking lot to the entrance, the sound of my heels on the concrete is extra loud - as if they're echoing in my head. I must be feeling extra self-conscious. I wonder if the students I pass are gossiping about me, or worse - if Frank suspects anything about me and Ethan.

"Hello Frank." I smile widely at him and take hold of his outstretched hand.

"Charlotte...I mean. Professor Rose" he leans in closer "I think it's best you call me, Dean or Mr. Fletcher; you know just around the students. There's some talk, I understand, after being spotted together at the party."

"Of course."

Oh great, people are gossiping that we're having an affair. He seems to think after our dinner together, that there's now some sort of intimacy between us that mustn't be revealed. He probably started the rumor about us.

"I trust you're feeling better, I was very concerned about you. Especially after you rushed out like that. I hope it wasn't dinner. I would feel terribly guilty if it was." He puts his hand on the small of my back and leaves it there, as he ushers me through the doors.

I want to say, *"No, actually it was a hot twenty-three-year-old that I had to go home and fuck, so please take your goddamn hands off me."*

"No Frank…Dean…Mr. Fletcher, I think it was a bug of some sort."

He gets closer to me and lowers his voice as we walk down the corridor together. "Now what I told you about Elaine, my wife, I don't want it to become common knowledge, not a good look for my wife to have left me." As if the whole school didn't already know.

"I won't tell a soul." We stop outside my classroom, and he places his hand on my arm, then looks at me intently as if he's seeing me for the first time today.

"You look different Charlotte; did you do something different with your hair?"

"No, I just put it up."

"Hmm suits you, you look like a stern school mistress." He winks as he says it.

Marvelous, the very thing that was supposed to turn him off has only encouraged him.

I laugh it off, "I must get into class and get things set up."

"Yes of course." He says that, but then leans against the door, resting his elbow on it, blocking my way.

"I hear through the grapevine that you've instilled a new love of poetry in our students." He hitches his pants up with his other hand and thinks I don't notice.

"Well, I introduced them to Neruda, amongst others."

"Ah yes, who cannot love *Neruda? The moon dwells in one's skin."* That isn't how the line goes at all. He says it in a voice that I suppose he thinks is poetic. I force a smile. Ethan read the actual line aloud to me in bed yesterday when I was going over homework. It had a vastly different effect on me, than Frank's bad attempt at it. I'm going to have to accept the fact that anytime I'm around Frank - my skin is just going to crawl.

"Yes, one of my favorite lines of his. Okay, see you later." I turn the door handle and open it, his arm falls, and he pulls himself upright.

"Ah yes sorry, goodbye. I hope we..."

I close the door behind me pretending I haven't heard him; I lay my books on the desk along with the photocopies of the poems I'm going to hand out today. My students really seem to be enjoying the lessons on poetry. I'm proud of the job I've done these last few weeks, despite what's been going on in my personal life. I have until the end of term to keep, as Franks says, *'proving myself.'* I'd forgotten how much I love teaching; it's so satisfying to introduce students to literature they otherwise wouldn't have considered - watching them come alive in class discussions. I've had a couple of students transfer to my class from the other English professor. That's not unusual at the start of a semester - but it works in my favor if I want to secure a full-time contract and the visa that comes along with it. I hope the school board gets to have a say and that the decision isn't entirely up to Frank. He's like Charles, in a way, but without the steely good looks or charm. I'd pitied him momentarily in the restaurant - but now I know he really is a total snake.

"Professor Rose?"

"Hmm?" It's Debbie, five minutes early for class. This is unusual, she isn't the most focused student I have, though she's trying.

"Hello Debbie. I didn't see you there, I was lost in thought. What can I do for you?"

I smooth down my skirt and perch on the edge of my desk, instantly seeing an image in my head from Friday - of Ethan *carrying me over here, putting his hands down the top of my dress, and pulling it open. He sucked my tits right here on this desk. Anybody could've come in. My God, his hands were tugging at my panties, and he nearly had them off. All I could think about was having him inside me.*

I hope my face hasn't gone red.

"I just wanted to say it was real nice seeing you at the party. You really are the coolest teacher here." She lowers her voice, "and I'm not just saying that because you're with the Dean."

Oh Jesus, we're officially a couple now?

"Thank you, Debbie, but there's nothing going on between me and Frank Fletcher. So, if you *are* saying it for that reason, then I'm afraid it won't do you much good."

"Oh, sorry."

"That's perfectly alright." She looks at me for a moment and then starts to fiddle with her hair.

"Was there something else you wanted to say?"

"Yes, but it's embarrassing."

"Go ahead." Now it's my turn to whisper. "I'm not easily embarrassed."

"It's just that you seem so together and beautiful, and men probably adore you."

Funny how someone can get the totally wrong impression. Mind you, if she knew what a hot mess I was, she probably wouldn't want me teaching her.

"I wanted advice from an older woman, and I can't talk to my mum."

That term, 'older woman' always feels good.

"Well, I'm here to help, so what advice do you need?"

She takes a deep breath. "I really like Delaney, I mean Ethan. He's sooo hot, I've never seen anyone as good looking as him. I think he likes me too. I mean, he came to that party on Friday after I asked him, and he definitely flirted with me. I mean you saw that, right?"

A chill goes through me. I put my hand on the desk to steady myself and accidentally knock a pot of pens onto the floor.

"Are you okay, Professor?"

"Yes, I'm fine, probably still recovering from a bug I had at the weekend. Go on." I crouch down on the floor and start picking up the pens. She bends down to help me.

"It's just that, Gina's my friend and she used to date him. I know she still likes him, and it feels awkward, ya' know? But I really want to ask him out on a date, is that too forward? Do you think it would put him off? He could have anyone he wanted."

I stand, place the pot upright and we both put the pens back in. My mind is racing, what am I supposed to say to that? *Keep your hands off him, he's mine!* Had he been flirting with her? I mean I thought he was when I saw him, but then I pushed it out of my mind. Just like I blocked out what Frank said about Ethan treating Gina badly. Debbie's looking at me anxiously - expecting some sort of wisdom. If she asks him out and he says yes, I don't know if I can take it. I know I don't have any hold on him. In my head I do, in my head he's about to fall madly in love with me. If she asks him out and he says no, then she'll feel rejected. So, I don't want to tell her to do that either. *Shit*. I walk over to the whiteboard so that she can't see my face and give myself time to think. It needs to be something neutral.

"Debbie, you have permission to do whatever you feel is the right thing for you." I turn around. Is that enough to get me off the hook? To end this conversation now. What if she asks him out in class today?

She beams at me "Thank you, that's really helpful actually."

Does that mean she is or isn't going to ask out the man I've just fucked the whole weekend?

"Great, glad I could help. I'm going to head to the bathroom, but if you could leave one of these on each desk, I would appreciate that."

"Of course!" I hand her the poems and head out the door with my phone in my hand, walking as fast as I can down the corridor to the bathroom. I throw open a stall door, turn and then lean against it. All I can think about is Ethan with his hands all over her, fucking her, waking up next to her and telling her she's beautiful. *Fuck! I slam my hand against the door.* I absolutely *cannot* spin out about this. For one, I have a class to teach in less than five minutes. Maybe I can talk to Ethan first, let him know that Debbie plans to ask him out. I'm betraying her confidence, I know, but I need to hear his reaction. I send him a text,

"Hey, you here yet?"

I wait a beat to see if he replies, but nothing. I go to the sink and splash cold water into my face. I hold onto the sink and look at myself in the mirror. *I'm pale as fuck.* It's lucky I told Frank that I had a bug over the weekend just in case I run into him again. I head back down the corridor and open the classroom door, it's already filling up, but no sign of Ethan at the back, still no text from him. Class is about to start. *Where the hell is he?* He said on the note that he'd be here. Panic washes over me, but just as I'm about to put my phone away, it lights up. It's Ethan,

"Sorry, got caught up at work, will have to skip class. I'll come over tonight, and you can give me my homework."

I sigh in relief. At least I won't have to watch Debbie ask him out today.

I'm exhausted after class. I'm too tired to cook, so, I text Ethan to see if he can pick up pizza on the way over. He texts back a thumbs up, *a fucking thumbs up, I hate those.* They always seem so dismissive, but it annoys me more than it should. I'm probably hangry, I open the fridge and peer inside. It looks pretty pathetic. We ate everything that was left in it over the weekend. I haven't been grocery shopping since last week. There's a bit of cheese left, about three olives in a jar and half a bottle of wine. That would have been a meal to sustain me back in college. I pull out the wine stopper and pour some in a glass. I unwrap the cheese and place it with the three black olives on a plate and take it into the living room. Perhaps I can watch some mindless crap on TV before Ethan gets here and relax a little. I take off my suit jacket, unbutton the top of my blouse and shake out my hair. My head aches from wearing it up so tight. I grab some lip gloss from the coffee table drawer and smear it on. Hopefully, I'm not still looking like a ghost and won't scare Ethan off when he comes in. I still haven't thought about how to broach the Debbie subject, without coming off as a jealous girlfriend. Maybe I'll just casually drop it in conversation - *"Can you pass me a slice of pizza? By the way Debbie thinks you're into her and is going to ask you out, are you?"*

"Hey." It's Ethan coming in the kitchen door.

"Hey!" I shout back with my mouth full after stuffing in the three olives, and a sizable chunk of cheese. I take a gulp of wine to wash it down, then stand, brushing cheese crumbs off myself. I've missed him since this morning and have to stop myself from skipping into the kitchen to see him. His stubble is thicker than this morning; it's almost a beard. I like it, it makes him look older. He has dark circles under his eyes, and his cheeks are pink from the sea wind. He closes his eyes as I kiss him and rub my fingers gently over his long lashes.

"Long day?"

"Very." He says it with a sigh.

I take the pizza box off him and lay it on the table. "Well, you're in luck, we've got just enough wine left to go with dinner."

"Not for me, thanks." He sits down at the kitchen table. He seems distant tonight, like there's a space between us that I need to carefully navigate. I don't like it, but I'm not sure what I expect. We still know barely anything about each other, despite him being in my thoughts twenty-four seven and him being inside me all weekend. I sit at the table with him and open the pizza box. I take out a slice and sigh contentedly as I eat it. I feel like there's something brewing and being hangry isn't going to help. I push the box over to him, and he shakes his head.

"On a hunger strike?"

He manages a tiny smile. "No, I'm just not ready to eat yet."

"Okay" I carry on eating the slice and desperately want another piece, but I feel self-conscious eating alone in front of him. I can hear myself chewing. We sit in silence for a few more minutes, but then my hunger gets the better of me and I grab the box.

"I'm going to take this in the living room to keep my wine company. When you're ready to talk, lemme know."

I get up and head into the other room, expecting him to follow me - he doesn't. I sit on the sofa, put on the TV and take a sip of wine. *Well, this is awkward, maybe he doesn't want to be here. I'm not going to beg him to stay though.* I make my way through most of the pizza in the box quicker than I should. When I go back into the kitchen, he's still sitting at the table in the semi dark. This is ridiculous, he might as well just go home. He's on his phone, texting.

"Glad to see you're able to communicate with someone."

Shit, that wasn't supposed to come out of my mouth.

"Hmm?"

"Nothing, I just thought you were in here because you wanted some space, not because you wanted to text."

"Sorry Charlotte, I'm not in the best spot tonight, I'm really tired."

"Why don't you go home and get some rest? We've been in each other's pockets since Friday."

I don't want him to go home, I love being in his pocket, but I'm not about to put up with him ignoring me or being on his phone all night! He still has his hood up on his sweater, and the light from his phone illuminates his face, I get butterflies again.

"I can't go home."

"What do you mean, you can't go home?"

He shifts in his seat, then takes his hood down. His blue-black hair spilling out like paint. He runs his fingers through it, but half of it flops forward as usual.

"Gina."

"What about her?"

"When I got home this morning, I found her in my bed."

"What on earth was she doing in your bed?" My stomach lurches. *Was there no end to these twenty something girls chasing him?*

"She said that she missed me. She was wearing one of my dirty T-shirts. It looked like she'd been sleeping in there all weekend."

"Oh my God." I sit down at the table. "Is she having some sort of mental breakdown?"

Ethan shrugs his shoulders "I don't know. I didn't cope with the situation well. She accused me of being with you."

Oh shit, that's the last thing I need right now.

"What did you say?"

"Nothing. I just left."

"Do you think she's going to tell anyone?"

He hesitates and runs his hands over his jeans. "No, I don't think so, it would be too humiliating for her. I think she's been telling people that we're still together."

"I'm not sure that people believe her."

"What do you mean?"

"Debbie said something."

His face goes blank.

"Debbie...the girl from class you were flirting with at the party."

"I wasn't flirting."

"Yeah, you were, but it's all right I get it, she's cute and as far as you were concerned, I wasn't interested. Anyway, the point is that she thinks you *were* flirting, and wanted my advice about asking you out."

"What?" He throws his head back and laughs, "That's pretty funny that she came to you for motherly advice about me."

"Yeah, hilarious Ethan, it actually made me feel like shit."

"Sorry. I hope you put her off?"

"How could I? I had to be neutral, so I just said she had my permission to do what she wanted."

"Great, thanks Charlotte now I have another girl to deal with."

"Oh yes how terrible for you to have girls falling over themselves to be with you. *Must be so difficult* being a man God."

"Man God." He laughs again "Is that how you see me?"

"No, most definitely not." I'm lying, obviously.

"That's good because Gods eventually fall from their pedestal, you know that don't you?"

"Is that your way of telling me you're going to let me down?" I pour the rest of the wine into the glass I left for him and drink it.

"It's inevitable Charlotte. I'm never going to live up to the image you have of me in your head."

"What image do you think I have of you in my head?"

"An unrealistic one." He looks right at me, and my heart threatens to jump from my chest to my mouth. I can't work him out tonight. I don't even know who he's being right now. He looks down at his phone again as it lights up with a text.

"Are you texting Gina now?"

His brow knits, "No, I'm messaging with her mother. She's flying in from Texas tonight, I was hoping she'd take her to a hotel, but she thinks it best for Gina's mental health, if she stays put."

"Isn't that a bit dramatic?"

"No, I can't just kick her out. I have to make sure she's going to be alright."

"Why does it matter to you so much? You told me she was just an ex you had no feelings for."

"I didn't say no feelings, I said '*those*' kind of feelings."

"It seems to me like you do." I can't stop myself from saying it. I wish there was more alcohol in the apartment.

"You're not listening. I owe Gina a great deal and it's important to me that she gets better."

"In your home?"

"Yes, if that's what's necessary."

"At least I know where your priorities lie." I know I'm being a *total bitch*, but I'm tired and far too attached to him already. He doesn't say anything, but instead puts his phone on the table and rests his head in his hands.

"I can't go through this again. Maybe it's best if I leave."

My head is spinning, I want to say no, stay and let's talk, but the words won't come out.

"Yes, I think it's best that you do."

He hesitates for a moment then stands and comes towards me. He brings his hand to my cheek and holds my gaze for longer than I'm comfortable. God damn those eyes, those black haunting eyes.

"I'm sorry Charlotte. I really am."

He goes to kiss me, and I want to yield to him, to give myself over so he will stay, but instead I pull away. "I don't understand Ethan, what's happening? Is that it? Was I just some sort of conquest for you? I bet you got a big kick out of getting your professor into bed. Well, fuck you!"

"No, that's not it at all, I just don't want to hurt you too."

"You are hurting me."

He goes to open the door, "It's better this way, believe me."

I watch him leave, his tall shadow just slipping out quietly like he was never here at all. There are clouds gathering over the horizon, it looks like the weather is going to break soon. A chill goes through me for the second time today. How can it possibly be better this way?

Chapter Seventeen

Ethan

"Stay out of Gina's life. You've done nothing but ruin it.
God, forbid you put anyone else through what you did to my daughter."

I keep re - reading the last text Gina's mum sent me. I'm on the sofa at the garage, it's hard and too short for me. I'm curled up and my back is *killing me.* It's usually Rob who stays on here - trying to sleep off the drink, before he goes home to his wife Mo. I could've asked to stay there, but I can't be dealing with the smug look on my brother's face - knowing I've fucked things up again. I didn't mean for it to go the way it did with Charlotte. I had every intention of staying at her apartment if she would've had me. But that last text from Gina's mother hit me in the gut. She's right, I shouldn't be with anyone. Charlotte knows nothing about my past, and it's better that way. I'll eventually fuck her up too, and I can't do that to someone again. Seeing that text on my phone, and Charlotte already getting mad at me proved it was best if I left. I know I hurt her by leaving, but surely it's easier now rather than later. A few months in and she'll find out what an asshole I am. It's cold in here tonight, and this blanket is thin and scratchy. Even pulling it tight around me doesn't help, my feet just poke out the end. I doubt Rob notices the shittiness of this sofa. He's usually passed out. I'm not sure how long I can stay here without Rob noticing. Not that he'd care. It's more that he'd enjoy seeing me sleep here because he predicted I'd fuck things up, and I don't want him to know he's right. Finally, I drift off to a fitful sleep. I have a nightmare that I'm in the ocean, slowly drowning, reaching out for something I've lost.

I wake up to a hand on my shoulder. For a minute I think it's Charlotte, and that I'm back in her bed, but I roll over only to find Mo, Rob's wife standing over me. She must've come into the office early to do the books, or the schedule that she does a few times a week.

"Hey" I rub my eyes and sit up. My throat feels like something died in it.

"Coffee?"

"Love some." I really like Mo; fuck knows why she stays with my brother. They were childhood sweethearts; they've been together since they were both fifteen. She's stayed with him through everything and has always treated me like a younger brother. If it wasn't for her, I might not be here. She helped me get my life back on track when I was throwing it all away. She brings me over a paper cup filled with black coffee, steam rising off it. It looks like mud, just how I like it. I take a sip and it burns my sandpaper throat as I swallow, but the pain is strangely satisfying. She perches on the edge of the sofa, like a little bird, waiting for me to explain myself. She takes small sips of her tea. Her brunette hair is tucked behind her ears, and her brown eyes open and close as she sips. The worry lines on her forehead are deeper than they should be, and I know that's mostly down to my brother and me. She has a pretty profile with small features, she looks as if she's built from hummingbird bones. This sofa would be perfect for her. I wonder if she chose this one on purpose just so Rob would be uncomfortable when he sleeps here. He told her he needed something nicer for the clients. But Mo knows that clients rarely come into the office. We're not that sort of business, people bring their cars here because we're good and we're reasonably priced. They drop them off and pick them up and that's it. I take a few more sips of my coffee and start to feel more alive. I rotate my left shoulder a few times, it got cramped up in the night.

'Is this the part where you ask why I'm sleeping in the office?"

Mo raises her cup to her lips "No, I'm more curious about how someone your height managed to get any sleep on there at all."

"Liar." I smile at her, and she smiles back. Mo reminds me of my mother; she might look delicate but can be tough as nails when she wants to be.

I'm guessing it's something to do with Gina?" She's up now, tying her hair into a ponytail; leaving a few wisps around her make-up free face. She scans the desk for papers to be sorted.

"You'd be guessing right, and yeah I know you told me not to let her stay, but I thought she was over me."

"That girl is never going to be over you Ethan."

"She will be."

Mo raises her eyebrows, and with papers in her hand, sits behind the desk and switches on the computer. "Why don't you go over to my place, take a shower, and get some more sleep? You do still have a bed there after all."

"Thanks Mo, but I'm up now and I can go take a shower at the gym."

"Robs not home, if that's what you're worried about."

I look at her quizzically, *why isn't my brother at home at 7.30 in the morning.* "Where is he?"

"He told me he had a business meeting in Santa Clarita last night, then phoned to say it went on late and so, he was staying over at the hotel." She takes a pair of glasses out of her bag and puts them on, before squinting at the computer screen. "Which means he had a game and got too drunk to drive home."

"You know about his poker games?"

She looks at me and rolls her eyes, "Of course I do. Why do you think I do the books? I'm not going to end up like your mother." She bites her lip and looks down. "Sorry, I didn't mean that."

It's been a while since we've spoken about my mom. "Don't worry Mo, I know what you meant. I'm going to grab my stuff and get out of your hair."

"I really wish you'd consider staying with us, you can have all the privacy you want in that annex. You don't even have to come into the main house. We left you alone as a teenager didn't, we?"

I grin, "Yeah you did. Most of the time...apart from when I was being a teenage douchebag."

She smiles crookedly at me, "Weren't you like that all the time?"

I laugh, "You got me there, Mo."

"Don't worry about your brother saying anything, he knows he's in for it when he gets home anyway. So, it's not you he's going to be concerned about."

I need to get out of these clothes, but it feels odd changing in front of Mo, it doesn't seem appropriate somehow.

"Thanks for the coffee." I crumple the cup up into the bin, and grab the bag with my clean clothes in.

"Anytime Ethan, but please don't stay here again tonight. Come home."

"I have a home Mo, but there's a crazy girl living in it." She smiles at me, but I can tell she's worried. I head outside to my car, and the sun hurts my head. I'll keep the roof up on the Mustang today, I just want to hide for a while.

Chapter Eighteen

Charlotte

It's been two weeks since the night Ethan left. It feels longer. I sat on the floor in the kitchen for a couple of hours afterwards. I thought he'd come back. I expected to see his tall shadow appear at the door, see him bend as usual to avoid hitting his head on the frame. See him step down into the kitchen and smile at me in that lopsided way of his. If only I hadn't been so hotheaded about Gina, things might have turned out differently. He hasn't been to class, though he has attended his other lectures. I checked in with the office administrator. He'll automatically fail English Literature now. I'm sad that I'm the cause of that. I'm sure he wanted more than working for his brother the rest of his life. I haven't seen him in the halls, or his car in the parking lot. The other day I thought I saw him leaving down the college steps; his unruly hair swept back, taking those long strides of his. But when I got outside, there was no one there. I'm not sure what I'd have done if it had been him.

After all, what did we really have together? Great chemistry, an incredible night under the stars and a weekend at my apartment, that's it. I was wrong about us having a connection. Lauren was right, I was an idiot to think there was any more to it. He was looking for a way out and I gave it to him. I've tried to lose myself in books and Netflix, and sunset walks on the beach. But it just reminds me that I'm alone. Melancholy has settled into my bones; it's a feeling I know well. I just hadn't imagined having that feeling in California. I envisaged exciting weekends with new friends, maybe even surfing like I did all those years ago in Brazil, and dancing again till dawn. I didn't think I'd be grieving over a twenty-three-year-old...*Damn oxytocin,* no wonder women bond with their partner so much after sex. Our body floods us with it. The *"Cuddle hormone,"* at least that's what Cosmo called it back in the day - when I thought reading that magazine would help my love life. That's the problem with hot men and mind-blowing sex; it pulls you inside out and then you're left hanging out to dry. My mother had warned me about boys like Ethan. *"Don't go for the looks darling, they're the bastards. Go for someone you feel is aesthetically beneath you, that way, they'll never stray."* She looked at my father when she said it, as if he was a wounded animal she had to tend to. *"You can always have affairs"* she'd added, in front of him, disappearing through a cloud of smoke from her pack of Virginia slims.

I haven't seen much of Frank these past couple of weeks, *thank God.* He's been busy in meetings and not looming outside my classroom like a ghoul. Although, he did slip a note in my cubby hole in the staff room with the schedule to the LA Philharmonic. As much as I would love to go to one of those concerts, I certainly don't want to go with him. No more word from Charles either. I told my lawyer about him calling me and she sent him another official letter, with a warning. I'm hoping that's enough to hold him off, for now. I'm trying, and failing, not to re live all the sex I had with Ethan. The first night under the stars when he kissed me. The way his abs tightened and rippled, as I sucked him off on the patio - his pre cum dripping on my lips. The way he felt inside me, how perfectly he fit as if we're made for each other. Yep, all these things play on a loop in my head like a movie I can't look away from. I haven't spoken to Lauren about it, I feel so stupid that I thought it was anything more than just a fling. I've kept my head down and focused on work - intercepted with sex flashbacks with the most gorgeous man on earth. I keep telling myself that I'm going to delete his pictures off my phone, but I haven't. He's not on social media - for that I'm grateful. I can't bear the thought of seeing him pop up on Facebook doing things *or someone*. I don't post anything on my page, for obvious reasons, and never accept any friend requests. Except yesterday, I got one from a friend I did my A-levels with. I haven't thought about Nathan Green in years- or *Nate* as I called him. Thinking about it now though, we always hung out together. We sometimes used to skip out on classes and go to the pub and smoke, and drink snakebite and black. Such a disgusting drink, but we thought we were so cool. I'm surprised I managed to get all four A-levels; with all the partying I did. We messaged back and forth a bit on Facebook. It felt safe to tell him I was in Los Angeles as we don't have any mutual friends. He doesn't even know Lauren as he ended up going to a different University than me. As luck would have it, he's in downtown LA for a couple of days. He's headed off to Peru for a research project and thought he'd take his layover here. He suggested driving down to Santa Monica to meet for a drink. I dismissed the idea at first, but the more I thought about it the more it felt like it might do me good to see an old friend. I've been wallowing in my own misery enough. We're meeting tonight at a little dive bar a few blocks from my place. I looked it up on Yelp and they have live music on Friday nights. It looks unpretentious - which is not an easy thing to find in LA.

I walk the four blocks from my apartment to the bar. It's been foggy the past couple of days, but tonight it's clear with a gentle breeze. I'm wearing jeans and a vintage T-shirt that I found at a thrift shop on Fourth Street. I've paired it with a leather jacket that used to belong to my mum. I'm surprised she ever owned such a cool thing; I grabbed it when she was going to throw it out - along with an eighties tight black knitted dress with diamantes on the shoulders. I brought that with me too. Most of my other clothes are still hanging in my wardrobe in London. I doubt I'll ever see them again. I push open the door to the bar and run my fingers through my hair. I let it dry naturally tonight, and for once it's not misbehaving - its sitting in soft waves on my shoulders. It's dark inside and I let my eyes adjust for a minute. Nathan texted about five minutes ago to say he was here. I'm glad it's not too busy as trying to find him amongst a sea of faces would've sent me into a mild panic. The place is pretty quiet for a Friday night, and the band is just warming up. Even in this low light though, I can spot who I think might be Nathan sitting in a corner in one of the booths with red velvet seats. The man stands and waves, *yep that must be him*.

"Charlotte, good Lord, you haven't changed at all."

"Yes, I have, I can legally drink now."

He laughs and puts his arms around me and gives me a hug. "It's been too long." He pulls back and looks at me, taking hold of my hands. It's all coming back to me now - his auburn hair, the kind green eyes.

"And you can grow a beard!" Something he never managed to do at college.

He puts his hand to his beard and scratches it. "Yep. This has taken me about a year."

I smile back at him, "It was worth it."

We take each other in for a minute. It feels so good to meet someone again who knew me pre-Charles, before my life completely went off the rails. I suddenly feel young again.

"Fuck, it's good to see you again, Char."

I squeeze his hands, "You too, Nate."

The band have finished warming up and start playing a version of Rod Stewarts, *"Maggie May."*

"Great, a classic cover band!" I slip into the booth and take off my jacket. I shake out my curls from the collar. "So, what are we drinking?"

"Snakebite and black?"

We both laugh. "I don't think Americans know what that is."

"Jack and diet coke?"

"Perfect." For the first time in weeks, I feel good. I'm with an old friend, and I plan to get wasted. We're not sure if it's table service, so he goes up to the bar to get our drinks. The small lamps on the tables are casting a romantic glow across the room. It would've been nice to come here with Ethan. He would've liked it here - it's dark and moody, and we could have made out quite discreetly in one of these little booths. I start to think about his hands searching underneath my t-shirt, and I push the idea out of my mind. *No, I bat that thought away like I'm pitching it across a field. I* will not allow any thoughts of that asshole to ruin my night. Nate comes back with the drinks and a plate of Nachos dripping with cheese. He places them on the table.

"I didn't know if you were hungry." He shouts it over the music, it's louder now and there are people piling into the bar, having heard the band from the street.

"You read my mind." I shout back and take one and stuff it in my mouth, the hot cheese melting down my chin.

"What?" He can't hear me now over all the noise. I grab hold of his arm and pull him into the booth beside me. "You're gonna have to sit next to me, so we can hear each other."

"Okay!" He slips in beside me and I bring both my legs up onto the seat into a cross legged position and press my back into the wall. I can be a pretzel when I want to be; something else that Ethan commented on. I take a sip of Jack Daniels and as I swallow it, it lights up my throat. I haven't drunk it in years. Not since my college days, I don't think. I down it quickly, loving the warmth of it in my stomach. Nate's sitting back and enjoying the band. He's wearing a pale blue linen shirt and jeans. His hair is cut short at the sides and a little longer on top, which seems the fashion of English men in their thirties right now. The beard suits him. It's a deep auburn color, like his hair. I've never been attracted to him, and I wish I had a friend here I could set him up with. He's such a great guy. A girl comes over and asks if we'd like more drinks, it must be table service after all.

"I'd like a double Jack Daniel's and diet coke please." I shout over to her.

He points at me, "I'll have what she's having."

I toss my hair to the side and flash a smile at him. He gives me a side look and raises an eyebrow cheekily. The waitress brings us back our drinks and Nate digs in his jeans for his wallet. She shakes her head and says something to him, then points over to the bar. He raises his glass at someone. I lean into him, "What did she say?"

"She said they were already paid for."

"By whom?"

He shrugs his shoulders, "By some guy at the bar."

My eyes can't focus now with so many people, and then suddenly, with pinpoint accuracy, I see him. *How could I miss him.* My heart leaps into my mouth. Even in the darkness, he's striking. He's wearing a scruffy biker jacket and jeans. His five-o clock shadow is thick, and his hair is messy, like it's been tousled in the wind. I can feel his soulful eyes bore into the very core of me. Time stands still as the band starts playing, 'Drops of Jupiter" by Train. The lead vocalist's husky voice sings into the mic about a girl falling for a shooting star; he wants to know if she missed him out there. I sink back into the booth.

"Hey, what's up? You look like you've seen a ghost." Nate puts his arms around me. I have seen a ghost. *What the hell is Ethan doing here?*

Chapter Nineteen

Ethan

Seeing Charlotte with another man's arms around her, makes my blood boil. I want to go over and haul his ass out of there, then just for fun - knock him the *fuck out*.

I spotted her the minute I walked into the bar. She was sitting cross legged in a booth, her t-shirt stretched tight across her tits. Her golden hair fanned around her like a fucking halo. I swear my heart skipped a God damned beat. I was about to go over, to tell her I'd made a *huge fucking mistake l*etting her go, when a guy leaned forward in the booth. He whispered something to her, and she laughed, throwing her head back. Her huge smile lighting up her face. She looked so happy. A waitress went over and took a drinks order from them. I stepped back into the shadow of the crowd so she wouldn't see me. I went to the bar and told them I would pay for their drinks and ordered myself a Jameson on the rocks. A girl at the bar beside me turned and asked if I wanted to buy her a drink, she was cute, with a pixie cut and wide eyes. The old Ethan would have said *hell yes*, but instead I ignored her, picked up my drink, and turned back towards Charlotte. I could've walked out of there without her seeing me, but something inside me wanted to see the look on her face when she spotted me. The guy she was with, turned to where the waitress was pointing and raised his glass at me. *Fucking prick.* That's when she saw me. I raised my glass at her, and the smile dropped from her face. She shrunk back into the booth, hiding from me.

"Hey Ethan, man thanks for coming. Great to see ya." Liam, the lead singer from the band, is slapping me on the back.

"Oh, hey man, yeah, no problem. It's great hearing you play again. Do you wanna drink?"

All I can think about right now is that some guy has his hands all over Charlotte.

"No, it's cool, Daisy at the bar is sorting me out." He winks at one of the barmaids.

Yeah, I bet she is. Some things never change.

"Catch you later man, yeah. Set finishes at ten."

"Sure, thing Liam."

I turn back to the booth, but Charlotte's gone. The skinny dude is sitting alone on his phone. I scan the room for her and see the back of her blonde hair go towards the restroom. I squeeze through the throng of people to where she's waiting in line.

"Charlotte." Her head turns, then immediately she looks away and folds her arms.

"Will you at least look at me?"

"No."

The other women in the line stare at me.

"Who's that guy you're with?"

"None of your bloody business."

I'm still talking to the back of her head. "For Christ's sake Charlotte, will you turn around?"

She doesn't move, just continues to stare ahead at the restroom door. The woman behind her taps her on the shoulder, "I'd turn around if I were you honey, this guy is the hottest thing on two legs."

Charlotte sighs and leaves the line, brushing past me. I grab hold of her arm and she shakes it off.

"I just want to talk to you."

She stops and turns, wedging herself in the crowd. "Talk to me? *Now* you want to talk to me? You could have done that two weeks ago, instead of just walking the fuck out." She makes a sweeping gesture with her arm, and accidentally knocks into the woman beside her.

"I wanted to talk to you, I just didn't know how."

She puts her hand on her hips, "It's quite simple Ethan, *you just open your mouth and words come out!"*

The band has started up again, Liam is singing 'Hey There. Delilah." by the Plain White T's.

I want to tell her that I'm sorry - that I've been a total dick, that I've done a lot of soul searching over the past couple of weeks, and I want to give it a go with her. Something I don't think I've ever considered with a woman. I still have a lot of shit to deal with, but it's her that I want to be with.

The music blasts out of the speakers next to us. Her face is flushed and her green eyes flash dark at me as she waits for an answer. I can't say all that here. She throws her arms up in the air and pushes her way through the crowd, back to her table. She mouths something to the man she's with and picks up her jacket. He looks over towards me, shifts himself out of the booth and stands. She's heading for the door, he goes to follow her, but I put my hand on his chest.

"Stay here, man. This has nothing to do with you."

"I don't know who you are, but I'm leaving with Charlotte."

"The fuck you are." I give him a little push and he falls back into the booth.

I catch hold of the swinging door as she lets it go in my face, having turned around and seen me instead of the posh English twat she came with.

"Where's Nate?"

"Nate? Is that your new boyfriend's name?"

"He's not my boyfriend and, even if he was, *it's none of your God damned business."* She screams at me like a wild cat.

"Just a fuck then? I know how much you like that." I didn't mean for that to come out of my mouth. *Shit.* I lower my head and she just stares at me. "I'm sorry." She doesn't say anything. but the hurt in her eyes gives me stomach pains. The bar door opens, and the Englishman comes out.

"Is everything all right Char?"

Char, fucking Char! Why is he calling her that? Who the fuck is this joker?

She puts her jacket on and pulls her hair from the collar. *The gorgeous hair that flowed down my stomach like a river when she knelt between my legs.*

"Everything's fine, thanks Nate."

He eyes me suspiciously from the side, like I'm going to shove him back again. "Shall we go somewhere else?"

I laugh, "She's not gonna leave with you, man."

Charlotte looks at me. Her eyes are wide and wet, and I know I've gone too far.

"Take me home please, Nate." She keeps her eyes fixed on me as she says it. He mutters, *"prat"* at me under his breath as he walks towards her. I take a couple of steps back.

I came here on my motorcycle tonight; it's parked out front. I was thinking about Charlotte as I picked it up last week at an auction —about taking her for a ride, her hands wrapped around me, her thighs gripping me from behind. I unclasp the helmet from the seat and slide it over my head. Throwing my leg over the bike, I start the engine, pull back hard on the throttle, and pull away from the curb. In my wing mirror I see Nate put his arm around her and she leans into him. I speed past them into the dark of night. So much for all my soul searching, I've totally fucked things up again.

Chapter Twenty

Charlotte

I always look forward to the last class of the week. The students are relaxed, ready for the weekend, and the class is more like an open discussion. We talk about our current favorite literature and share any books we've been enjoying. Often students will read extracts from the ones they're reading at home, and I will also introduce some new ones. It gives them a break from the curriculum, and it encourages them to read more and continue learning outside of class. It was quite popular at my old university. It became an unofficial, 'Friday Afternoon Book Club.' Students from other majors also joined. The local coffee shop even started sponsoring us and laid on hot drinks and pastries. Charles *hated* the book club and put a stop to it. He couldn't stand that my classes were more popular than his. He took it to the board and told them it wasn't educational. I didn't know that it was him who'd instigated its demise. I argued that it encouraged the pupils more in their studies. It inspired lively and intellectual discussion, and that reading more could only help them in their other classes. But I lost my case, and the Friday afternoon book club was disbanded. Charles sympathized with me. He told me that he'd done everything he could to swing it in my favor - but alas his hands were tied. It was Penny who let it slip, that it was Charles who convinced the board to put an end to it. We were out for end of term drinks, back when I believed she was my friend. She said she thought I knew. I'm still not sure if she did it on purpose - or to further drive a wedge in my marriage. When I confronted him, he just laughed it off and said, "*Oh that silly book club,*" as if it was nothing. "*I did it for your own good, Charlotte. The other Professors didn't like it. I was only protecting you.*"

"Afternoon class." Everyone is already assembled and chatting, and I instinctively look to the back to where Ethan used to sit. I instinctively do it still, even though it's now three weeks since he sat in that chair.

My mind goes back to last Friday when I was at the bar with Nate, and Ethan showed up. Fuck knows what he was doing there. I saw him talking to the lead singer when I slipped out of the booth, to try to get away from him. So maybe he knows him? I was so shocked when I saw him, and so freaking angry that he expected me to just bat my eyes and listen to him. The nerve of him to ask about Nate! He was so rude to him too. He acted like a brat, and I was so embarrassed. Nate walked me home and I cried in his arms before I went to vomit in the toilet. We picked up more Jack Daniels on the way home. I'm not used to liquor; I usually just stick to wine. Nate slept on the couch, and I crawled into bed around 2am, after falling asleep hugging the toilet. I'm mortified about the whole night! I apologized profusely to Nate the next morning. He took it in his stride, but he was probably just being polite. I still can't get over what an absolute piece of shit Ethan was. I hate myself for it - but when he got on that sexy motorcycle, and roared off into the distance, I wanted to run after him. Ugh - he looked so hot. Also, since when does he have a motorbike?

I sit and grab some books from my bag. I lay them on my desk and bring my focus back to class. "I hope you've all brought some interesting reads with you today. I am especially hoping that some of you brought some poetry books. We made some great discoveries of poets last week, and as much as I love a good story, poetry can reveal life to us in layers - it can tell us something about ourselves."

The door opens and I look up. It's Ethan. All eyes turn on him, not only because he's late - but also because he's bloody breathtaking. He hasn't shaved since I saw him last Friday and his already thick stubble is now a beard. He must have ridden here on his motorbike, as his hair has that same disheveled look it had in the bar. He's wearing a gray t-shirt and his muscly arms are even more tanned - it must be from the bike. As he passes my desk, I catch his earthy scent. I close my eyes for just a second and remember my tongue on his skin in the shower, licking drops of water from his torso and then down to his...

"Sorry I'm late." His voice jerks me back to reality, as he takes his old seat at the back of the classroom. He tucks his long legs under the desk and sticks his pen behind his ear. He's even more stunning with a beard - *if that's even possible.* He reminds me of the woodcutter on the book cover of, *'Estonian Fairy Tales.'* I've had a copy since I studied literature as an undergrad. It's one of my most loved, dog-eared books. For many years that woodcutter stared out at me from the cover of that book. I kept it on my bedside table. He was always there, faithful, even when my husband wasn't. I take a minute to gather myself, my hands are clammy, and my throat is suddenly dry. I take a sip of water.

"As I was saying, poetry can open up language to us in ways that we hadn't thought of. Did anyone want to say something about any poems they've read recently?" The only person that raises their hand is Ethan. "How about poetry in general?" My class appears to be mute this week and it's still only Ethan's hand that it's in the air. He's rocking back in his chair. *I hope he falls out of it.* "Anyone?" I say through gritted teeth. He never said anything during a lecture before. *Now he wants to talk, and not just do stupid doodles?* I want to tell him not to bother, that he's failed the class anyway so he might as well *go the fuck home.*

"Ethan, have you read any poetry lately? You haven't been here for three weeks. I'm surprised you want to contribute. Unless you've spent that entire time with your head in a book? Which I doubt." There's muffled sniggering around the room. I know it's mean, but I don't, particularly care.

"Actually, I've been reading more of Neruda."

I sit back on my desk and fold my arms, whilst he digs into his bag for something. He pulls out a thin book, then opens it to a page he's bookmarked. I realize that he's holding one of *my* books, the one that I'd read to him from that weekend we were together. I was taking a break from our sexathon and was spending an hour going through some homework. He laid his head in my lap and asked me to read some poems from it. I'd felt like something out of Pride and Prejudice - stroking the head of my dashing dark-haired suitor. He just wanted to hear my voice, he said, to listen to the way my mouth cradled the words. *What a crock of shit, and now I've found out that he stole my book! So, he's a thief as well as a prick!* I'm fuming, I manage to hide it under a veneer of politeness.

"We're all familiar with Neruda by now, he is, I believe, a class favorite. What did you want to share with us?"

"Well, take one of his love poems for example. In this one he talks about how much he's craving this woman, as if he's starving for her. You can really feel his pain in the words."

He's talking about one of the poems I read to him that weekend. It was right before he pulled me down to him, kissed me and peeled off my clothes. I remember him kissing me in each place my dress fell from me, before fucking me slowly on the sofa. My face feels hot, I don't want the whole class to see me go red. I get up and go back behind my desk and pretend to rearrange some things.

"Yes, his words are so simple and yet so incredibly deep. Why did you choose that poem in particular?"

To taunt me, to make fun of me?

"Because of what you were saying – that poetry can offer a way into language that we hadn't thought about. Here, Neruda presents images describing how much he wants this woman, and it's much more powerful that way. It's visceral, it stays with us, haunts us."

Wow. who knew the man of so few words could be so freaking eloquent. He certainly hasn't revealed that side of himself to me before. The girls in the class are all looking at him gooey eyed, especially Debbie.

"That's very astute of you Delaney, thank you for sharing. Why don't I write some of the lines from that poem, on the whiteboard. We can discuss what techniques Neruda used here and come up with images of our own on the subject of passion and desire. The poet shows both the light and dark sides of them in his work. So, let's uncover the negative as well as the positive forces these emotions can sometimes unleash." I direct that bit at Ethan. He holds my gaze for a second, before sitting forward in his chair and taking the pen from behind his ear. *Probably to go back to doodling.*

The remainder of the two hours seems to go mercifully quickly. Ethan's quiet for the rest of the time and, as predicted, he appears to just be scribbling in his book. He keeps his head down, only looking up occasionally. He's not paying attention at all. I don't care what he does though, quite frankly. I don't know what he's playing at bringing in that book - or even what he's doing here in the first place! If he was hoping to embarrass me or upset me, he hasn't. I've been teaching for more years than he's been an adult; I can handle worse than this.

"Charlotte." I'd hoped he'd leave before I did, or that Debbie making goo goo eyes at him would catch his attention. I have nothing to say to him.

"Ethan."

"Have you got a minute?"

"No." I don't look at him. I refuse to get lost in those deep eyes of his and be pulled into whatever pathetic excuse he's about to come up with for his behavior.

"I'm sorry."

"Which thing exactly are you sorry for?" I lower my voice. "For walking out on me, for threatening my friend at the bar or for stealing my poetry book?"

"Yeah, I'm sorry about that. I planned to give it back to you today."

"*That's the thing* you're most sorry for?" I raise my voice louder than I should. I look around to see if anyone's noticed. There are some students chatting at the back of the room, but they're not paying us any attention.

"I shouldn't have bailed on you either, I was going through some stuff."

Bailed? He makes it sound like he just forgot to show up for something.

He looks like a puppy dog standing in front of me, but I'm not going to feel sorry for him. "Not a problem." I begin to shove things into my bag, but the more I stuff - the more things keep spilling out. *Damn it,* this is the time when I need to be one of those organized women who compartmentalize their handbags. *What's that? Half a chocolate mint melted.* I pick it off the desk and shove it back in. *One of those, 'got it all together' women wouldn't be carrying melted chocolate around in their bag. My mother was right, I should have gone to finishing school. By now I'd be wearing pearls and sashaying around some country estate, counting all my ponies. Instead, I'm here with chocolate stuck to my hand, with bits of fluff and a dented straw and what looks like a dead hamster falling out of my bag - yuck- what the actual fuck is that?*

"That's quite the treasure you carry around there." I look up at him and expect to see him laughing at me, but instead he looks concerned. His brow is knitted, and his eyebrows hang like a blackbird's wing. No, I will not get seduced by his beauty, Ethan is not my Estonian Woodcutter, *he's a total and utter shit bag.*

"Well, ya' know, got to be prepared for anything." I just scoop everything back in my bag.

"Yes, I can't leave the house without my essentials either."

Sarcastic bastard.

I'm about to reply when Debbie appears at the desk.

"Hi."

She's looking at Ethan and I don't even think she's registered that I'm still here. She looks down then up at him through her eyelashes.

How very Princess Diana of her.

"I just love what you were saying earlier about poetry, it was just ...so sexy."

Really? This is happening right now in front of me. Really?

"Alright. I'll leave you to it. I have a date with the sunset and a bottle of wine." *God, I sound sad.* Ethan puts his hand out and touches me on the arm. It feels like a bolt of lightning shooting up my spine. Not having had his hands on me for three weeks has, apparently, sent my body haywire.

"Actually, Professor Rose and I have to talk about something."

Debbie looks over at me and pouts, finally acknowledging my existence. "I need to talk to you about something too. I've missed you in class these last few weeks, and you haven't responded to any of my texts." She's fiddling with her hair again and balancing one hip against my desk. She's wearing tight jeans and a tiny white crop top, and her glossy red hair falls to her waist. She looks like a siren, meanwhile, I'm just standing here like a twat with a bag full of crap in my hands. She maneuvers herself in front of me, to block me from his view.

"Yeah, I've had a lot going on, and so really it's quite important that I talk to the professor."

"Okay I'll just wait for you outside the door. We can go grab a coffee or something when you're done."

Ethan put his hands in his hair to push it back, something I understand now that he does when he's uncomfortable.

"Sorry, but I have to rush off straight after class."

"How about we meet up over the weekend then?"

Damn, she's persistent, what's he going to say to that?

"I have a full schedule this weekend, can you just tell me what it is now?"

Is he that dim not to see she's trying to ask him out? I'd even warned him when we were last together, for God's sake.

Debbie stops leaning against my desk and gathers her books closer to her chest.

"It doesn't matter."

This is awkward *as fuck*. I feel like I should say something to make her feel better. "Great work today in class Debbie, some lovely contributions and thoughtful talking points." I smile at her, but she's too lost in her disappointment to hear what I'm saying. She sighs and takes one last lingering look at Ethan before leaving.

"Well, that's another heart you just broke."

"Another one?"

"Isn't that what you implied when you walked out on me? That you had a litany of them all over the city, like little cracked eggshells."

"That's not what I said."

"No, but that's what was *inferred*."

"Can you at least let me explain? I wanted to the other night, but you were too busy with that English Dude. What was his name…Nut?"

"His name is Nate and you God damn know it is. Anyway, there's no explanation necessary. You disappear for two weeks, then show up at a bar and threaten my friend. You've failed class by the way so I've no idea what you're doing here today. You made it clear when you left that you didn't want to be with me. I'm a grown up." I shrug my shoulders, "I've dealt with worse heartache. So, you see, there's nothing more to say." He looks at me under those ridiculously long lashes, those soul-searching eyes of his seeing right through me. I turn to wipe the whiteboard, *I do not want him,* I say to myself as I furiously scrub it. "Why couldn't you throw Debbie there a few breadcrumbs? Make her weekend?"

"Why would I do that?"

"I don't know, maybe because it's the kind thing to do, something like that."

"I'd only be leading her on. Best to cut it off now."

"Like you did with me?"

"You're upset."

"Me? Upset? Why would I be upset? You take me to see a meteor shower and then proceed to make out with me under shooting stars - *which was clearly your intention all along, by the way.* You tell me I'm the most beautiful thing you've ever seen. I nearly let you fuck me right here on this desk and risked losing my job! We have one incredible weekend together, where you tell me you want to make a go of it, and yet at the first sign of trouble *you just fuck right off!*"

Well, that all came out of nowhere.

He puts his hands in his pockets and looks down, his hair flops forward into his eyes. He pushes it back, it flops again.

"I'm sorry Charlotte, but you're wrong. I never had any intention of anything happening between us that first night. I fantasized about it, yes, but had I planned it? No."

I snort like a horse and instantly regret it. "You actually said to me - *and I want to laugh now at the cliche of it* - You said to me, before you put your hand down my jeans that *I was the only girl you had taken up there.* No doubt you say that to all of us, just to make us extra wet. I'm sure Debbie would look fabulous spreadeagled on the hood of your sexy little car!"

I sit back down on my desk; *I said way more than I planned to.*

"Wow, is that really what you think of me?" I was about to say yes, but the way he's looking at me nearly floors me. He looks like the lost boy in the painting again - the one he reminded me of when I first saw him. There must have been something innocent in him then, that I'm seeing now. All the color has drained from his face, and his eyes are so black - it's as if he's disappeared into them. I lean forward and close my eyes for a minute, my head is spinning.

"Can you blame me for feeling that way, Ethan?"

"I know I messed things up between us, but I thought you knew that everything that happened between us was real. I don't know how you could mistake that for something else."

I'm tired and I'm emotional. I can't take much more of this rollercoaster with him. "I don't know what's real anymore. Everything moved so fast, and then you were gone. All I know is that I've had a few weeks to get you out of my system, and yet you're still lodged here." I put my hand on my chest, my heart's pounding. "You're stuck inside me, and I can't get you out."

"You make me sound like a ghost you want to exorcize."

"Aren't you? You drift in and out of my reality like you are one."

He raises an eyebrow and sighs, then rubs his beard. The only thing he's missing is an ax and a lumberjack shirt.

"Why pull that little stunt in here today with the Neruda poem? Also, can I have my book back? *The one that you stole."*

"I was always going to give it back to you. I took it because I wanted to impress you. I was gonna learn some poems and recite them to you, like you did to me. It sounds cheesy as hell I know." He puts his hands in his pockets and looking down, shifts on his feet.

It doesn't, it sounds romantic and thoughtful. He sits on the opposite desk and clasps his hands together before taking them apart. He doesn't know what to do with them.

"I had every intention of seeing you again. When I came over that night, I didn't plan for it to go the way it did. I just saw a look on your face that I've seen before, and I knew I'd disappoint you. I'd have ended up ruining everything, and it scared me. So, I ran. Then I saw you at the bar and I was gonna come over, but then I saw you were with someone and my jealousy kind of...got the better of me."

Hearing him say out loud that he was jealous makes me feel way happier than it should.

"I've got news for you Ethan, you did disappoint me and ruin everything."

He looks up at me, those long lashes sweeping the apples of his cheeks. His jaw set.

"Not as badly as I would've done if we'd continued. I did a lot of reflecting in those two weeks, and by the time I saw you last Friday I knew I wanted you back." He stands, "But it's clear to me now, after hearing what you just said, that I am no good for you."

I hate him in this moment - *I hate him* for being too scared to take a chance. He reaches into his back pocket and hands me the book of Neruda poems.

"Here, I'm sorry. I truly am. I'm sorry that I skipped so much class. I'm just sticking with math and astronomy for now. I'll take English again with another teacher next semester."

I take the book and our fingers touch briefly. I swallow any pain I feel about those fingers, never feeling their way around my body again.

"Thank you."

He nods and puts his hands back in his pockets. "I guess this is goodbye then."

He gets up off the desk and slings his bag over his shoulder.

"I guess it is. Goodbye Ethan."

I watch him walk away, hoping he turns back, but he doesn't. I blink back any tears that are brewing and push down a hiccup that's threatening to emerge. I go to put the book in my bag but notice something sticking out of it. I pull it out, it's a piece of paper torn from his notebook. It's a sketch of me, sitting at my desk. He's drawn me as I've never seen myself before. The way he's captured my features is striking. I didn't even know he could draw. So, that's what he's been doing when I thought he was doing stupid doodles. I flick through the book, and there's another one scribbled on the back of an old take-out receipt. It's a tiny pencil drawing of me in bed, laying on my side smiling at him, it's exquisite. I carefully put both sketches together in the middle of the book and close it. There's a side of Ethan that I never knew existed.

Chapter Twenty-One

Charlotte

"He drew you?"

I skype Lauren as soon as I get in. I ended up calling her last weekend after the incident at the bar and told her everything. She never said, *"I told you so,"* about any of it. I don't know why I thought she would.

"Yeah, they were in the poetry book. There was a drawing of me sitting at my desk. Then I flicked through it and there was another one. I thought he was just doodling in class today, but he was doing a portrait of me."

"So, it's a good picture?"

"It's amazing Lauren. He drew me at my most beautiful - or more beautiful than I could ever hope to be. He captured the light and the shadows and the inner part of me. Does that make sense?"

"Yeah, it does. He obviously meant for you to find them."

"Yes, he must've done, but why? Also, I had no idea he could draw like that, he's like a proper artist and I thought he was just this gorgeous sort of ethereal mechanic."

"I wish my mechanic was gorgeous and ethereal."

"Lauren, don't make me laugh, we're trying to do some serious analysis here."

"Well, you have to go and talk to him."

"Why? He made it perfectly clear he was afraid of hurting me. Typical excuse from a guy who's trying to get out of any kind of relationship. You said yourself that twenty-three-year-olds don't want anything serious."

"Hmm, I know, but maybe there's more to him than I thought. I mean, he draws you these stunning pictures and leaves them in your book. He turns up in class and starts talking about that poem. Why would he do that?"

"To fuck with me?"

"I mean, possibly? But I don't think that's the case. I'd never normally advocate calling a guy who broke it off, but I sense there is more to it. Maybe he's scared. Things did move extremely fast between you."

"You're seriously encouraging me to call him? Wow, that's a turn around."

"If nothing else - I want my regular installments of the Ethan saga. If it stops now -how am I supposed to keep living vicariously through your sexy relationship? I want the next episode."

I laugh, "So basically, I'm just cheap entertainment for you."

"Yep, that's basically it."

"Very funny."

"Charlotte, last night was the first time Paul and I even attempted to have sex in months. Just as I'm about to have an orgasm, his mother, in the midst of her dementia, wanders in - asking which aisle she can find the bacon in."

"I'm sorry." I stifle a giggle.

"No, you're not, but that's okay. I'd find it hilarious too. Anyway, have a think about what I said, it might be worth talking to him."

I do want to speak to him, to ask him about the sketches. Even if it's the last time I see him – at least I'll get some answers.

Chapter Twenty-Two

Ethan

I'm working under Old Blue again. I'm so lost in my thoughts, that I don't hear someone come into the garage. Everyone else has gone home, and I'm glad to be working in solitude. Under an engine, everything's familiar to me. There's an order to things. Maybe I've been foolish trying to get my school credits - to want something more from life. I should be grateful to be here, to have a job and an apartment. The world under here - I know how to navigate. Not like the one out there. It's clear to me now how numb I've been these last few years. I thought I was doing okay, just getting on with life. I wasn't getting into any trouble and was having fun with girls here and there. But I wasn't feeling anything. I know that because this thing with Charlotte has thrown me. It's made me *feel* something again.

"Hey." A voice interrupts my thoughts.

I ignore it and continue to work under Old Blue. I've been talking to the truck. I've been telling her about the road trip we're going to have, and how good she's gonna feel to be back to her old self. I can see Charlotte's feet from here, delicate low-heeled shoes, and bare legs. I look up to see she has a small scab on her knee, and I remember how clumsy she can be. There is a pool of water forming around her feet.

"Either it's raining outside, or you're melting."

"The former."

"Well, that's a relief."

"Are you going to come out from under there?"

I take a minute to think, "No, probably not."

"I'd like you to."

I don't particularly want to leave my little cave under here. "Did your car break down again?"

"No, I wanted to see you." She's bending over now, her blonde hair draping like fronds around her face. It's dangling over the small pond forming around her feet.

"I saw you this afternoon. I thought you were done with me." I know I'm being difficult, but she annoyed me earlier - implying that I was leading her on. I'll admit that in the past I haven't been the perfect gentleman, but Charlotte is a whole new ball game for me. A terrifying one, which is why I had to stop it in its tracks. She's standing back up now and rummaging in her bag, no doubt having to navigate the fluff farm she's cultivating there. She's bending down again, shoving something at me under the truck, it's the picture I drew of her in class today.

"Explain this."

"Well, what you have in your hand there is called a piece of paper, and I took this thing called a pencil and made marks on it."

"Why are you being such a shit?"

"Because that's what you think I am, so I might as well live up to expectations."

"Okay forget it, see you around Delaney." She begins to walk away, her heels clip clopping on the floor. I quickly slide out from under the truck; I don't want her to leave. Not least of all because I can hear the summer storm now rolling in off the ocean.

"Do you want a towel?"

She stops and turns, her hair dripping onto her white blouse that has turned slightly transparent from the rain. I can just make out the shape of her nipples poking through, and the outline of her breasts. Does she own any item of clothing that doesn't end up sticking to her? *Don't get distracted Delaney, going there will get you in trouble again.*

"Yes please."

I walk past her to the bathroom. I'm still unsure why she came here to show me the sketch I did of her. I hand her the towel. She's lost a little weight. I didn't notice earlier, but I can see it in her face. Her jaw is finer, and her cheekbones are more pronounced, cat like.

"Thank you." She takes the towel and starts rubbing her hair. The first time I saw her do that was when I picked her up to take her to class. The last few weeks seem like a blur.

"Did you walk here?"

"Yes, I didn't think it would rain. I suppose the black clouds rolling in should have given it away. I wasn't planning to come here. I was just out walking, but when it did start raining, I was close by." She shrugs her shoulders, "Sometimes you work late on Fridays, and I just wanted to get out of the storm."

The whole garage lights up and within seconds the sky around us rumbles. The rain is now coming down in sheets, smacking on the tin roof of the garage.

"Lucky you came in." I'm not sure that I believe what she's saying though. Was she on her way here anyway, and is now just using the storm as an excuse? "You should get out of those clothes."

"What? I'm not taking my clothes off Ethan."

"It's not like I haven't seen it all before." I raise my eyebrows at her, and she scowls back.

"I mean we have a spare set of coveralls in the back you can put on. You can get changed in the bathroom, or you can just stay there dripping in your wet clothes."

"I'd rather stay in my wet clothes thanks."

Why is she always so fucking stubborn?

"You're not worried about catching a cold?"

"I never catch colds. I'm British, I'm used to this weather. Not like you Californians who think that every time it rains it's the apocalypse."

"I'm just trying to be helpful."

"Don't."

She folds her arms and shivers, then sneezes.

I walk past her into the office before she sees me getting hard at the sight of her body through that shirt. I've talked myself out of an erection by the time I'm back with the coveralls. I throw them at her.

"You can put these on in the bathroom, or just stay in your clothes and catch pneumonia. Either way, I'm going to keep working here." I slide myself back under the truck. She's silent for a minute, then I see her weight move to her back foot.

"I don't think it's going to fit me."

"Of course, it's not going to fit you. It's made for a large hairy mechanic."

'Is it clean?"

"Let's hope so." Silence again, except for the sound of the rain splashing on the roof.

"I think we should talk."

"Before or after you get changed?"

"Before." Great, now I've got to stand here looking at that shirt clinging to her, her tits straining at the wet material, her shorts sucked into her skin. But I can restrain myself, for now. I push myself out again and stand. I lean back against the truck and fold my arms. It's taking every ounce of willpower for me not to get hard. I see that she flits her eyes briefly between my legs.

"I have some questions."

"Should I be taking notes?" She ignores my sarcasm.

"Why did you draw me?"

"It was something to do."

"You shouldn't have drawn me without my permission."

I laugh, "Should I have written you a note? *Dear Teach...Is it okay if I draw you a picture?*

"Shut up."

"What's the problem, don't you like them?"

"That's not the point."

"What is *the fucking point, Charlotte*? Why are you here?"

"I told you; I was just out walking!"

"You were just out walking with my sketches?"

"Why did you leave them in the poetry book for me to find?"

"I dunno, thought you might like them."

"Why are you so afraid of being with me?"

Woah, I still haven't got used to how direct she can be. How the fuck am I supposed to answer that?

"Go and put on those coveralls Charlotte and I'll take you home."

"Is that it?"

I want to say no, I want to give you everything, but I can't.

"That's all I can give you."

She bites her lips. Her pillowy, *I want them round my cock,* lips.

"All right if that's what you want. But I don't want your coveralls. I'm going to get wet again so I might as well stay wet."

I want to make a crude joke, but now's not the time. I just nod and shove my hands in my pockets to stop me grabbing hold of her, hoisting her up onto Old Blue and ripping her clothes off.

The wipers have to work extra hard tonight, it's only a short ride to Charlottes, but the windshield is foggy. The rain just keeps on coming. We need it though, at the end of a summer drought us Angelenos are glad for it. The Mustang isn't though. There's water pooling in the footwell of the passenger side, and Charlotte has to crouch on the seat to keep her feet up. I forgot that the roof sometimes leaks, it hasn't rained for so long. The car's stalled twice now at traffic lights, the engine must be cold and damp. This car is twenty years old. I guess she has the right to complain now and then. I've slowed down to a crawl; the roads are treacherous. Los Angeles isn't built for rain; it can't cope at all. We both got soaking wet just running from the garage to the car. My hair feels like a slippery mess. I've just pushed it as far back as I can, but the odd drop keeps trickling down my forehead. Charlotte keeps shivering as the heater has decided not to work. We'll probably both come down with colds after this.

Finally, we pull into the carport. I daren't turn the engine off in case I can't get it to start again. Charlotte's hair's stuck to her head and is now a dark golden color. Her face is pink, flushed, and rosy from the rain. She looks worthy of her last name. I'm not looking forward to the drive home. I'm still staying at Rob and Mo's and their house is another thirty minutes away. It'll take even longer in this weather. Maybe I'll just wait it out at the garage.

"I don't think you should drive in this." She's not looking at me, but straight ahead instead.

"I'll be fine."

"Seriously? We barely made it here and the roads are oily. Just at least wait until the rain eases off a bit."

"I think it's here for the night."

She sighs then and I feel bad, I've been a bit of a dick with her tonight. "Okay, maybe a coffee will be good, wake me up a bit."

She pulls hard at the handle and the passenger side door lurches open. A deluge of water cascades off the roof as she swings her legs out, covering them.

"I just can't catch a break today, can I," she mutters as she gets out of the car.

I tell the Mustang that it'll be okay, that I'll fix her roof and look at the engine. I pat the steering wheel as I leave. I can see Charlotte looking at me quizzically. I guess not everyone talks to their cars like they're people. I remember I still have the blanket in the car, and I take it out of the trunk.

"Why are you getting that out?" She purses her lips at me.

"We can put it over our heads whilst we go up the stairs. Besides, it needs a wash." *Again, not a time for jokes, Ethan.* I hold it out over our heads like a tent.

"Okay on three, we run. One, two, three!" I start to run and the rest of the blanket flops over me.

"I said on three!" I shout at her, the wind off the ocean filling my mouth with water and salt.

"You said after three!" She's still huddling in the carport and then I hear her say, *"Fuck it"* and she joins me underneath the blanket. We fly up the steps like a weird four-legged creature. I hold it above us still as she fumbles for her key in her bag. Amazingly, with all the crap in there, she finds it quickly. She unlocks the door, and as she pushes it open, a crack of thunder splits the sky open above us. Startled, we both fall inside the door. I throw the blanket on the floor in a mushy heap. We both bend over to catch our breath, then she starts laughing - which makes me laugh. Both of us are hunched over in hysterics as the sky outside flashes white. For a moment we freeze, staring at each other. She reaches over to the wall and flips the light switch on; the moment gone.

"You should probably take a hot shower. I can run downstairs to the laundry room and put your clothes in the dryer."

"Thanks, but you should shower first. You've been in wet clothes longer than I have." Though I don't want her to change, I want to keep looking at that shirt, clinging to her tits. I can't stop thinking about how soaked her panties must be by now.

"Oh no, your sketches! They'll be ruined!" She reaches into her bag and pulls out the book of poems, it's soggy and wet. "No, no no," She flicks through the pages to find them, before putting them on the table and flattening them out. There she is in charcoal, laid out in front of me. She's leaning over looking at them, her eyes wide with concern.

"Don't worry, I can draw some more."

"How can you draw me some more if I'm not going to see you again?"

She picks one up and starts to shake it out. There's another flash of lightning and the lights flicker on and off. She's standing here in front of me, soaking wet, her soft hair flowing down her back. She looks like a mermaid. I want my hands and mouth all over her, but I've told myself that I can't. *What if I'm making a huge mistake though? What if these feelings I'm having for her are the real thing. She's not Gina and I'm not a kid anymore. Do I want to keep running away my whole life? She's right, the minute things got difficult I left. I don't want to do that anymore. I don't want to be that guy, that's not who I really am.*

I take a step forward, my mind still at war with itself, but I can't resist her any longer. I walk up behind her and lower her hands. She doesn't move as I put my face to her neck and kiss it. I lick off the tiny droplets of moisture that have gathered there.

"What are you doing?" She whispers.

"What I should have done earlier."

The sketch falls out of her hands onto the floor, as she leans back into me. I start to bite at her neck, slowly at first then lick her again up to her ear. I want to sink my teeth in further, to taste her blood, to claim her in some way. She turns her face to mine and her breath feels warm. Her eyes are opal-like, her lashes are wet and black. The freckles on her nose are like her own little constellation of stars. I bite her top lip gently, and her lips part as my tongue finds its way inside. I run it along the inside of her lips, before seeking out the rest of her mouth which she presses into mine. I'm tearing at her blouse now, not caring about ripping it. It feels like cobwebs in my hands, and I pull it off her shoulders. I unclasp her bra with one hand at the back. She helps me pull the straps down, and as it falls, she tips back slightly- as if she's putting her tits on display for me. I run my fingers over them, remembering the curves of them that I've drawn. Her nipples are hard. I roll one between my fingers; its pinkness just asking to be sucked. I sit on the table and pull her to me. I tease her nipple with my tongue as I pull her little shorts down over her hips, taking my time over the slope of them. She's wearing flimsy black lace panties and the sight of them makes me groan.

"You always wear the tiniest panties" I whisper into her tits and snap the string on one side as I say it. I hook my fingers through them and tug them down to rest just on her thighs.

"Don't take them all the way down" she whispers, "It feels dirtier not to." Hearing her say, *"dirtier"* in her accent makes my dick strain even further to get out. I grab hold of her behind her head and kiss her hard, pulling her body between my legs. I want to consume every inch of her. She's pulling my t shirt off now and running her hands across my chest. She takes her hand down to the tail of my dragon. She follows the line of him down to my pants, before feeling the outline of my cock under her hands. I tilt forward as she pulls my jeans off, and I can't help but stroke my dick at the sight of her naked body with her panties half pulled down.

"I want you in my mouth and in my pussy." She kneels and begins to lick up and down my shaft, before wrapping her lips around its head as I swell in her mouth. I close my eyes and throw my head back, as she brings her mouth round and down my cock and up again, swirling her tongue as she does. I press my hands into the table and watch her. I'm hypnotized by those soft lips moving up and down my hard dick, and her heavy breasts pushing up against each other. I've never had anyone suck my dick like she does. I won't be able to stop myself from coming though and I want to fill her sweet little cunt. I want to stuff it full of my cum until it floods out of her. I grab hold of her hair and pull her up, bringing her face to mine and kiss her. I can taste my own pre cum on her lips. I turn her around and she leans over the table.

"Is this what you want Delaney?"

She pushes her ass high in the air, and I moan loudly.

"Yes, that's exactly what I want." Her panties are still just below her thighs, and I pull them down a little as she parts her legs further. She looks back at me as I enter her and takes a sharp inhale of breath.

"I'd forgotten how big you are."

"Rookie mistake," I reply, thrusting into her again as she spreads her legs more. The lace of her panties rubs up against my thighs. I pull her hair off her face, and she turns to look at me. I feel like a wild thing, a creature that has climbed out of the depths to hunt her down and fuck her. I thrust harder, wanting to fill every inch of her gorgeous little pussy. "You're so fucking wet."

"I'm always wet when you're around."

"Fuck, now I'm thinking of your little panties getting wet when you teach me in class."

"They were soaked." she turns to me and licks her lips as she says it.

"Oh, my fucking God" She pushes her ass up to me then and starts gyrating on my cock. My eyes disappear into my head. She's about to cum all over my dick as she moves faster. She's going to pump the cum out of me.

"Oh Ethan, I've missed your cock so much. I want your cum inside me, I want to carry it around in me all night." She pushes down hard on me then, breathing fast. Her body begins to pulsate as she orgasms on me. I explode, feeling her cum makes me grab her waist and pull her to me, and I shoot my load up her until I see stars.

I hear myself saying her name again and again, until I collapse on top of her. My face in her hair, before she turns her cheek to me. I lick the sweat off it like a dog as another clap of thunder erupts, and the lights in the apartment flicker again and go off.

Chapter Twenty-Three

Charlotte

I light another candle; dried wax is stuck to the brass like something out of medieval times. Lorraine, the owner of my rental, likes her candles. She has dozens of them, the drawer in the living room coffee table has at least twenty. Some are in boxes, some half burned. These brass candlesticks adorn the mantlepiece. If only I'd got some wood, we could be laying in front of a fire by now, getting warm. The coastal air is thick tonight, swarming with the mood of the storm. I wonder if it's as cool inland.

"Mo says their electricity is on, we can go there."

I wander back into the kitchen, "Stay with your brother?"

"We don't have to see them. I'm staying in the guest house out the back. It's cozy, we can have a shower then snuggle up in bed. You can see where the seventeen-year-old me lived and slept, dreaming of women like you."

I still can't believe that I just had sex with him on the kitchen table. The last time he sat at that table, he walked out. *Are we really going to give this thing a go, between us?*

I move the candle to the kitchen windowsill, the wax dribbling down and hardening.

"I dread to think of how many times you jerked off in that bed."

"The mattress is new, if that helps."

"Marginally." I can just see Ethan in this light. He's standing with a towel around his waist, his torso highlighted by the candlelight. We still hadn't managed to have a shower; the hot water's powered by electricity. "What are you going to wear to go to your brother's in?"

"What's wrong with this towel?" The rain has eased off, but the sky still looks threatening. I roll my eyes at him, only someone in their twenties would be happy leaving the house with just a towel around their waist. *Though he does look pretty freaking phenomenal.*

"I'll borrow one of your sweaters, you've got a couple of oversized ones. If that will make you feel better."

"It would." I'm wearing my silk kimono. I didn't imagine when I bought it that I would wear it after sex with a beautiful man. I sit on the edge of the table. He comes over and kisses me on the head. Everything suddenly feels so different from the last few weeks.

"Maybe we should just wait it out here?"

"Charlotte, did you also forget that we just put a bucket in the bedroom to catch the drips from the leaking roof. I'm pretty sure if there's one spot, there will be more. We can't sleep here."

"You can keep me warm." I put my arms around his waist and lay my head on his stomach, it rises and falls to his breath. I love the line of hair that runs down from his belly button. I rub my face against it. I can feel his cock under the towel begin to get hard again. His phone lights up on the countertop with a text.

"Mo says the electricity will be out on the coast for the night, and another storm is expected with possible flooding. We should leave soon."

I hope Mrs. Lebowski downstairs is alright, I should probably check on her before we go.

"Your car probably won't start."

"That's why we're taking yours."

"Like mine is reliable…"

"Well, it can't be in worse shape than the Mustang."

I put my arms round him again and bury my face. "I don't want to drive right now, I'm exhausted."

"I'll drive."

"You could just leave me here. You forget that I'm from England. We're damp ninety nine percent of the time." I know I sound ungrateful, but I really don't want to risk running into his brother. He seems like an ass.

"I don't want to be apart from you, we've wasted too much time already."

I look up at him, "I've wasted? You're the one who went AWOL! Are we going to talk about this or is it just sex and then carry on as usual?"

"I was hoping for that, yes."

I give him a sharp dig in the ribs. "Seriously Ethan, are we going to talk about what happened? Why you got so freaked out? How do I know it's not going to happen again?"

He comes to sit next to me on the table and grabs hold of my hand.

"All I can tell you Charlotte, is that I will do everything I can to make sure it doesn't happen again. Some shit happened in my past that I'm not proud of. It was after my mom got sick, I kind of self-destructed." He trails his fingers through his hair. "Ever since then, I've been running from anything or anyone that makes me feel something again." He hesitates for a minute. "I guess I was so afraid that eventually I'd lose you as well. So, I put a stop to things before I could fuck things up. I know it doesn't make sense. I thought I would eventually forget about us." He squeezes my hand, "But you're all I could think about."

A lump forms in my throat. "What if you feel like running again?"

He looks at me, a small smile tugging at the corner of his eyes, "Then I'll remind you to keep my feet on the ground."

I bite my lip; *I still haven't told him what I'm running from.*

"I'm scared too."

"I know you are." He leans in and rubs the tip of his nose against my cheek.

"Eww, your beard is tickling me."

"I didn't hear any complaints earlier." He rubs his beard against me purposely before I push him away laughing.

"Okay professor, go get changed, and let's get out of here before the next storm rolls in."

I give him a little salute as a drop of water falls on my head. Any conversation about my past will have to wait until later.

I wake up as we pull into the carport of his brother's house. I don't even remember falling asleep. The heater must have lulled me into it, thank goodness it's working in this car. I sit up and rub my eyes. I'd been dreaming that I was living in a cottage in the woods with Ethan but was too afraid to go outside. I was convinced that something was out there, watching us in the dark. I look across at him in a towel and my sweatshirt and the nightmare falls away. I'm in my pajamas, they seemed the coziest thing to put on. We must look quite the pair. My hand fumbles for the door handle, but his hand presses gently on my shoulder indicating for me to stay put. He undoes my seat belt and kisses me on the nose. I relax my head back and close my eyes again. I don't know why I'm so tired, but I expect it's the last few weeks catching up with me. Ethan gets out of the car and opens the passenger door. He scoops his arms underneath me, and I put my arms around his neck. He lifts me out of the car, and I can hear his heartbeat as I lay my head on his chest. "I hope your towel falls down," I whisper to him.

"You wish." he replies, carefully shuffling between the car and the side of the carport. He walks into the back yard. The rain has mercifully stopped, and I snuggle into his warmth. I feel so safe. He holds the keys in his mouth, finds the right one with his free hand and unlocks the door. He pushes it open with his foot and carries me in. He switches on a lamp, and I see that it's a simple room with whitewashed walls. It's sparse with just a closet, a desk and a bed covered in a blue blanket. There is a statue of Madonna and child on the wall with a candle perched above it.

"I didn't know your brother was religious."

"He's not. Mo put it there when I moved in after my mum died. She said it was to watch over me." He puts me down carefully on the bed.

"So, Mo is the religious one?"

"My mom was, she believed in all that. Took us to church on Sundays, and I think Mo wanted to carry on part of that tradition."

"It's beautiful." It really is. Madonna's gown is painted ruby and her mantle a cornflower blue; the babe is pink and fleshy in her arms. The sconce above her is like a halo, that probably shines when the candle's lit. I would've liked that above my bed as a child - a reassuring mother, rather than the one I had. There's a plain wooden chair at the desk, it looks like something a quaker would have. I sense this room has been a refuge for not only Ethan, but perhaps even for Mo since he left.

"Do you still want a shower?" Ethan opens a door that leads to a small kitchenette, and then another door to the bathroom.

"Mm, yes please, that sounds nice." Even though my pajamas are cozy, my earlier walk in the rain means that my bones are still rattling a bit. I miss the summer heat I'd been complaining about.

'I'll just run it until it gets warm for you." He's talking to me from the bathroom now and I can hear the rushing of water and the gurgling of a drain as it swirls down.

"Are you not having one?" I take off my socks and sneakers and stretch out my toes, wriggling them to get the feeling back again. He's back in the room now, his hair moist from the steam of the shower.

"No, you go first."

I lean back on my elbows and look up at him. He looks like a peaceful giant. "That beard suits you." He rubs it, and the image of the Estonian Woodcutter comes to me again.

"You think so? It's getting a bit itchy now." He scratches underneath his chin.

"It's like a black forest. I wouldn't mind getting lost in there." I tip my head to the side and grin up at him.

He laughs. "I'd be okay with that."

"Why don't we take a shower together?" He knows what I'm implying.

"I thought you were tired."

"I am, but maybe it will wake me up, come." I extend my hands towards him. He pulls me up and I press my face to his chest, I feel safe again.

The bathroom is small with a step down to a good-sized shower for the space. The tiles are beige and white and look as if they haven't been changed since the seventies. The room is steamy already and Ethan's body is camouflaged by wisps of vapor as he pulls the sweater, he borrowed off me, over his head. I'm already out of my pajamas and putting one foot into the shower. It feels so welcome on my skin. I stand under it and lift my head to catch some of the heat in my mouth. Ethan is behind me now. His hands on me, gliding down my hips, pulling me to him. My skin is slippery under his touch as he brings his hands around to my breasts and cups them. I tip my head back towards him and kiss him on the mouth. His lips are warm, and we catch droplets between us. I can feel his erection at the small of my back. He puts his arms all the way around me and reaches for the soap that's sitting in its dish. It's a dark forest green and as he brings it to my body and down between my breasts, I smell him. This is what his scent is, pine trees and clear skies and rich earth. He takes it down to my belly button, then between my legs where he circles it, washing me there as it foams white. Then he takes one hand off the soap and takes the foam, and gently strokes it on my ass, up and down so tenderly it's almost too much to bear. I turn around to him, his long lashes have tiny beads of water on them, like early morning dew. I push his hair back and hold his face. I can see the tiny amber flecks in his eyes, and his cheeks feel sharp beneath my fingers. He looks up to the shower head, and I lick his Adams apple. I run my tongue down the stubble on his neck, lapping at the moisture as it runs down him like a waterfall. I know what I want as I take the soap off him. It feels smooth, like a pebble polished by the sea. I run it across his chest, and it leaves a creamy froth as I move it down towards his navel, and then to his groin. I bring the soap underneath him and around his balls. I kneel, his rock-hard dick standing proud. I lather around and lick his cock from the base to the tip; it's my turn to worship at the altar. He lays his hand on my head as if in a blessing and pushes his hips to me. My mouth opens and I take him in, my lips molding their way around his cock, as it swells even more in my mouth. He's groaning and saying my name as I hold his dick still. I suck gently on it like I'm enjoying an ice pop on a hot day. I bring my lips back up his shaft and then down and up again, pressing my tongue against it as I do. I reach down and touch my pussy as he moans again. I can't distinguish my wetness from that of the shower, everything feels fluid. I want to be fucked again, to be thrown against the cool tiles and ground into them. My lips, though, can't seem to let go of his glorious cock. I pull it out then put the tip of it inside the cheek of my mouth. I tap the bulge and he leans into it, "Holy fuck, Charlotte. That—" His breath sounds strained. He can't even seem to get the words out. "That's the hottest fucking thing I've ever seen in my entire fucking life." I pick the soap back up and sweep around his balls, before tipping my head back and easing him in, I want him deep.

I want to feel his orgasm all the way down my throat. I put my hand back to my pussy and press my fingers in. I stroke my clit as I deep throat him. I have one hand on the floor to support me, and the other between my legs as I eat his cock. He's so focused, the water is falling down his body and hitting me in the face. He's looking down into my eyes and then he moves faster, and my hand between my legs does the same. He grabs hold of my hair then arches his body back and his legs begin to shake. I rub small circles against my clit, moving quicker and quicker and my climax rushes at me, building like a wave until it ricochets through my body as his cum splashes at the back of my throat. I swallow. I look up at him, and his mouth is open as if in a silent roar, his dick is still hard in my mouth. I slowly take it out and rest my face between his legs. He turns the shower off, and we stay like that for a moment, me knelt between his legs. He puts his arms underneath me and pulls me up to standing, our wet bodies find each other in the fog, and I push my tits into his chest as his hands cup my ass and pulls me to him.

"You give the best head, Miss Rose."

"Well, look what I had to work with."

He tugs gently on my bottom lip with his teeth, and I yield to him, our skin slippery against each other's. He gets out of the shower to pass me a towel from the rail. It's blue, like the blanket, and soft. I wrap it around me like a sarong, as he slides open the window to try and clear the room of the steam. He gets a towel for himself and ties it around his waist, his chest slick and bare.

"Are you hungry? Do you want me to get anything from the kitchen?"

"I'm good, I think I'd just like to get cozy in bed."

He opens the bathroom door for me, and we walk through the small kitchenette back into the bedroom. I sit on the bed, opening the towel and bringing it down to dry my legs.

"Can we light the candle on the Madonna?"

"We can do whatever you like," He opens a desk drawer for a lighter and flicks it with his thumb to check it's working. He walks over to the statue and lights the halo on Mary's head, and it sparks for a second. I take off my towel and slip into bed, the sheets feel fresh and clean and the blanket comforting. Ethan puts the lighter back in the drawer, then clicks the desk lamp off and tucks himself into bed beside me. He pulls me close as the Madonna glows, her gown shimmering jewel like, as she shines her light over us. I feel more peaceful than I have in weeks, but there's also a knot in my stomach. I know this can't last forever. Eventually, it will come to an end. I'm still married, and my visa will only last as long as Frank says it can. I'm falling for a man that I know I can never really have. I close my eyes and pray that someone isn't watching me in my dreams again.

Chapter Twenty-Four

Ethan

Something has woken me up and it takes me a minute to figure out what it is. Then I hear it again, it's a light tapping on the door. There's a single stream of sunshine coming through the crack in the curtains. Motes of dust are swirling in it, creating its own little galaxy. I stretch for my phone, it's already nine thirty. Charlotte is still sleeping. I cover her breasts with the sheet, and she rolls onto her side, mumbling incoherently. I pick a t-shirt off the floor and pull it over my head, before going to the door. Mo is on the other side of it. I step outside and quietly close it, putting a finger to my lips. I rearrange my hair to make it less disheveled from sleep. I want to look a little bit respectful whilst talking to my sister-in-law, especially since she would've seen Charlotte sleeping in my bed when the door opened.

"Sorry I didn't know you had company. I just thought you might like some coffee." I like my sister-in-law a lot, but I know when she's lying. She knew I was bringing Charlotte home and she probably wanted to get a look at her.

"You checking up on me big sis?" Mo feels like that to me, like the sister I never had. She has the same kindness and consideration for others, as my mom did. She clasps her hands together.

"No, no of course not, I just heard your car come in late and wanted to make sure you were okay after the storm."

"You're a terrible liar." I grin at her, before taking a sip from the hot coffee. It lights up my veins instantly.

"I *did* just want to make sure you're all right."

I arch an eyebrow at her. "Right."

"I'm being serious, Ethan. You know you're playing with fire here, and—"

"And how exactly am I playing with fire, Mo?"

Exasperation pinches her features. "Why do you always have to be so difficult?"

"Is it because Charlotte's older than me?"

Exasperation turns to annoyance in a flash. "Come on. You know me better than that. What does anyone's age matter? It's not like you're below the age of consent—"

I can't help but let out a huff of laughter at this; Mo swats my arm, scowling.

"It took a lot for you to go to college, you stubborn asshole. You're not like your brother. You're too good to spend the rest of your life working at the garage. You have all of these dreams! If you get kicked out of school now—"

I hold my hand up, stopping her in her tracks. I have to. I don't like where this conversation is headed. "Thanks for the coffee, Mo. I appreciate you checking to see if I'm okay. I—*we*—are both fine."

"You know I just love you, and I care what's best for you, right?"

Fuck. I hate seeing the concern on her face.

"I'm a big boy Mo."

"Yes, sweetheart, I know you are, and I also know you've had plenty of women."

"Inappropriate for this time of the morning, Mo."

"Sorry, I'm just trying to say that I know you're more sensitive than you make out. You are your mother's son." I look at Mo in the early light, her dark hair tied back in a ponytail, the small wrinkles forming around her eyes, her tiny frame. She looks older than she should.

"My brother doesn't deserve you."

"He does his best."

"Does he?" Mo takes a sharp breath in, and I take the hint.

"I just put another pot of coffee on, and I have some fresh bagels and pancakes if you and your... friend would like some."

"That would be nice, Mo, thanks." I kiss her on the cheek and watch as she makes her way back to the main house. I don't think it will be nice at all, not with Rob there, but I don't want to offend her.

Charlotte stirs as I open the door and come back in, there's something so right about her being here. I put my coffee on the desk and dive onto the bed. She screams, then laughs as I land next to her. Her hair is up in a messy bun and blonde tendrils of hair are feathering her face. The little galaxy of light is highlighting the freckles on her nose. She looks ageless, the curve of her neck elegant, her skin pearl like. "You're beautiful in the morning light." I hear the cheesiness of the line as I say it.

"I don't believe you, but I'll take it." She takes a little bite at my neck, and I want to wrestle her down to the bed, but we don't have time. I get up and look for a change of clothes.

"Who was that at the door?"

"Mo, my sister-in-law. She's invited us for breakfast."

"Will your brother be there? I don't think he's my biggest fan."

"Rob isn't anyone's biggest fan."

"Great, a tough audience at breakfast."

"Charlotte, you teach at a community college. This will be a walk in the park."

"If you say so."

"I do."

I feel bad lying to her, I have no idea what we could be walking into.

Chapter Twenty-Five

Charlotte

I tuck myself into the breakfast nook as Mo places plates of bagels, pancakes, toast, and a pot of hot coffee onto the table. I feel conspicuous being in a stranger's kitchen, especially wearing Ethan's clothes. I hadn't thought past the coziness of my pajamas last night, and so now I'm wearing a pair of his tracksuit pants and a, *'Go Dodgers'* sweatshirt. I splashed my face with water and refashioned my hair back into a messy bun. I haven't got any makeup with me, and any remnants of yesterday's has been washed off. It's not the ideal time to be introduced to Ethan's family. I've met Rob before and spoken to him on the phone, but we've never had an actual conversation about anything other than my car. The first time I met him, he kept leering at me. So, I'm relieved to see that he isn't up yet. It's Saturday so the garage opens a bit later. I'm hoping he might stay in bed longer, so that I can avoid him completely. Mo seems nice though and Ethan always talks highly of her. The place is clean and has a country kitchen feel. There are fresh flowers on the table and paintings and photographs on the wall. There is one of a woman with dark hair kneeling in between two boys. One boy has his arms folded, and is a foot taller than the other, he's squinting at the sun. The other has black curls like the woman and is holding her hand. It must be Ethan, Rob, and their mother. Even from here I can tell she was stunning. She's obviously where Ethan gets his good looks from. He rarely talks about her though, and I don't want to force the subject. I only know that he was awfully close to her. Ethan grabs a piece of toast off the table and bites into it, before sliding his long legs round the bench to join me. He nudges me with his elbow when he lands and winks - it's his way of reassuring me. I probably look very uptight, which doesn't sit well with my English accent. It can make me seem stuffy. I try to relax my shoulders. Mo was busy cooking when we came in and so, it had been a quick, *"Good morning."* Now she's joined us at the table. Everything suddenly sounds very loud; the clinking of the coffee cups, the scraping of the cutlery. I know it's because I feel self-conscious and nervous about meeting his family. Looking at myself through Mo's eyes; older than her, teacher to her twenty-three-year-old brother-in-law and wearing his clothes. It can't be a great first impression. I feel short of breath and realize it's because I'm not actually breathing. *It's just breakfast*, I tell myself and stick my fork in a pancake before flopping it on my plate. I smile politely at Mo, really wishing this would be over.

"So, you're from England, Charlotte?"

I nod, chewing on a piece of pancake.

"How are you enjoying California, so far?"

"I love it. It's such a beautiful state. I'd love to take a road trip up the coast - I hear Big Sur is beautiful."

"We should do it. We can take Old Blue and camp out in the back under the stars." Ethan grins at me and I blush. I know what he's implying by, *"under the stars."*

Mo laughs "That old truck you're working on? I doubt she'd make it off the forecourt."

"Please Mo, that's the love of my life you're talking about." He grabs another piece of toast.

"I'm sure Charlotte will be pleased to hear that." Mo raises her eyebrows, spooning sugar into her coffee and stirring it.

"Oh, don't worry. I'm well aware of Ethan's car obsession."

She smiles at me, "That's good to hear. Now, why did you choose to stay in Los Angeles?"

I take a sip of tea, "I was offered a teaching job here."

"Oh yes, you're an English teacher…that's how you met Ethan."

"Yes, that's right." I stuff a large piece of pancake in my mouth and look at Ethan. He's too busy filling his face to hear what Mo just said. So, I nod and chew another mouthful. I'm waiting for her to say something else, but first she takes her time spreading some jam on a piece of toast.

"I loved English at school – reading all those classical novels. I always have a book by my bed, but by the time my head hits the pillow I'm out."

Okay so maybe this isn't going to be too bad.

"I think a lot of people struggle to find the time to read these days."

"Yes, you're lucky you get to read for your job. Ethan's been telling me how much he loves your classes. I even found him reading poetry the other day."

He obviously hasn't told her that he skipped three weeks of classes.

Ethan stops inhaling his food for a second. He leans back and puts his arm around the back of the bench. "She did." I'm grateful that he's rejoined the conversation.

"You must be a good influence on him then." She's searching my face when she says it and I know she's looking for something to mistrust. Clearly, she's very protective of Ethan and he seems completely ignorant of her prying.

"I hope so." She holds my gaze for a moment longer than necessary and then breaks it to take a sip of her coffee.

"Perhaps you could recommend some books? If I know there is a good book by my bed, I might be inspired to stay awake longer."

"Since when could you stay awake past nine?" Rob has entered the kitchen. His hair is sticking up and he's wearing a t-shirt and pajama pants.

"Nice of you to get dressed bro."

Rob turns his back to his brother, "Didn't know we had company. Where's the coffee?"

"On the table, you just need a cup." Mo's voice is low, clearly annoyed by her husband.

Rob opens the cupboard above his head and pulls out a mug, then walks over to the table, and pours himself some coffee. Everyone is silent.

"Scoot," Mo moves round the table as Rob wedges himself in, his belly bumps up against the table and a vision of Frank in the restaurant comes back to me.

"Hi Rob, I'm Charlotte. We've never been formally introduced." I stretch my hand out across the table. He ignores me and grabs a bagel.

"Ethan's teacher. I know who you are."

"Easy brother." Ethan shoots Rob a warning glance.

Rob shrugs "What? We already met, no need for *formalities*."

He says formalities in a fake English accent. I feel my cheeks get hot. Ethan squeezes my leg.

"What are you two doing today?" Mo's trying to soothe the situation.

"I'm going to try and do a temporary fix up of Charlotte's roof now the rain has stopped."

"Isn't that her landlord's job?" Rob's talking about me like I'm not here, so, I look directly at him and answer.

"Yes, but I'm subletting, and that's not really allowed."

He mutters something about *there's something else that's not allowed*, but then shuts up. Mo must have kneed him under the table. I serve myself another pancake. If I'm going to sit through *the breakfast from hell* -I might as well, make the most of it.

"I was just telling Charlotte how Ethan is always reading these days and that it's good to see him engaged in school again isn't it?"

"What's the point in you reading poetry anyway?"

At first, I thought the question was directed at me. but then I see that he's looking at Ethan.

"Maybe if you learned some poetry, big brother, then Mo here might get a little bit more romance from you."

"She gets all the romance she needs." He dips his knife in the cream cheese, takes a big dollop, and smears it on a bagel.

Mo gives a nervous smile and pours herself some more coffee. We all sit in silence for a bit. Rob devours his bagel in about two bites, then goes for another. When he's finished, he sits back and belches. He really is a pig.

"So, you're not coming into work today?" Rob looks across at his brother, then wipes his mouth on the back of his hand. A lump of cream cheese is still visible, dangling from the corner of his mouth.

"No, I told you, I need to fix Charlotte's roof. I've put plenty of hours in these past few weeks, and I didn't notice any overtime in my paycheck."

Rob laughs, "You think you should get overtime? I'll tell you what. Why don't we get Mo a second job, so that we can pay you overtime." He whispers, *"Jerk"* under his breath, then goes to refill his coffee, but it's empty. Mo gets up, but Ethan puts his hand across the table to stop her.

"Finish your breakfast Mo. Rob can get his own coffee if he wants it." She freezes for a minute, unsure what to do, but then sits back down. I don't know how she would've squeezed past Rob anyway. There isn't any daylight between his belly and the table. I know that the two of them didn't get on, but the fact that they managed to work together - made me think they were at least civil to each other. Rob stabs at a pancake and plops it on his plate. He squeezes half a bottle of maple syrup on it. "Hey Mo," he says louder than necessary, seeing as she's right beside him. He eats with his mouth open. "Your precious little Ethan here, thinks you should get another job." He looks directly at us, "So, that he can keep his new girlfriend in the *style she's become accustomed to.*" He says the last part in a bad English accent again. I glance at Ethan - his body stiffens and his eyes narrow. He sits forward.

"We all know Rob, that if you hadn't wasted half your life savings on card games - then your wife wouldn't have to work her shitty job in the first place. You're a pathetic drunk and gambler, just like dad."

I know Rob's an utter pig but why bait him like that? It's only going to make things worse.

Rob stands, making the table jerk as he does. He slams his fist down and the condiments all shake like miniature buildings in an earthquake. Rob and Ethan glare at each other and for a minute, I'm worried that Rob is going to lunge across the table, but Mo puts her hand on her husband's arm. I can see by his face that just her touch has steadied him a little, he must love his wife enough for that small action to affect him.

"I'm not going to sit here and take this!" He maneuvers himself from the breakfast nook and out of the kitchen. Mo's lips are tight, and her head is down as she plays with the fork on her plate. She sniffs, looks up and smiles. "Sorry about that, his bark is worse than his bite."

Ethan reaches out his hand and puts it over hers. She puts the fork down and squeezes it back. It seems that this isn't the first time this sort of thing has happened. Mo removes her hand from under Ethan's and pats his. I feel a little uncomfortable, it seems very intimate. They're obviously very close. That must be why it felt like she was interrogating me earlier. She gets up and refills the coffee pot. Ethan watches her the whole time, with a look of worry on his face. When she comes to sit back down at the table, he speaks to her softly.

"Are you okay? I'm sorry if I made things worse for you."

She looks up at Ethan and smiles. I feel as if I shouldn't be here - as if I'm intruding on private family time. At the same time, to see him being so loving towards his sister-in-law, makes my heart melt a little.

"I'm fine, you know me - tougher than I look."

Ethan nods, "I know Mo, but still..."

Mo shakes her head and blinks back tears. I sense that she's heard enough for today. She takes out her ponytail and pulls her hair around her shoulders.

"Any idea when Gina is moving out?"

Gina, I'd forgotten about her. That's the reason we're here though and not at Ethan's. It annoys me to think that he's letting her stay there still. It doesn't make sense to me. Why give your apartment over to someone like that? It's as if she has some kind of hold over him.

"I dunno, I haven't spoken to her in a few days."

A few days, so, they're still in touch regularly. But then, she's staying at his place, so I suppose they have to be.

Mo leans forward and rests her arms on the table, "I think you need to be firm with her, she's winding you round her little finger, just like she used to. You can't give up your apartment out of guilt."

"I have no intention of giving up my place, I honestly thought she'd be gone by now. You're right though, I do need to sort it out. I'll talk to her today."

I don't know what Gina's playing at or why Ethan feels so guilty about her. Mo picks up her plate and gets up from the table.

"You know I'd have you stay here as long as you want sweetheart. I just think you need to sort this out."

Ethan follows Mo and gets up from the table. I scooch round the bench with my plate and cup in my hand. I notice a book on the kitchen counter as I put my breakfast things down. My brain freezes for a second, as if my mind doesn't want to take in what it sees. I pick up the book, and it falls open on the inside back cover. Charles's face stares back at me. They've photoshopped his eyes to be even bluer and painted in his receding hair line.

"I haven't read that one yet, my friend at work recommended it to me. Got great reviews on amazon. Maybe that will keep me awake. Have you read it?"

My mouth is dry and, at first, no words will come out. I close the book and try to get his image out of my head.

"No, I haven't." I try to swallow, but my throat hurts.

I'm lying, I know that book inside out, I wrote most of it, like I did Charles's previous two books. I wrote all the recent ones that made it to the New York Times Best Seller list. To see it here in this kitchen seems so out of place. I feel unsteady, as if someone's playing a trick on me. But I know that can't be possible. It was a bestseller book recommendation, why shouldn't it be here?

"Are you okay Charlotte? You look like you've seen a ghost?" Mo's studying me now, as if she's suspicious of something.

"I'm fine thank you; I just got a bit hot."

"She has a habit of swooning when I'm around." Ethan comes up behind me and kisses me on the cheek.

"Ha ha, very funny." Feeling his kisses on my face instantly makes me feel better.

"Well, I'll let you know if it's any good. Perhaps we could do a book trade or something? We could have our own little book club?"

Great, a book club on the book *I wrote*. It will likely never happen though; we both know that. She's just making a show in front of Ethan to make him feel better. So, I smile and go along with it.

"What a great idea." I pull Ethan's arms around me, and a shadow passes across her face, so quickly, that I think I might have imagined it.

We walk back to the guest house hand in hand. Ethan's quiet, probably thinking about having to talk to Gina, or still reeling from his brother being such a *giant fucking asshole*. I want to tell him that Mo doesn't like me, but I know he won't believe it. Men are often blind to things like that. I also think it's because she wants to protect him, rather than any specific vitriol towards me.

"Sorry about Rob. I thought he might behave. I was wrong."

I shrug it off, I don't want him to know how much the whole experience has rattled me. "Don't worry about it."

"We're staying at your place tonight, right?"

"Are we?"

He was about to pick up his overnight bag, but pauses, "Don't you want me there?"

How can I tell him that I'm still worried that he's going to leave again, especially when he finds out what I've been hiding from him. I want him there though; I want to wake up with him in my bed every morning.

"Of course, I do, I just want to make sure we're doing the right thing."

"I thought we'd been through this?"

"We have. I'm sorry, I just need some more reassurance I suppose."

He comes over to me and puts his arms around my waist, and squeezes my ass, "I can give you all the reassurance you need."

I push him away, laughing. 'Not *that kind* of reassurance."

He puts his hands in the air, "You can't blame a guy for trying."

I sit on the end of the bed and watch him move about the room. His long taut body looks so sexy as he grabs clothes to put in his bag.

"Were you your mum's favorite?" It's out of my mouth before I can catch it, a habit of a lifetime is hard to break.

"Hmm?"

"Between you and your brother?"

"Why would you ask me that?"

"I just wondered if that's where all the animosity stems from."

"I don't know, he was always closer to dad."

"You never talk about your parents."

"What's there to say?" Ethan opens the door to the small bathroom and starts to pack his toiletry bag. I pick at the snags on the blanket on the bed that have gone bobbly.

"I just thought you might want to share that with me. I feel like I know you, and yet I don't. Does that make sense?" I get up and follow him into the bathroom.

"I suppose so. I could say the same about you."

"Probably, but it feels like when I ask you stuff like that, you shut down. Like that scar on your chin for example, you must know where you got it from." I can see both of our reflections in the bathroom mirror.

"I keep telling you Charlotte, that I don't remember. I probably fell off my bike or something as a kid."

I want to believe him, but then I look down and notice his hands are gripping the sink, his knuckles are white. He still isn't ready to tell me what happened to carve that lightning scar in his chin, whatever it is still haunts him.

Chapter Twenty-Six

Charlotte

Three Weeks Later

"Is he here?"

"Is who here?"

"You know damn well who."

It takes me a minute to register who I'm talking to at 8.30 am on a Sunday morning. I pull my kimono tighter and adjust the glasses on my nose. My eyes are still blurry from getting out of bed to answer the door. I should have just ignored it. There's an angry 5ft nothing girl on my doorstep, and I'm not at my best first thing.

"It's Gina, isn't it?" I hear Mrs. Lebowski's door below creak open. No doubt. She's listening through the crack. I thought she might cut me some slack after I gave her lots of candles and matches on the day the electricity went out. She didn't.

"It's Professor, isn't it?" Gina puts her hands on her hips and cocks her head. No one should be this sassy at this time on a Sunday morning. She's wearing a tiny summer dress that just covers her ass. It looks like something I dressed my barbie dolls in as a kid.

"If you're looking for Ethan, he's not here."

She pouts and squints her eyes at me "So you do know who I'm talking about?"

I sigh, "How did you get my address?"

She pulls a piece of paper out of her purse and waves it at me "The genius wrote your address down the first time he picked you up when your car was in the garage. I knew that English woman had to be you." She gives me the once over, "I just didn't think he'd still be fucking his professor, but here we are."

Wow, this girl's a piranha. I consider planting my hand in her face and shoving her away. I need to be careful though, Ethan must have his reasons for letting her hold his apartment hostage. He's been staying with me for three weeks now. He unofficially moved in after the night at his brother's. I assumed that he'd spoken to Gina, and that she'd be out of his life soon. I haven't asked him about it, as the subject seemed so sensitive. Last time I asked, it blew up in my face. Obviously, nothing has been sorted out at all. I adjust my hair, it's doing its usual, *"I refuse to be tamed,"* morning routine. I'm not appropriately dressed for dealing with, what appears to be, my nemesis at the door.

"I knew the minute he looked at you at Carl's party, that something was going on! You pretend to be all classy and la dee da" she said the last bit in a surprisingly good British accent, any other time I would have complimented her on it. I'm not sure what she's expecting, a cat fight maybe? I could probably pick her up and toss her in the ocean, she's so minuscule. The thought is tempting.

"What do you have that I don't?"

I mutter, *"Sanity"* under my breath. "Look Gina, I'm sorry that you felt you had to come here today and have a showdown with me. I'll let Ethan know you came over, and he will call you."

I go to shut the door, but she wedges her foot in it. *Fuck her!* I know though, that in the state that she's in, any kind of altercation is not the answer. I've dealt with enough troubled students to know to stay calm in this kind of situation. Maybe the best thing would be for her to wait here for Ethan, let him deal with her. He should have done that weeks ago, instead of hiding from her. I walk back into the kitchen and let the door swing open, I fill a pot with water and pop it on the stove to boil for tea. I still don't understand Americans and their lack of kettles. This disarms her; she was probably hoping I would escalate the situation.

"Tea?" I ask, turning the dial for the gas and listening to the click, click, click as it comes on. I reach into the cupboard for two mugs, not waiting for an answer. She's still standing in the doorway, looking unsure of her next move. I only hope it doesn't involve throwing anything at me or hair pulling. I continue my tea making and take two tea bags from their box and place one in each cup. Ethan went out early to go to the

Jewish bakery to get the, "*Best bagels and cream cheese you've ever tasted.*" I look up at the clock on the kitchen wall, he's been gone forty minutes. These bagels better be bloody good. I hear Gina come into the kitchen; she closes the door behind her. I hope it wasn't a mistake letting her in.

"Do you take milk or sugar?"

"I don't want any tea."

"Suit yourself. Is your mum still here?" I want to keep her talking until Ethan gets here. I don't want to give her a chance to lose it again.

"No, she went home yesterday."

Ah, so that was why the patient was let out of the loony bin.

"You must miss her."

"Not really, I'm moving back to Texas next week, so I'll see her then."

Thank fuck for that.

"I thought you're from Los Angeles?"

"I am, we moved there when I left high school. Mom thought it best I get a fresh start."

She must be referring to her relationship with Ethan. Six years is a long time to not be over someone. It's pretty obvious that she's never dealt with the pain it caused her when she was a teenager. Perhaps she thinks her life took a bad turn when she split up with him, and wants to feel the way she did before? Is that why she moved back here? To try again? I know they got back together for a couple of months, and it didn't work out. Ethan said it was pretty awful, and that it felt as if she was punishing him the whole time for past mistakes. I've counselled plenty of students to know that it's likely therapy she needs, not Ethan. However, I'm not the person to tell her that.

The water on the stove is boiling, I turn off the knob and pour it into my cup. "Are you sure you don't want one?"

"What kind of tea is it?"

"Earl gray."

"What's it taste like?"

"It sort of tastes like London - on a foggy day -with the sun trying to break through."

She screws up her face, "Sounds weird."

I smile, even though I want to strangle her. "It's an acquired taste."

"Does Ethan like it?"

"He does."

"I'll try some." I pour the rest of the water into her mug and carry them both over to the table. I set hers in front of the chair opposite. I sit down and after hesitating for a minute, she pulls out the other chair and sits. I blow on my tea. It makes a thin whistling sound and small bubbles appear. My gran always said that when lots of bubbles form in tea it means good fortune; I hope she was right.

"Ethan tells me you play the piano."

"Did he?"

"Yes." He said her one redeeming feature was that she played like a dream.

"Do you do it professionally?"

"No, I haven't played for years."

Another sign that she's forgotten how to be happy by herself. "Maybe you should start again."

"What's it to you?" There it is; the snap from the little crocodile across the table here. Part of me had started to feel sorry for her, but that's the mistake Ethan keeps making.

"I just think that we all need creative outlets."

"What's yours?"

"I write."

"Books?"

I want to say that I ghost wrote most of my husband's last two books, largely because he was too pissed to get through them. "No, just my own stuff. Poems and short stories."

"Sounds lame."

"Thank you." I take a sip of my tea and smile. I refuse to let her get to me. She takes a sip of hers.

"Ugh that's gross."

"I told you it was an acquired taste" *Much like you,* I add under my breath.

"How old are you?"

"I'm thirty-five."

"That's old."

"Is it?"

I regret inviting her in. I thought I could rub some of her rough edges off - but she has the personality of a piece of sandpaper. What the hell had Ethan seen in her? I mean, I suppose she's pretty and petite - with those big brown eyes, olive skin and a perfect body.

I feel like a gangly giant next to her, or worse her mother; even though she's Ethan's age. I sneak another look at the clock, he's been gone nearly an hour now. How long can this bagel line be? I feel like I'm stuck babysitting an annoying child. I want to go get dressed, but don't want to leave her unsupervised. I don't trust her not to poison my tea or something.

Finally, I hear the purr of the Mustang, Ethan's back. He shuts the car door and sprints up the stairs. Gina tenses then tosses her hair back. She pulls her legs out from under the table and crosses them.

"Sorry it took so long, I ended up..." He stops dead when he sees her. The top of the paper bag with our bagels, is rolled over and crumpled.

"I believe you two have met" I say, raising my eyebrows at him. I sip the last of my tea before, putting the cup in the sink.

He runs his hand through his hair, "What are you doing here Gina?"

"I was going to ask you the same thing, Babycakes." He visibly cringes when she says it, as I did at Carl's party. I grip the counter and start to count from one to a hundred in my head. *Don't lose it now.*

"Charlotte, can you give us a minute?" As much as I want to hear what he says to her, I don't want to be in the little witch's company a moment longer. I need to get in the shower and wash her disdain off me.

"Sure" I say, before glancing at Gina. She looks at me and smirks. I walk over and kiss Ethan. I rub my thumb gently across his cheek. I leave the room confident that Gina knows that he's no longer hers.

Chapter Twenty-Seven

Ethan

"I'll ask you again Gina, what the fuck are you doing here?"

"That's no way to greet a lady." She walks across to me and brings her hand up to my face, but I move just out of reach. I'm about to say something snarky about her not being a lady, but I stop myself. I don't want to antagonize her further. I can't believe she's showed up here. What the fuck must be going through Charlotte's mind right now?

"Seriously, what's your game?"

"I'm not playing any games." She turns and slides herself up onto the kitchen counter, I take a couple of steps back. "Unless you want to play? You always used to." She leans back on her elbows and licks her lips What *does she think is going to happen right now?* I look away.

"Get down from there."

"Why? You used to love fucking me in the kitchen, bending me over something. Does your professor know about that? Maybe I should tell her."

I take her by the arm and pull her down. I open the door and bring her outside. "I don't care what you think about me, but leave Charlotte out of it. Do you hear me?" I let go of her wrist. I didn't mean to drag her out like that. "I'm sorry, I just don't know how to make you understand."

She folds her arms and pouts up at me, "Understand what? That you'd rather fuck anyone than be with me?"

"That's not what I mean, and you know it."

"I love you, Ethan." She grabs my arm, but I shake her off and turn away. I look out across the horizon and close my eyes. I don't want to look at the ocean, churning and moody today.

"You don't love me Gina, you love the idea of me. You love the eight-year-old boy who used to promise you stupid things."

"Stupid things like marrying me?"

"What?"

"Don't you remember?" She puts her hand in the pocket of her dress and pulls something out. A tiny paper ring lays in the palm of her hand, yellowing and wrinkled. "You made me this out of a page from your schoolbook. You told me you were going to marry me when we grew up, that we would always be together."

Fuck, I'd totally forgotten about that ring. I can't believe she's still got it. I run my fingers through my hair and put my hands in the pockets of my shorts.

"Gina, we were kids. We also used to pretend I was Batman, and you were Wonder Woman. I'm sorry that I hurt you so badly, but you must realize that it's time to move on."

She closes her hand on the ring and looks down. Her eyelashes are wet. I feel like such a shit right now.

"Why did you go out with me again then? If you didn't believe we were meant for each other - why try again? Why put me through that?"

I look across at Charlotte's apartment, the door's closed but I don't know how much she can hear. "C'mon, let's take a walk on the beach." She follows me down the steps and we cross the cycle path, onto the sand. It's early enough for it to be quiet still, no tourists, and a warm Santa Ana breeze. We walk in silence for a bit. We used to go to the beach together a lot when we were kids. For a moment, it feels like we're back there again, before everything changed - before we both did.

"Do you remember that time my mom took us to the beach, looking for sea glass and you swore that you saw a mermaid in the water?"

She smiles, "Yeah, I was obsessed wasn't I."

"Yep, you wouldn't stop going on about if for weeks. I kept telling you there were no such things as mermaids. Then, my mom told me not to say that. She said that it was good to believe in something magical. When I asked her why, she said, "*because sometimes we just need to.*" I look across at Gina.

"That sounds like something your mom would say. I miss her."

I shove my sneakers in the sand, "I miss her too."

I look up at the sky, anything to avoid looking at the ocean, the sun is breaking through the clouds. "I needed to believe in something too. Especially after she died." I take a few steps away from her. "I hurt you Gina, I totally fucked things up the first time around. I wanted to give it another chance because I still wanted you to believe in something. I thought I owed you that."

She looks past me towards the horizon. I can tell she's fighting back tears. I feel like total shit.

"It was never going to work between us, was it? You were only getting back with me because you felt sorry for me. I don't want your pity, Ethan. I just want you to love me."

I turn to look at her. She looks like a tiny doll; her eyes are wide, searching my face.

"I do love you Gina, just not in the way you want me to."

She folds her arms across her chest, "Do you love her?"

My gaze drifts up towards Charlotte's apartment. She'll be in the bedroom now, drying herself from the shower. I picture her pink warm skin against mine, kissing her soft lips, how my heart skips a beat when she enters the room. I put my hands in my pockets and turn back to Gina. "Yeah, I think I do."

Gina chews her lip and makes small circles with her toes in the sand. "My mom booked us flights back to Texas on Wednesday. I wasn't sure if I was going to go, but now I am. I never want to see you again Ethan Delaney, do you understand?"

I nod and we take each other in one last time, before she turns and heads back up the beach. I watch her small figure until she becomes just a blur, then is out of sight. I look up at the sky, its eggshell blue and clear, and the waves sound calmer in the distance. The beach is starting to fill up with tourists. I head back up the beach. I want Charlotte close to me, in my arms. I don't want, Gina or my past to ever come between us again.

Chapter Twenty-Eight

Charlotte

"Hello! It's so good to see you!" Lauren's face smiling back at me from the screen, makes me instantly happy.

"You too! How are you? How is Paul and the kids and the mother-in-law?"

"Infuriating, challenging and needy. In that order."

I laugh and am reminded again that, although things are hard right now - Lauren has a lot more on her plate than I do.

"So, where's the crazy girl?"

I'd messaged her and told her about Gina. I take a sip of wine and relax back into the sofa. "An hour away from getting on the plane back to Texas to go and live with her mother."

"You must be relieved."

"Not until that plane takes off, I won't be."

"Have you got the full story from Mr. Sexy yet?"

"Not yet."

"So, all you know is that they were childhood sweethearts, and she thinks they're Romeo and Juliet?"

I sigh at the absurdity of it. "That's pretty much it."

"I still don't get why she was living at his place still. Why didn't she move out when they broke up again?"

"She'd given up the lease on her apartment, without telling him. So, I guess he felt bad. They were together through high school, and she was there for him when his mum died. So, he just felt guilty about the whole mess."

"And nothing happened between them, after they broke up the second time? Even though she was living there?"

"He says not."

"Do you believe him?"

I hesitate. What business was it of mine even if he had slept with her before I came along? I push the uneasy feeling down. "I do."

"So, how's it going with Ethan? You said he's been living with you for a few weeks?"

I feel warm inside just thinking about how wonderful these last few weeks have been. Waking up with him every morning, making love all over the apartment - on this couch. I smile "It's been going pretty darn well."

Lauren laughs, "I know *that* face! You've been fucking each other's brains out."

"Yep." I giggle and hide my blushing behind my glass.

"Is it serious, or just sex?"

I snap off a piece of dark chocolate from the bar on the table and place it in my mouth. It feels rich and velvety on my tongue. "I'd say it's serious. He says he wants to make it work."

"Wow, you've gone from hating each other, to being all loved up in just a few weeks. I can't keep up." She tops up her glass with wine.

"I know, it sounds nuts. I think we're just trying to make the most of it as I don't know how much longer I'll be in the States for now."

"Shit, I'd forgotten about that. When does you visa run out?"

I go cold, I don't even want to think about it. "End of next month."

"Can you get it extended?"

I shrug my shoulders "My boss hasn't mentioned it, I haven't dared bring it up. I've been avoiding him; he's desperate to get in my pants."

"Ugh gross!" Lauren screws up her face, "How are there men still like him in the system?"

I sigh, "I'm married to one."

"You've told Ethan now though, right?"

I bring a cushion up and hug it to me. "No, I'm sort of hoping I won't have to."

"How does that work?" She jerks forwards as something hits her in the back of the head. It falls onto her lap, and she picks it up. It looks like a large furry sea creature.

"Paul, Paul! Alfie is using Mr. Lobster as a projectile again! Can you do something? This is my time, we agreed!" Her husband comes into the room as she puts herself on mute. All I can see are two people mouthing angrily at each other. I remember their wedding. It was such a beautiful day; they had a marquee on the lawn of a beautiful country estate. They couldn't take their eyes off each other in the first dance. Is this what happens to all couples? They end up fighting all the time. I'm not sure I ever want a relationship again. Maybe a short love affair is better, that way it will always be frozen in time as something wonderful.

"Sorry, the boys have both been out of hand lately and Paul needs to *lift a fucking finger* to help." She says the last bit loudly for the benefit of her husband.

"I still don't get why you haven't told Ethan that you're still married."

"Honestly, I think I'm in too deep now." I bite my nails, "How the hell do I say, by the way I still have a husband."

"You could say it just like that, you don't usually have a problem being direct."

"Very funny. Honestly, I'm hoping that Charles will sign the divorce papers and my visa will be extended. In an ideal world, Ethan never has to find out."

"In an ideal world, Charlotte, I'd be sitting in the Caribbean right now with a hot naked man bringing me a piña colada."

I clutch my stomach, "Don't make me laugh. I did Pilates for the first time in forever yesterday and my stomach muscles are killing me."

"At least you still have stomach muscles."

"True."

"Didn't you say you met his family?"

"His brother and sister-in-law."

"You said he was close with her right?"

"Yeah, very. Why?"

"Well maybe she can fill in some holes for you. You said he lived with them when he was a teenager. She must know more about what happened with Gina, and why Ethan hates talking about that or his mother."

"I can't go behind his back."

Lauren shrugs her shoulders, "You wouldn't be. You'd just be inviting her over for a glass of wine and a chat, getting to know her. These things would just naturally come up."

"I don't think she even likes me."

"She probably thinks of Ethan like her son, and you're his teacher. She's bound to be a little apprehensive about you. More reason for her to get to know you, and have her fall in love with you too, like the rest of us have." She winks at me, her eyes bright even though she must be exhausted.

I feel a wave of calm wash over me. It sounded like a good idea. I could kill two birds with one stone. I could get to know Mo - which would please Ethan and find out why he's so closed off about his past.

"I'll get her number off Ethan and text her."

"And you're going to tell him this week about Charles?"

My heart thumps twice in my chest. "I can't, not yet."

Lauren nods. "Okay my sweet friend, I'm off to pour my husband a glass of wine and see if we can spend the evening without one of us murdering the other."

I smile, "Good luck!"

"I'm gonna need it."

I pick up my phone to ask Ethan for Mo's number. I tell him it's because I want to invite her round for some wine and book chat. I feel like a hypocrite wanting to find out more about his past, when he doesn't know anything about mine.

I text Mo and invite her round on Friday. I'm nervous just thinking about it, but it would also be good to get to know her better. I can't wait to get Charles out of my life and feel secure here. I run downstairs to pick up the mail. I'm waiting for something from my lawyer, that I need to sign. I open the mailbox and pull out a handful of letters. I run back upstairs as I flick through them. The one from my lawyer is there, a couple for Lorraine and another one for me marked, 'Department of Immigration.' My fingers fumble, ripping it open. I scan through it and it's to remind me the date my visa runs out. It says no other application has been received to extend it and once that date expires, I will need to leave the country within two weeks. My palms are sweaty, and I feel dizzy. I knew this would be the case but seeing it here in black and white makes it worse somehow. I can't go back to England, not before Charles signs the divorce papers. I lean my head back against the cupboards. I'm in love with a man twelve years younger than me and trying to run away from a man I hate. To top it all off, the very thing that has kept me safe here, my job, might end soon. I need to get a handle on Frank. He's been avoiding me recently, but I'm going to pin him down for a meeting early next week. I'll see Mo on Friday, hopefully, and get some answers about Ethan. I put my face in my hands, why does everything have to be so complicated?

Chapter Twenty-Nine

Charlotte

Mo is sitting on the sofa opposite me. She's wearing a floral dress with a long cream cardigan. Her hair is styled into dark curls around her face, and she's wearing makeup. She looks vastly different from the Mo I met a few weeks ago. It's as if a gray cloud has lifted from her, I wonder if that cloud is her husband. Ethan says that Rob's *"away on business"* right now, so she's probably enjoying some time to herself.

"You have such a lovely apartment." Mo is smiling at me and sipping the wine I've poured her.

I kick off my heels and tuck my feet underneath me in the armchair.

"Thank you. Though, unfortunately none of the furnishings are mine. I'm just subletting. I only rented the apartment for a few months."

Mo leans forward and rests her glass on the coffee table between us. "Oh? Where are you going after that? Are you planning to move in with Ethan?"

This isn't something I've allowed myself; to imagine what comes next. What if my visa is renewed? What if Frank gets over his ridiculous crush long enough to see that I'm a great professor and these kids are actually engaging *with me. What if California becomes my home, and I get to wake up every day to palm trees and the sound of the ocean? What happens if Ethan and I aren't bound by the college's stupid rules? Even though he's not in my class anymore – I'm still a teacher at the college he attends. What if we overcome the odds? What if we did live together? Waking up to him with his body pressed to mine. Making each other coffee in the mornings, kissing each other before we go about our days. Meeting each other to grab a quick lunch. Locking the door of my office, Ethan sliding himself inside of me, clasping his hand over my mouth to stifle the desperate sounds he pulls out of me. Dancing together in the kitchen, sliding all over the place in our socks, his arm locked around me, strong and secure, keeping me up...supporting me in every way. Then what?*

A ring.

Vows.

A child.

A complicated, messy, beautiful life.

I shake myself so hard out of this fantasy, I almost give myself whiplash. What the hell am I doing to myself? Charles is never going to sign those papers. It'll be a cold day in hell before Frank sponsors me. I'm not fucking him to return the favor. I'm only hurting myself, picturing a beautiful future that just can't be.

"Charlotte?"

Mo's staring at me, still waiting for an answer. I tuck a piece of hair behind my ears. "No, that's not something we've discussed." I'm sure my face is crimson.

"I was going to say that would be a bit quick." She raises her eyebrows and helps herself to a handful of chips.

"Once I know whether my contract at work is extended, then I can think more about where I'm going to live."

"Is it likely to be extended? Ethan tells me the students love you."

"It's going well, but that's really up to my boss."

"Is that still old Frank Fletcher?"

"You know him?"

"He was the principal of my high school, still there when Ethan attended too. *'Fletch the letch'* we used to call him. He had this long-suffering wife, *Elaine.*

"She just left him actually, but he's trying to keep that quiet."

"I bet he is." She takes another sip of her wine. "Mm this is delicious. Where did you get it?"

"Just from the liquor store across the street, it's become my favorite though. Here, have some more." I reach for the bottle, and she holds out her glass. Perhaps with some more wine in both of us we can both relax a bit more. She's wary of me, but I must remember, like Lauren said, that she's bound to have reservations. I find some relaxing music on my phone and turn on the wireless speaker. Norah Jones starts playing. Mo melts back into the sofa as we both take in the sound of her voice for a moment. I light one of Lorraine's many candles, and the scent of summer jasmine and cedar drifts over us.

"Did Ethan tell you that Gina showed up here?"

"He did."

I'm waiting for her to say something else, but she doesn't. She's tapping her foot to the music and seems to be lost in her own thoughts. I guess I'll have to lead the way on this one.

"I wanted to ask you about her actually."

"Oh?" Her foot stops tapping.

"How well do you know her?"

"I haven't spoken to Gina in a while. Rob said she stopped by before she left, but I wasn't home. I told Ethan it was a mistake letting her stay at his apartment. She's always been a little, how shall I put it...unhinged, even in high school. She used to get into these jealous rages with him."

"And he put up with it?"

Mo takes another sip of wine. I can see she's deliberating whether to tell me something or not.

"He put up with it, until he didn't."

What sort of answer is that?

"So, you weren't surprised when Ethan told you about what happened the other day?"

"No, in fact I've been expecting it. As much of a good-looking guy he is, Ethan's very naive when it comes to women."

She looks directly at me as she says it and for an instant, I think she knows my secret.

Wow. I am stone cold, certifiably paranoid. How the hell would Mo ever know anything about Charles? Ever? There's just no fucking way. What, has Ethan's petite little sister-in-law hired a P.I. to dig up dirt on me? Has some guy in a trench coat been rifling through my trash? Hacking into my email? I've never heard of anything more preposterous in all my life.

I bring my legs out from underneath me and sit more upright. I need to address the elephant in the room - the fact that I'm his English professor.

"You don't approve of my relationship with Ethan, do you?"

If she was shocked at me saying it, then it doesn't come across. I've noticed that some Americans aren't used to how direct Brits can be - and I'm especially blunt. She just puts her glass down and holds my gaze.

"If you mean, was I happy to find out he was sleeping with his English professor? Then, no."

She's being direct back. I think I'm going to need more wine for this. I pick my glass up from the table.

"It took a lot for Ethan to go back to school, and I'm not sure if you understand that. He's an intelligent, talented boy and he deserves more than ending up like my husband." She looks down at her hands. "Ethan was struggling, and I did everything in my power to make it better for him. I promised his mother that I'd take care of him. To see him risk his chance to do something with his life, by having an affair with his teacher..." She shakes her head, "When Rob told me, I couldn't fathom it."

I'm not sure what to say, she makes it sound like we've done a terrible thing. I think again about Charles and how he took advantage of his students - *is that me? I haven't let myself think about that possibility for a while.*

She takes a sip of wine and runs her fingers around the stem of the glass. "Though, he does seem less lost since he met you and that can only be a good thing." She shrugs her shoulders. "He's an adult now though, and I have to trust that he knows what he's doing."

"Lost?"

"You don't see that in him sometimes, the lost little boy?" I did see it, but I thought that perhaps it was something only I saw.

"Yes, I see it." I consider telling her about the painting in the national gallery. The one called *'The Lost Boy',* that for some reason reminds me of Ethan. But I stop myself. "I'm sorry that you feel that way about us. I tried to stop it from happening... But, it's more than an affair. Ethan and I care for each other a lot."

Her hazel eyes study me. For as delicate as she looks, I can see that Mo is not someone to be messed with. I'm surprised that she's still with Rob, but I know from my own experience, that women often stay with men for all the wrong reasons.

Her face softens a little, "I can see that. He's a boy with a big heart, but he doesn't give it away easily." The lines around her eyes are deeper than they should be. Taking care of Rob *and* Ethan couldn't have been easy.

"I bet Ethan was adorable when you met him."

She smiles, "The lashes on him...Iris, his mom, said that when he was a baby, people used to think he was a girl, he was that beautiful. He was the perfect kid, really, just so sweet. He would play by himself for hours, always painting something or making things. Then when Iris got her cancer diagnosis, he lost his way." The corners of her mouth quiver a little. "She was everything to him. She used to call him her little shadow. I know that as teenagers, kids go off the rails...but I never thought Ethan would. He was too sensitive, too good."

"What did he do?"

Mo opens her purse and pulls out some lip balm. She applies it thoughtfully, as if she's mulling over my question.

"You should ask him, not me."

"I've tried, but you know how closed off he can be. If I know more about his past, then I can understand him better. Help him if he needs it."

Mo lifts her eyes to the ceiling and bites her bottom lip. I can tell she's conflicted as to whether to tell me anything. We sat in silence again for a moment. I don't want to push her further.

"He blames himself, you know, for what happened to his mother."

I sit forward, "Why? He said she had cancer, that she found out quite late; so there was nothing they could do for her."

"Yes, she did, but she didn't die from that." My skin goes cold.

"What happened?"

Mo takes a sharp inhale of breath, as if to prepare herself to tell the story - for her body to be able to hold up under the weight of the words.

"Ethan had always been the perfect kid, like I said. I met Rob when I was just fifteen. Ethan was only seven. Arthur, their father, had totally checked out by that point. He was drinking all the time. One day, he came to pick Ethan up from school, and he was so drunk that he fell out of the car when he opened the door. A parent reported him to the Principal and Social services were called. They said if it happened again, they would take Ethan away. His mother couldn't give up work, she was working two jobs just to keep their head above water. So, I helped out with Ethan. I picked him up from school and hung out with him until she got home. Sometimes Gina came round to play. I never took to her, even as a kid, but she adored Ethan and he seemed to like her. He was a little angel, he spent most of his time with me and Rob. Iris worked in a supermarket six days a week and in a bar some nights. Her only day off was Sunday and she used to take him down to the beach. They'd swim together; he was like a little seal, she used to joke." Mo stops and takes a big sip of wine. She puts the glass down and places her hands in her lap.

"This went on for years, even when Ethan was old enough to be home by himself. By that time, Rob and I were living together, and he'd always come straight to our house after school. He hated being around his dad. By the time he was fourteen, Iris started feeling unwell and missed a lot of work, and they were struggling. Rob helped where he could, but he was working for someone else at the time. I persuaded Iris to go and see the doctor, but it was too late. The cancer was everywhere. *"Tumors all over,"* he told her, too late to do anything. He gave her just a few months to live."

"Oh my God." I get a pain in my stomach, just thinking of what this must have done to Ethan.

"Yeah, but Iris was never one to give in. She kept working the hours she could. Ethan wanted to help his mum and started working forty hours a week at a cafe just to make ends meet."

"Forty hours and in high school?'

"Yep, crazy isn't it. That's when he sort of lost it, I suppose."

"What do you mean?"

"We thought he was coping. Kids adjust, everyone says. Gina was his girlfriend by then, so he had her, but we'd forgotten how sensitive he is underneath it all. He's like his brother that way - though you wouldn't know it with Rob these days." She takes another large sip of wine, then points to the bottle.

"Yes, yes of course help yourself." She pours herself a large glass.

"Anyway, the next thing we know, Frank's calling Iris into the school. Apparently, Ethan's grades had dropped, and he'd been picking fights. The police brought him home after he'd been caught spray painting public property and hopping the freight trains coming into LA. Iris found drugs in his school bag... It was like he was a different boy. He was moody and rude to his mother. She tried to talk to him, and he just asked her what the point was."

"What the point was?"

"What was the point in going on? On him getting good grades at school and doing well in life if his mother wasn't going to be there to see it? If the God she always talked about didn't love her, or her family, enough to keep her alive - then there couldn't be a God. So, nothing mattered."

"Wow." I try to get my head around how fourteen-year-old Ethan must've felt.

"He was exhausted from working and going to school. That would account for his grades to drop, but not the fighting or the other stuff. Then one day about a year after her diagnosis, they had a massive argument and he stormed out." She pulls at the hem of her dress, stalling for a minute.

"When he came home that evening, his mother wasn't there. Arthur, his dad, hadn't even noticed she'd gone, and by this time, she wasn't supposed to go anywhere alone. She'd stopped working by then and was no longer supposed to be driving. She left a note on the kitchen table - telling her boys that she loved them, but that everything had just become too hard, that it was better for everyone if she wasn't there. She said she needed to find peace." Mo wipes her eyes with the back of her hand. I take a packet of tissues out of the coffee table drawer and hand them to her.

"Thank you." She whispers it, her voice barely audible.

"You don't have to tell me anymore."

"No, it's important. If you're going to be in a relationship with him... this is going to come up... Ethan is traumatized by this still."

I nod and let her continue.

"The only place his mom ever felt peaceful was in the ocean. The doctor had forbidden her to go swimming there. I guess Ethan, intuitively knew that's where she'd gone. He probably should have called us, but he didn't. He wasn't thinking straight. He got in his dad's car and went looking for her. He was just fifteen. He didn't have his license yet but had driven his drunk dad home from bars before."

"Arthur sounds like a shit."

"He is. It's a shame, he and Iris were both very talented artists. They could have been something, but Arthur drank his life away and so Iris had to work at least two jobs to keep the family afloat."

"So that's where Ethan gets his artistic talent from?"

"Yeah, but don't waste your breath trying to get him to use it. He thinks all artists end up drunk and broke, thanks to his dad."

That explains why he never told me he could draw.

"Anyway, he drove to the little beach she used to take him to. Her car was parked there but it was dark by now and there was no sign of her anywhere. He called her name... but nothing. So he went into the water, to look for her. He climbed up on the rocks to see if she was further out. He said he kept diving and diving, until eventually he gave up. He walked in his wet clothes to a nearby house. He asked them to call the police, and then us."

Mo looks down at her glass. "They found her body a week later."

"She'd drowned?"

Mo nods, blinking back tears.

"She washed up a week later, on the full moon. I remember that specifically because that's what they told us would affect the tides. Rob had to identify her. Arthur couldn't cope; he left the day after the funeral and never came back. Ethan blamed himself. He shut down from us and went to live with Gina and her family."

"Gina?"

"Yes, he lived there until he was seventeen. He felt too ashamed; he believed that Rob blamed him for his mother's death."

"Did he?"

Mo squirms a bit in her seat "I think Rob always resented Ethan for taking his mother's attention. He also thought that if Ethan had called him that day, instead of going by himself to the beach, that he would have found her, but his mother had likely been gone for hours by then."

Now I understand why Ethan sometimes wakes in the night with those nightmares about being in the ocean, his body shivering, but dripping with sweat.

"Ethan would come and stay with us occasionally. But he never went home again. Rob and I packed up the family home.

I managed to track down Arthur and he agreed to sell, so the mortgage could be paid off. He said to give the little that was left to the kids. It's probably the one redeeming thing he's ever done. We were able to put the deposit down on the garage and start the business. The other half was put away for Ethan. When he was eighteen, he began helping Rob out at the garage. He broke up with Gina at the same time and moved in with us. He got back on track, stopped doing drugs and breaking the law. He kept his head down and got his own place a couple of years ago."

Wow, no wonder she was concerned about him fucking up college.

"So do the boys ever get on?"

"Only when they're working on cars together but, lately things seem to have got worse."

"Why didn't Ethan tell me all this? I know he has these nightmares about the ocean, but he never told me why."

"He probably wasn't ready."

I feel sad when she says this. He's been holding this burden for so long; it's such a huge part of his life and he hasn't told me. I subconsciously twist my finger where my wedding band used to be, then stop. I hope Mo didn't register it. She reaches for her purse and stands.

"I've already said more than I should."

"Thank you, I do appreciate you telling me all this." I go over to the shelf and pick out one of the books I brought with me from England. I hand it to her.

"Here, we didn't get to have our book chat. But this is one of my favorites, so you can borrow it if you like." I smile kindly at her, "Perhaps when we get together again, you can let me know what you thought about it."

"I'd enjoy that, thank you."

She smiles quickly back at me as I open the front door. She's about to step out, but before she did, she turns to me.

"Ethan deserves someone special. I hope the two of you can make it work. Secrets aren't any good in a relationship, they eat away at it." Her eyes are still wet from crying.

I close the door as she leaves and rest my head against it. I now know his secrets, but he still doesn't know mine. Mo's right, if you're not careful, they can rot things from the core.

Chapter Thirty

Ethan

"Mo came round the other night." Charlotte's sitting on the end of the bed. She's wearing her kimono, and it's fallen open at her cleavage, I can just see the outline of her breasts. One leg is up across her body and the other is straight, she's reading. I press the charcoal to the page and draw the curve of her thigh.

I don't want to think about my sister-in-law right now, I want to concentrate on Charlotte's body, on the glide of her limbs and the softness of her flesh. Once I've finished drawing her, I intend to pin her to the bed and explore every inch with my tongue.

"Yeah, I know."

"She told me some stuff."

"Oh yeah," I smudge the charcoal with my finger for the crease on her inner thigh. I wish Charlotte would take the hint and shut up about Mo already. I wasn't that keen when she asked for her number in the first place. I love Mo, but I don't want her nose in our business just yet.

"She told me what happened to your mom. I'm sorry Ethan."

I look at her, *did she just say what I think she did?* It's stifling in here. I put my paper and pencil down and reach for the collar of my t-shirt to pull it away from my neck. I feel like it's strangling me. I need some air. I get up off the bed.

"I've been wanting to say something for days and..."

"That's enough, Charlotte." She's saying something else, but I can't hear it, there's just ringing in my ears. I grab my pants, put them on, and storm out of the bedroom.

"Ethan, wait!" She's follows me as I head into the kitchen and open the front door. I go up the couple of steps to the balcony and place my hands on the wall. I take a cigarette and lighter from my back pocket and light it, staring out towards the horizon.

"Ethan, I..."

"Just give me a minute, will you?"

She sinks back, "Please don't leave."

I don't say anything but wait for the cigarette hit. I take a few more drags, watching the smoke curl and float away. I haven't spoken about this in years. Mo had no right to do this behind my back. *I'm so fucking mad at her.* I exhale the last of the smoke and stub the cigarette out on the wall. Then I light another one. Charlotte moves towards me. She looks up at me as if she wants to say something but takes hold of my hand instead. She rubs the charcoal that's etched into the ridges on my thumb.

"I love how your hands always show the work you've been doing, there's something so beautiful about that. To see who you are in your hands."

I take another drag of my cigarette and then close my eyes for a second. I smoke the rest of it in about two minutes, before putting it out next to the old one that's still smoldering. I turn and put my head on hers, there's a faint smell of her perfume lingering in her hair. She smells like wild figs and summer. I bury my face in it and she puts her fingers on my chin. My beard is gone, and she can see my scar through my stubble. She circles it. I know she wants to ask me about it again but is stopping herself.

"I'm sorry."

I close my eyes again and bring her hand down from my face. "I have this scar, because I scraped my jaw on a rock when I was diving to find my mom. It's a constant reminder of how I failed her, of what I did."

"It's not your fault."

I want to believe her, but I can't. I turn away from her.

"She was in a lot of pain, my love."

"I thought about doing the same thing after she died. I wanted everything to just stop. I thought I could just walk into the ocean and…" I can't finish the sentence; I can taste bile in my throat, and the sounds of the waves thrashing in the distance make my head throb.

"Ethan that scar is a reminder of your love for your mother. It's a testimony to it."

"It sure doesn't feel like that."

She puts her hand to my face again and I kiss it.

"I have to go get ready for my meeting with Frank this morning. I can cancel it if you need me here?"

Just the sound of his name makes me angry, but I know she has to keep that meeting.

"I'll be fine, I'm going to stay here and smoke myself to death."

"Don't say that."

She leans in and kisses me. She tastes of salt and cherry lip balm.

"I'll come and say goodbye before I go."

I stay outside watching the ocean swell, and for the first time in years, I don't turn away.

Chapter Thirty-One

Charlotte

I smooth down my skirt before taking a seat in Frank's office. I've chosen my clothes carefully, knowing what he likes. Should I feel guilty about that? Or am I just leveling the playing field? Ethan whistled and raised an eyebrow at me when I left. He didn't come inside - just stayed on the patio and smoked another cigarette. He never chain smokes like that. I didn't mean to blurt out the question about his mother this morning, but it's been brewing in me since I spoke to Mo. Who am I to ask for the truth when I'm still lying to him about being divorced? I really need Frank to come through for me right now. He hasn't looked up from his desk since I've come in. His secretary told him I was here, and yet he still made me wait a good twenty minutes before he let me in. Normally he'd open the door immediately and greet me with a hug and a, *"How is my favorite English professor today?"* before ushering me into his office with his hand too low on my back, telling his secretary we're not to be disturbed. I had put up with it to keep on his good side. I've never told Ethan how handsy Frank is. There was no hand on my back today though, no quick sniff of my hair. His secretary seems off too. She always looks disapprovingly at me, but today there's also a smugness there.

I walk in with a huge smile, expecting Frank to come out from behind his desk to greet me. instead, he keeps on working and just says, "Sit down professor, I won't be a minute."

It's been more than a minute now though and I feel uneasy, something isn't right. The air is thick as if something visceral is bearing down on me. I can hear my own heartbeat as loud as the clock ticking on his desk. I have to say something.

"Sorry Frank, is it better if I come back another time? You seem so busy these days; I hardly get to see you." He stops moving his pen and looks up at me from under his glasses. He gives me a look that I've seen him direct at unruly pupils - but never me. He puts his pen down and reclines back in his chair, crossing his arms behind his head.

"I would have thought I was the last person you'd want to see Professor Rose." *Professor* again, not Charlotte. Something's going on.

"I'm not sure what you mean Frank?"

"Do you remember that night I took you to the seafood restaurant and bought you dinner? You wore that low cut lemon dress, and you even took my hand at one point?"

I shift in my chair, where is this going? "I took hold of your hand because you'd just told me that your wife had left you. I was being kind."

"Were you being kind when you left me alone at the party afterwards?"

"I told you I was sick. I knew you were worried about your nephew, and I thought it best if I just left."

He sits forward in his chair again and rests his elbows on the desk. The whole room smells of leather and perspiration, I feel nauseous.

"You know I spent that whole weekend trying to figure out why you would just leave like that and not ask me to take you home. Especially as you'd been ... so accommodating at the restaurant. I couldn't fathom where I'd gone wrong. But now I know it was nothing to do with me at all, was it?" A cold sweat comes over me. I straighten my back in the chair and fold my arms, I'm not just going to sit here and let him speak to me in riddles.

"Okay Frank, what's going on?"

"Why don't you tell me Charlotte, why don't you tell me what has been going on since the first day I employed you."

Fuck, he knows. "I don't know what you're talking about."

He takes the document he's been working on and pushes it across the desk towards me.

"What's that?"

"Your contract Charlotte, or rather the termination of it."

"My contract isn't up yet.'

He stands and walks round to the front of the desk and sits on it, fixes his tie then reaches into his top pocket and pulls out a pen. "You broke your contract, Charlotte, when you had intercourse with a student."

Shit, of course, this was always going to happen. It was inevitable.

"I still don't know what you're talking about."

Frank laughs. "Oh my dear Charlotte, now I see your penchant for deceit eluded me. I had a phone call last week from Gina, lovely girl, an old student of mine. Told me everything about you and Delaney."

Fucking Gina, of course it was her. I knew I was right not to trust that Ethan had dealt with her. Frank's looking at me like he's a cat about to torture a mouse.

"If you sign this new contract Charlotte, then your little indiscretion will not go further than this room. Delaney will, of course, be suspended. One small detail, though is that you will come back to teach at the College open house next week. Your class has been extremely popular, and it looks good for me that I took a chance on you. It puts me in the running for 'Dean of the year' and that's a shiny little trophy I'd rather like to sit on that shelf behind me." He looks behind him as if he's picturing it there already. "Not to mention the opportunity to hire another little English rose after you. One that is less ... how shall I put it? Ah yes, less disappointing."

"If you think I'm going to come back and help you out after your fire me, you can think again!" I'm standing now, picking my bag up off the floor.

"I don't think you're in any position to negotiate, professor. If you don't want me to report this to the board, then I suggest you sign the contract and show up next week. Preferably wearing another low-cut top and a big smile on your face. Just like today, when you thought, I was going to extend your contract." He looks me up and down as he says it, like I'm a piece of meat.

I've never wanted to punch someone in the face so hard. I have to force myself to pick up the pen and sign the contract, before throwing it at him. I go to the door and open it; I want to make sure his snooty secretary hears what I have to say.

"I thought about giving you a pity fuck Frank, but just the thought of that made me sick to my stomach. You repulse me, and I expect you repulse your wife too. No one's surprised that she left." His face drops for a second and it gives me a little satisfaction, not enough, but a little.

"You know he's just a fuck boy, don't you."

"What?" *What crap is he saying now?*

"Delaney. A fuck boy."

"No. he's not."

"Oh, don't tell me he's manipulated you too? I mean look what he did to Gina, led her on for years.

"He was a kid."

"Why do you think she moved in with him?"

"She didn't move in with him, she was just staying there until she found a new place."

He smirks, "Don't tell me you believe that! I bet he fucked her all over his apartment. That sweet little ass served up on a plate... No man could resist that."

My god he's gross, the way he talks about women - especially as he used to teach Gina.

"You're disgusting."

"You're the one fucking a student, not me."

He's really enjoying this. The more excited he gets, the shinier his face is.

"Ethan isn't some kind of teenage idiot, incapable of making his own decisions. He's a grown man and last time I checked - way over the age of consent."

"It doesn't matter how old the piece of shit is, sweetheart. It doesn't matter if he consents. He was your student, and you were in a position to use your authority over him in return for sexual favors. It's *unethical* is what it is, and you're *this* close to being sued by the school - so I would go quietly and nicely if I were you."

"Ethan's no longer in my class, and you fired me so he's not my student anymore and we can continue our relationship freely."

Frank sits back down in his chair and smacks his hand on the desk and laughs. God he's repugnant.

"Relationship? Oh Charlotte, don't tell me that's what you think you're in? That boy doesn't know what the word means.

You're not his first rodeo and you certainly won't be his last, not at your age."

I slam the door. I can still hear him laughing as I walk down the corridor. I hold my head high until I get outside. Once I'm in my car, I sink into the seat. I have never hated anyone as much as I hate Frank Fletcher right now.

———ele———

I don't go home straight away. I head to a bar a few blocks away from my flat. The same bar that I met Nate in. It's dark inside, just some dim light from the old-fashioned lamp shades that cast an orange, surreal glow. I take a seat at the far end of the bar and order a glass of red. I want to be alone with my thoughts. I can't believe how that meeting went. I *knew Frank was a dick ... but, wow.* The bartender comes over with the bottle of merlot and I just nod, lost in thought staring at my glass as he refills it. I can feel him watching me, wanting to catch my attention. He's probably bored and wants to chat. The place is empty except for a couple cozying up in one of the booths, and an old man sitting at the other end of the bar. But I'm in no mood for small talk. I say thank you once the glass is filled and take a sip, still avoiding his gaze.

"Australian?"

"No, British."

"It sounds the same to me."

"It's not."

He raises his eyebrows and backs away with one hand in the air, turns and recorks the bottle. I feel bad. Just because my day was shit doesn't mean I have to make him miserable too. I take him in now. He's tall, clearly works out, fair hair that sits just above his shoulders. Probably about the same age as Ethan.

"I'm sorry, I've had a bad day, I just lost my job." He doesn't turn around at first, just picks up a cloth and begins polishing glasses.

"I didn't mean to be rude." I offer. "It's probably better if I just finish my wine and leave."

"That's okay, we all have bad days." He turns back to me, and grins and I can see now how good looking he is in an all-American boy sort of way. He's probably an actor working in a bar until he gets his big break, they all are.

"I'm Luke." He extends his hand and I take it.

"Charlotte."

"Well, if it helps, you're the prettiest lady I've seen in a long time." It's a line, he's chatting me up. I consider whether I should call him on it, but I'm too tired to complain.

"It doesn't, but I appreciate the compliment."

"So, was it a good job? The one you lost?"

"It was."

"Lawyer?"

"Sorry?"

"You look like a lawyer, in your suit."

"I'm not a lawyer." I take another sip of wine and circle the stem with my fingers, my mind already back to Ethan.

"Are you going to make me guess?"

I'm regretting starting this conversation. "I'm a zookeeper."

"That was going to be my second guess."

I smile, despite myself.

"Okay, I won't ask again. But I get off in thirty minutes if you'd like me to take you somewhere to get your mind off the shitty day you just had?"

The wine has already gone to my head. I haven't eaten much today and the stress of that meeting with Frank had got my adrenaline going, now I'm suffering from the crash. I look at Luke's smooth skin, his perfect teeth. No doubt he has a rippling six pack under that shirt. I take my wallet out of my bag. The thought of being with anyone else but Ethan at this point literally makes my skin crawl.

"Maybe another time Luke." I leave him a generous tip and walk out of the bar. I just want to get home to Ethan.

Chapter Thirty-Two

Charlotte

I leave my car parked on the street and walk the few blocks home. I don't even care about the ticket I'm going to get when I return in the morning. The sun is going down, and mist is coming off the ocean, turning the air cold. I pull the collar of my blazer up and curse my high heels. I saw on my phone that I had two missed calls from Ethan, but it's better if I explain everything face to face. When I get home, his Mustang is still parked in the carport. Perhaps we could just go to bed, have sex and I won't mention how Frank rattled me. Then it dawns on me that lately all I do is try to solve everything with sex. Ethan and I didn't talk about getting back together, we went straight back to fucking.

I climb the steps to my apartment. The vase on the outdoor table has fallen over in the wind and some of its cloudy water has spilled onto the tablecloth. The single rose Ethan bought me is now lying on its side, stranded. I pick up the vase and the rose and remove the tablecloth that's already half off. I take a deep breath and open the door. Ethan is sitting at the kitchen table, his face lights up when he sees me. He prises his long legs from under the table and stands to greet me. Why does he have to be so goddamn sexy? His hair flops forward which as usual fails to stay back when he sweeps his hand over it. He's wearing his light blue sweater that I sometimes wear in bed on the nights he stays at home, just so I can smell him. I put the vase and rose in the sink and throw the tablecloth on the side, before going over to him. I bury my face in his sweatshirt and burst into tears. He kisses the top of my head.

"Sshh, ssh it's alright." But it's not alright. I step back and wipe my hand under my nose, then I hiccup.

"He fired me."

"What?"

"Frank, he fired me."

"Why?"

I say nothing, just look up at him.

His eyes darken, "Because of me?"

"Because of us."

"He can't do that!"

"He can and he has. He also suspended you."

"Fuck!" He begins to pace, his hand moving up and down his chin. "Okay, you'll get another job. Any college or university will be proud to have you, or you could tutor privately! I bet there are loads of parents out there who would jump at the chance of an English professor teaching their kids."

I sit down at the table; I want to rip my suit off. It feels dirty somehow. I take off my jacket and put it on the back of the chair. I close my eyes and hold my breath, counting slowly in my head.

"It's not as easy as that. If I don't have a job, I don't have a visa and I have to..."

"No, don't say that." He kneels beside me, his hands holding mine on my lap. I open my eyes and wait for another hiccup, but holding my breath seems to have worked.

"We will figure this out, there's always a way."

I'm exhausted. The emotional toll of the day has been too much. I feel as if I've been treading water for so long - waiting to know if I can stay or not.

"How did he find out?"

"Gina."

"Fuck! No, fuck." He shoots up from the floor with his hands on his head. "Mother fucker!" He kicks one of the cupboard doors before leaning on the counter to steady himself. He shakes his head, "Why the fuck would she do that?"

"She could never forgive you Ethan, you broke her heart. She wanted to hurt you back."

He turns to look at me, "I trusted her. I let her stay at my apartment for months. Fucking hell!" He brings his hand to his jaw and rubs it.

"I don't think that helped Ethan. If anything, it gave her hope."

He shakes his head. "I'm sorry, I really am Charlotte. This is my fault."

'No, it's not. Were you a little naïve? Yes, but you were trying to do the right thing."

I refuse to fight with him about this, it's exactly what Gina wants. I get up and walk across to the sink. I rinse the vase, fill it with fresh water and put the rose back in it. I put it on the windowsill, its petals ruby in the overhead light. "We can talk about what we're going to do in the morning. Right now, I'm tired and all I want to do is lay on the sofa with you."

He takes hold of my hand, and pulls me close, he rubs his face in my hair. "You always smell so good, like a summer's day or something."

I look up at him, into those opal-like eyes of his. "Whatever happens Ethan, all I know is that I want to be with you."

He pulls me tighter. "I'm not going anywhere, Charlotte. You're stuck with me now. I won't let anything come between us again."

I just want to stay with him here, forever. I'm going to go and teach that open house next week, and then I will tell him everything. He deserves to know. For now, though, all I want is to feel safe in his arms.

Chapter Thirty-Three

Charlotte

"Morning."

I rub my eyes. Ethan is sitting on the bed next to me handing me a cup of tea. "Morning." I yawn as I say it and sit up slowly. "You're up and about early." Normally we wake early but have slow mornings in bed together. I take the cup from him and sip it tentatively.

"Yeah, I didn't sleep well." He has half-moon circles under his eyes.

"More nightmares?" I understand now why he has them, but I don't want to push him about it.

"No, it was because of what happened yesterday with Gina and Frank." His eyes are seal like this morning and wet, like he's just surfaced from the ocean. "I suppose I just realized that we might not have much time together."

"Don't say that." I'm not ready to talk about this right now, I need to wake up properly before I face the absolute fuckery of my life.

"I need to tell you stuff, I feel like I need to get it all out." He takes hold of my free hand and rubs my fingers gently.

"What stuff?"

"About Frank and Gina. It might explain why I fucked everything up for you."

I put my cup of tea down on the bedside table. "We talked about this yesterday, you're not to blame."

He lets go of my hand and stands up. There's an urgency about him today, like he's ticking. "I want us to make a fresh start Charlotte. I want us to figure out a way that you can stay, but before we do that, I want you to know everything. Don't you think it's important that we know a bit more about each other?'

Of course I do, I've been holding back from him now these past couple of months. That little white lie I told in the beginning has been eating away at me, but how do I tell him the truth? It's only a piece of paper that says I'm still married, would it hurt him that much if I told him?

"Okay but not here, I need some fresh air. Just let me get dressed." I feel like we need more space for this conversation. I get changed into a pair of shorts and tank top whilst Ethan waits in the kitchen. I can hear him pacing and the floorboards are complaining beneath him. We head out of the apartment and across the strip of sidewalk that separates my building from the beach. We have to wait for a cyclist to pass in neon orange spandex, and a family of seagulls that waddle by us squawking. The sand isn't too hot at this time of the morning, it feels powdery between the slats in my sandals. I take them off before we head down to the shore. Ethan's been quiet, he looks deep in thought. He is probably mulling over what he wants to say. I know I have stuff to say too and maybe today is the day to say it, under a cloudless cobalt sky. The kind of sky that anything can be forgiven under. We still say nothing though as we near the shore and sit on the top of the dune. I certainly don't want to open the conversation with, *"By the way, I'm still married."* So instead, I push my feet further into the sand bank that's wetter and colder here.

"I want to explain why I didn't just throw Gina out. Also, about Frank."

"Alright." I put my hands in the sand and bring them up over both my feet and start to pack it around them like I'm molding something out of clay. We're both sitting with our knees up, except Ethan has his arms around his. He looks like a small boy who got lost at the beach.

"Gina and I became friends in elementary school. She was the new kid, with a weird haircut and bottle glasses and the other kids picked on her. So, I stood up for her, and sort of, looked after her I suppose. Nobody bothered her when she was with me and back then she was sweet. We hung out after school, and she came over for dinner. She used to say that we'd get married one day. I made her a ring out of paper, or something, when we were eight. It was just something silly. She's still got it though. She showed it to me the other day. It was all crumpled and dirty, it was sad."

He pauses and looks out onto the horizon. The sea is calm today, glass like even. I wonder if he thinks about his mother when he looks at it. I'm silent still, just listening, piling a mountain of damp sand onto my feet. That's something I used to do to my dad as a kid at the beach; bury his feet then the rest of him. He'd make out that he couldn't move and then he'd turn into the sand monster, and chase me down to the sea and pretend to throw me in. I loved that game. My mum would lay on her towel, covered in tanning oil, reading a romance novel. The cover always had some heroic man on it, usually sitting on a horse with a tiny boned woman swooning in a bodice. I used to sneak a read of them sometimes from her bedside drawer. They were full of terms I didn't understand, like *'Passion moistened depths'* and *'Love's sweet arrow.'* I'd write the words in my diary and draw flower petals around them.

Ethan leans back on his elbows and kicks off his flip flops. "We went through school together and somewhere it turned from just being friends to kissing each other and making out. Then it was just assumed we were boyfriend and girlfriend." He shrugs his shoulders, "It was easy, I went along with it. It was hard at home with mom and dad fighting a lot. Gina had a great family. Her parents didn't argue, there was always food in the fridge, they took me away on trips. It was like I'd just slotted in with her and that's how it was. She lost the glasses and the weird haircut, but she also lost her sweetness somewhere along the way and I think that might have been because of me."

"Why would that be your fault?"

"I think she had our future all planned out and other girls, well, you know..." He looks down.

"They liked me. Gina would get jealous even though I never did anything. I wanted to, but I didn't want to hurt her. She got bitchy and controlling and was constantly asking me where I had been and who I was with. Then my mom got sick, and I started working full time to help her out. Life really pissed me off, I got into trouble, and Fletcher threw me out of high school."

"He's the reason you didn't graduate?"

"Well, I was being disruptive. I always got good grades and was usually top of the class. But that didn't count for anything, and you know Frank being Frank, he wanted something in return for not kicking me out."

"What do you mean?" I look at his achingly beautiful face and there is so much sadness in it.

'He wanted my mom." He leans forward and draws something in the sand. "She was beautiful."

"I saw a picture of her on the wall at your brothers. She was stunning."

"Mom could have had anyone she wanted; fuck knows why she chose dad." He starts flicking little bits of sand up with his feet. "Frank always had a thing for her, made a beeline for her at parent evenings as my dad never bothered to come. We used to laugh about it when she got home, but she also felt sorry for him. My mom felt compassion for everyone and everything, she was a much better person than I am."

"You're a good man, Ethan."

He makes a face and goes back to doodling in the damp sand. "Anyway, he said he'd keep me in school if he could take her to dinner."

"Dinner?"

"Yeah, well we both know what *dinner* means in that asshole's head."

"What did she say?"

"She agreed."

I pull my feet out of their sand burial. "How do you know this?"

"I found her diary after she died. I shouldn't have read it, but I did."

"Wait a minute...your mother slept with Frank to keep you in school?"

"Once. He took her to a motel room and..." He shook his head. "I wanted to kill him."

"I'm not surprised. Jesus. This is so fucked up Ethan!"

"You know what else is fucked up? He still kicked me out of school anyway after he got what he wanted."

I can picture Frank's face in my mind, and I want to smash it in. He's a vile, vile human being.

"I can't even begin to imagine how you felt finding that out."

"I set fire to her diary. I mean looking back I should have kept those pages and handed them into the school board or something, but I just wanted to see it burn. I needed to see what he'd done just turn to ash. I wish to God that I never read it."

I stretch out my feet. I'm chilled to the bone after hearing that and need warmth from the sun. I give Ethan a minute.

"Does Rob know?"

"Christ no, he would have hit him with a crowbar. Then Fletcher would have destroyed another one of us."

"So how on earth can you stand being around Frank? How do you not want to murder him every time you see him?"

He tips his head up and the sun hits under his chin. "I need to do something with my life, I can't go on working for my brother forever. This college was the only one I could go to and still get to work. He couldn't deny me entry, community college is for everyone. Also, I'm a constant reminder to him of what he's done. I guess I hoped it might cause him to have some sort of, *'Come to God moment,'* but seeing how he has been with you – he obviously hasn't."

"The man's a total snake, Ethan. He's never going to change. No wonder you got so mad when I went to dinner with him."

"Yeah, I felt like he'd won again."

"There was never a chance of that. "I say it softly and he nods, then stretches his legs out like mine.

"Anyway, I found all that out after my mom died. I was such a fucking mess then; my entire world had fallen apart. I felt totally alone. Dad left, not that he was of any use anyway. I knew that

Rob blamed me for mom's death, so I moved in with Gina's family. She was there for me. Her family were there for me, but I ended up letting them down. I started getting heavier into drugs, I wanted to escape from reality as much as I could. I got into trouble with the cops. I started calling the girls back who gave me their number at work. I began seeing them behind her back. I didn't see the point in relationships." He looks at me from under his lashes, "I'd lost the most important person in my life, so nothing felt sacred anymore. I was either numb or high. I kept sleeping with different girls to see if I could feel something. Eventually Gina's father kicked me out. He should have done it long before that, but Gina kept begging him not to. I was oblivious to all this; I was just living in my own head."

"That's when you moved in with Mo and Rob?"

"Yes, Mo's someone else I owe a great deal to. If it wasn't for her, I think I might have ended up like my dad or on the street or not even here."

"What do you mean not here?"

"Like I said yesterday. I used to go down to this little beach where mom died. I thought it might be better if I just went in the ocean and never came out. I felt like I was a burden to everyone. I used to imagine what it felt like to drown, to let go, to feel that release. I could never bring myself to go into the water though, it was like my feet just wouldn't take me in."

Hearing him talk like this makes my stomach churn. "I'm glad they didn't."

"Yeah, well at the time you might not have said that. I was an awful teenager. I lost my job at the cafe and so Rob took me on as an apprentice. Mo watched out for me and eventually I stopped getting high and just continued feeling numb. I thought that was how I was always going to feel, and I had come to terms with that, but then you came along." He looks at me with his dark hair falling over his face, like the night closing in. The lost boy in him is visible, but also the man who overcame so much.

"That's why I got so scared. Those feelings terrified me and were sudden. I didn't know what to do with them. Then, when Gina reacted how she did, I thought you'd also be better off without me, so I left."

I rest the side of my head on my knees and reach out for his hand. Now would be the time to tell him, wouldn't it? When we are both in that space to open up. Tell him that I'm still married, but reassure him that's its him I want to be with. I want to say something, but the words stick in my throat. He brings my hand to his mouth and kisses between my fingers.

"I'm sorry that you had to go through all that, that you felt you were better off not here. I wish I had known you then, been there for you."

"You wouldn't have wanted to know me then, though at seventeen I would still have flirted with you."

"Well, you could have tried..."

He's grinning at me, but I know how much this all hurts him inside. The sun is casting a halo around him. He's my angel now.

I close my eyes as he leans in and kisses me with lips that taste of salt and sand. We will work all of this out, I know we can.

Chapter Thirty-Four

Charlotte

"So, he hasn't responded at all?"

"I'm afraid not."

"So, what happens next?"

I'm on the phone to my lawyer Stephanie. She sent Charles another letter last week, asking why he had so far failed to respond to any of her requests. A week has passed and nothing.

"He is legally bound to respond within 30 days. If he doesn't, we can apply to the court for a default."

"What does that mean?" I flick through the legal paperwork on the kitchen table.

"It basically means the court can decide the case without your spouse's input. In a divorce by default, the court will make decisions based on the information you file and what the law says. It's not ideal, and we usually advise against it. However, in this case we may have no choice."

I sigh and sit on the edge of the table. "What does that mean for me?"

Stephanie doesn't say anything for a minute, I can hear her moving papers around. When she speaks her voice is weary. "From what you've told me about Charles, he's not someone who fights fairly. I would imagine he would hide his assets, plead poverty, and essentially leave you with nothing."

The vein on the side of my temple begins to twitch, "How can that be possible?"

Stephanie sighs, "It's the way things can go, unfortunately. I must also advise you that if you fight the court's decision and lose. You will end up with all the legal bills."

"So, you're telling me I'm fucked, basically." I run my hands through my hair and walk towards the window, hoping the sight of palm trees and a blue sky might calm me down.

"No, it just means it's probably better if we just give him a little more time. We discussed the plan for you to stay in the States, didn't we?"

"Yes." The grace period for my work visa runs out in a week. Ethan and I are going to take a week's vacation in Mexico. Then I can come into the country on a tourist visa for three months and start looking for work, and a new visa sponsor. It's risky, but it's the only way to do it. Lorraine is staying in Brazil longer and so I can come back from Mexico to her apartment.

"And you're sure you don't want to come back to the UK to see if you can move things forward that way?"

"I'm sure." I don't ever want to see Charles again.

"Okay then Charlotte. He still has a few weeks to reply, let's hope he does. I'll let you know if I hear anything and if he contacts you at all, let me know immediately."

"Thanks Stephanie, I appreciate it."

Once I'm off the phone, I pace the kitchen for about an hour, biting my nails. I have an ominous feeling in the pit of my stomach that I can't shake. The open house class is tomorrow, and I still need to go over what I'm going to present. My mind is whirling right now, but I have to focus. I sit at the table and look at the pile of legal papers. I take them to the closet and shove them in the shoe box with Charles's letter. I can't risk Ethan finding them. I close the door and cringe at myself; do I really think I can hide this from him forever? I can't think about that now though, I have to keep my end of the bargain with Frank and do the open house, then he's supposed to give me a reference. I've thought about private tutoring. I'd likely be in high demand because of my resume, but I'd miss teaching in a classroom. I already miss my students. I wonder who's been teaching them this past week and whether the progress we made so far this term, has been wasted. Maybe they all know about Ethan, it's bound to have come out somewhere. Though Frank would have wanted to keep a lid on it, for his own ego's sake, if nothing else. At least tomorrow, I can leave my students with some final materials and perhaps give them an inspirational talk, if there's time. Frank texted me yesterday to tell me there's now a guest speaker as well. I resent the fact that they'll take up some of my time. I go back into the kitchen and take my laptop off the chair. I need to go to the printers and get all the papers prepared for the College open house. I sit down, exhausted from worrying about Charles and my visa. I just need to get through tomorrow.

It took me longer than I thought to research everything I wanted to. The printers was a disaster, it was short staffed as usual and the one printer that was working kept getting a paper jam. I didn't get home until a couple of hours ago, and I've spent the whole time since putting all the materials together. Ethan is staying at his place tonight, and I've been so focused on work that I have no idea what time it is. I look up at the clock on the kitchen wall, it's already ten pm. My stomach gurgles, I suppose I should eat something, but when I peer into the fridge it's very disappointing. We've been getting takeout most nights or staying at Ethan's. His place still feels haunted by Gina even though he took Mo's advice and burned some sage. Maybe I can try lighting some again and wafting her energy away with it. There's some Thai curry and rice left in a container, and I put it in the microwave to heat up. I really need to go grocery shopping, all this take out or eating out is lovely, but not the healthiest and I've definitely gained weight. I take my phone out of my bag whilst my dinner is heating up. There are three missed calls from an unknown number and one voicemail. I press the speaker button and listen to it as I grab a plate out of the cupboard.

"Charlotte, it's Penny. Call me as soon as you get this. I'm sorry about what happened last time, but I need you to call me back. Charles is missing." My heart leaps into my throat. What does she mean Charles is missing? Someone always knows where Charles is; he's like a demanding child and needs constant attention. *"Too spoiled by his nanny"* Lauren used to joke. My phone lights up again and it's a text from Ethan,

"Getting an early night baby. I'll see you tomorrow. Don't stay up too late!"

This is when him knowing about my past would help, now I must hide all this too. I send him a heart emoji back. He's coming to class tomorrow to support me. There's no way Frank will make a scene with prospective students there. I press call back; it takes a while for Penny to answer. It's only six am in the UK, and the missed call was an hour ago. Hopefully she's found Charles by now, or perhaps he's just balls deep in his new fling somewhere.

"Charlotte, thank God."

"Hi Penny, what's going on?"

"Well first off, thank you for calling back, I'm so sorry about what happened last time, you know, when Charles answered."

My jaw tightens. 'You said Charles was missing?"

"Yes. No one has seen him; well, no one's seen him for three days and I can't get hold of him."

"Is he at home?"

"No, I went round, and the cleaner was there, but she hasn't seen him. Nothing was packed, he was just gone. Not turned up to teach, not even Beck's has heard from him."

"Becks?" Silence on the other end of the phone then the sound of swallowing. Clearly, Penny has said something she shouldn't.

"Sorry yes, that's just his new... intern." She coughs. She meant to say *his new fuck*.

"When was the last time Beck's saw him?"

"Three days ago, she said goodbye to him in the morning when he left for work. "She pauses again, Penny's crap at keeping secrets for her boss.

"Go on."

"He said he'd see her in class, but he never showed up."

I have that gnawing feeling in the pit of my stomach again, like something nefarious is lurking there. I'm not sure why I care that Charles is missing, it would solve all my problems if he just never showed up again. Maybe an ex-student had it in for him. It wouldn't surprise me, or perhaps Beck's had a boyfriend she never told him about and he was out for revenge. Still, I had been with the man for most of my adult life, I couldn't help but be a little concerned. Charles was routinely on time, was anal about things like that. He planned his days meticulously, Penny had his calendar down to every half an hour, even to what book he planned to read in bed that night so she could tick it off his reading list that week and order the next one on the list. I'm surprised she didn't wait by the toilet to wipe his ass.

Then suddenly it dawns on me; what if he's here? What if he's found me? I turn around as if he's at my door. My heart starts to palpitate, and my legs go weak. I hold onto the counter.

Think rationally Charlotte. Your lawyer said there was no indication that he had anything other than your PO Box number. Even if he was in California, there's no way he could easily track you down.

"Are you still there?" Penny's voice is panicked on the other end of the phone.

"Yes, I'm still here. Just give me a minute." I go to the fridge, take out a bottle of water and take a drink to cool myself down. I sit at the table.

"Was there anything unusual in his calendar three days ago? Any gaps unaccounted for?"

"No, everything is accounted for, you know what he's like Charlotte. He just disappeared." Penny is sounding increasingly frantic.

"Have you told the police?"

"Yes, but they just told me to file a report. They said he's a grown man, give it a week."

"Well, they do have a point."

"For someone other than Charles, yes." Penny has a point too.

"So why are you calling me Penny, what do you want me to do about it?"

"I thought you might have heard from him, you're the only person we haven't spoken to, and you are, after all, still his wife."

Still his wife, my stomach lurches again at the thought that some people in this world still think of us as a couple.

"I'll let you know if I hear anything Penny. He'll turn up eventually."

"The police asked about you."

The police? "What? Why?"

"When someone goes missing, the first person they suspect is the spouse."

"Suspect? Do you think I flew home one night and did away with Charles?"

"We don't even know where you are, Charlotte. I only know by the dial tone on the phone that you're abroad."

"If the police want to contact me, Penny, give them my number." I hang up then, what else am I supposed to say? I probably sounded like a cold-hearted bitch, but I don't care. Penny's betrayed me enough times to lose any right to be offended. My fingers instinctively look for Charles's in the contacts on my phone. *Unblock caller?* What would be the point in that? I can't retrieve any previous messages, I already looked that up. If I unblock him, it means he can contact me anytime. The virtual security fence I've put up around myself would be gone. I close his contact on my phone and put it down. Should I be worried that my husband might be lying dead somewhere? Or that he's going to turn up on my doorstep? I'm not sure which of those ideas I find worse. I hadn't even flinched when I heard he had a, *"new intern."* I want to call Ethan, but he said he was getting an early night and I don't want to disturb him. Besides, what would I even say to him? *"My husband that you don't know about is missing. and I'm feeling a bit uneasy about it?"*

The thought of the Thai curry makes me feel sick now. I take it out of the microwave and throw it in the bin. I pour myself a glass of wine and pace the kitchen instead. I should probably try and get an early night too, but I know my dreams will be full of Charles - and that's a nightmare I can't stomach.

Chapter Thirty-Five

Charlotte

When I get up in the morning the Santa Ana winds are banging the shutters. It spooks me and I get out of bed to close the window. I hardly got any sleep. I'm nervous about today and the uneasy feeling about Penny's phone call kept me awake most of the night. I'd hoped to hear that she had found Charles by now, but my phone has remained silent. I need to focus all my energy on today. In a few days I will be lying on a beach in Mexico with Ethan, and all this will be over. It's a two-hour class today, it's a sort of taster for potential students. English is always a popular department. I know Frank wants to promote it and show off the progress the students have made in the short amount of time I've been there. I know he will also want to capitalize on my name, and the fact that I taught at one of the top universities in England. I am to give the impression that I will be teaching next term. I'm not allowed to tell anyone that I'm leaving, because Frank wants that stupid award. I feel sad today, not only because it's my last class, but also because I feel I've let my students down. I'd never change what happened with Ethan, and I know I will teach again, but today is going to be hard.

I want to look good, mostly as a fuck you to Frank. I decide to wear the outfit I wore on my first day of class. The short skirt and the jacket and heels. I text Ethan to let him know that I'll see him there, he sends back, *"Just like old times Professor. Maybe we should recreate me undressing you on the desk."* I reply, *"You wish."* I put on my glasses and take a last look in the mirror. I feel confident that I can get through this. I step outside and head to the college for the last time.

Frank's waiting for me on the steps, and I have Deja vu, but this time he doesn't take my arm and fawn all over me. He escorts me to the classroom, like I'm a prisoner at the police station. He's obviously worried I'll go off script and speak to the students, or worse, the school board.

"You will open the class and talk a bit about what you've been doing with the students. A few of them will read out some of their work, and then I will introduce the guest speaker." He says it through gritted teeth, smiling at anyone we pass in the corridor.

"Fine." I don't want to talk to Frank, I don't even care who the stupid guest speaker is crashing my last class. I'm going to enjoy being with my students again, and then get the hell out of here. Frank opens the door to a packed classroom, there are even more people than I imagined. My students greet me with smiles. The others I assume are prospective students, parents, members of the school board - including the award adjudicator. I put my bag on the desk and look up instinctively towards Ethan's old desk and there he is, with his boyish grin, pencil behind his ear, wearing a white t-shirt, blue jeans. He must've thought it would be cute to wear the same outfit he wore on his first day too. I look to my left to see Frank smiling, he must have spotted Ethan, but it doesn't get the reaction I was hoping for. He almost looks happy to see him there.

I take in the room "It's good to be back with my favorite students."

"We missed you." One of them shouts and I sense Frank twitching in the corner, he won't want people to ask where I've been this past week.

"As I said on my first day here, stories shape our lives, and I wanted us to share old and new ones together. So, a few of the students are going to share what has particularly inspired them so far this semester." I take a seat at the front of the classroom and watch as, one by one, some of my students come to the front and talk about their work. I'm proud of them, and all the stress of the last few months fades away and I'm reminded of why I came here. I found the love of my life, but it's my passion for teaching that brought me here, and it's not something I am prepared to give up. I will get another job at a university or a school, or private tutor until I do. I will never waste away like

I did in the last two years before I came here. The students finish with their presentations, and I thank them. I give out the materials I printed, and then hand the class over to Frank. He comes over and shakes my hand, squeezing it too hard. I smile through it; I don't want to give him the pleasure of knowing that I'm uncomfortable. I go to take my seat again at the front of the class, but he stops me, his hand on my waist. I look over at Ethan and his lips are pursed, I'm sure his hands are fists under the table.

"Thank you, Professor Rose, for your wonderful words and for doing such a great job with this class. You certainly know how to make your students feel special."

I know that's a dig about me and Ethan, but I don't rise to it. I smile broadly and thank him for being such a *'hands on'* boss.

"However, now it's time for us to show you how much we appreciate you. We've been keeping a secret from you like you've kept from us" I'm confused, what's he talking about. I want to look at Ethan, but my smile is frozen on my face, and I can't move.

"We know you came halfway across the world from one of England's top universities to teach at our little old community college. You wanted a chance to give back to students who weren't as lucky or privileged. You didn't tell us, though, the kind of people you rubbed shoulders with in England, or the life you left behind for us."

What the fuck is he talking about? Class is over and he needs to be wrapping things up.

"So, we've brought that world to you today, to say thank you for everything. We know you must have missed him…"

Oh shit, no, no, this can't be happening.

"Our guest speaker today is none other than your husband, the infamous author Charles Armstrong." The name that comes out of his mouth sounds like a slow bell knocking inside my head. The door opens and he's walking towards me. No deep black eyes, just the cold steely blue ones that I'd run away from.

"Darling, I knew you must have missed me but didn't think you'd swoon."

My legs have buckled. He grabs hold of me and whispers in my ear. "Hmm you've put on weight, more to grab hold of, I like it."

I must be dreaming, right? I open my mouth to make a sound, but nothing comes out. In this slow-motion state, I turn to look at Ethan, but his face is blank. Charles brings my face back round to his and kisses me on the lips. I don't stop him. I can't, I'm too numb. I've completely checked out. It's a coping mechanism I learned as a kid when my parents argued, and in my marriage when Charles was abusive. Frank has a Cheshire grin on his face, I expect him to start licking himself any minute now. How long has he been planning this? How long has he known that I'm married? The whole class is applauding, and I don't know why.

Does it look like I'm enjoying this? In my head I'm not even here, I'm running in a field, through long grass. I'm a kid again and I'm going down to the old pond to visit the little tadpoles and the damselflies, the place I go to when my parents argue, it's safe here, and I'm watching the adult me open and close her mouth. She's saying something but I'm not sure what's coming out. I hope it's the truth, that Charles is a monster, and that adult Charlotte says she no longer wants him to be her husband, that she is in love with someone else. But the class is smiling so it can't be that. I see one person leave though, get out of his seat at the back of the class and walk out. I want to follow this person, I don't know why, but I have a feeling that I just lost the one thing that matters to me the most.

I'm not sure at what point I came back into my body. Class is over, except for a few straggling students asking for Charles's autograph. I tried to call Ethan twice when Charles was entertaining his fans, but he didn't answer. I was going to text him, but what would I say?

"Did you like your surprise?" Frank has sidled up to me and I put my phone down. My skin crawls.

"I knew you hated me Frank, but this?"

"I don't know what you're talking about. I thought it would be a lovely surprise for you."

"Bullshit." I say it under my breath as I wave goodbye to one of the students. I want to know how he pulled this off. "How long have you and Charles been in touch?" I go over to the whiteboard and start wiping off Charles's notes.

"Not long. It all worked out perfectly really. I'd already fired you, but knew you were contractually bound to come back for the open house. Charles called the college a few days ago, asking for you. When my secretary told me that your husband was on the phone, I was shocked. I thought about telling him about your sordid affair with a student, but then this idea popped into my head, and it seemed so much more..."

"What, cruel?"

"Yes, that's it."

I want to slap him, hard. Instead, I wipe the board more vigorously pretending it's his face.

"Oh, c'mon Charlotte, you kept it a secret that you were married to a famous author. I couldn't let my students miss out on such a great opportunity to meet him."

"An opportunity to humiliate me, you mean?"

"Why of course not. Yes goodbye, thank you for coming." He waves and smiles at someone as they leave. I don't bother to turn. "No, it was an opportunity for the college to have a famous author come and give a talk to the English literature class. The board was extremely impressed that we have such connections."

"You won't have for much longer, you fired me, don't forget."

"Oh, didn't I tell you? Charles has agreed to become an honorary board member. Of course, he won't be able to do much from England, but it looks good for us and for him to show that he is giving so much back to the community. Looks like I'll be getting that award after all."

I want to rub that smile off his face with the cloth. "You two are a match made in heaven."

"Like you and Mr. Delaney? Or is that off the cards now after today? He didn't look very happy when he left. Did you forget to tell him you were married, like the rest of us?"

I square up to Frank now, I don't care who sees. Charles is engrossed with the remaining throng of adoring fans, and they with him.

"Ethan told me about how you propositioned his mother, how many women have you done this to, hmm? I'm sure I could dig up more than a few. I could certainly add myself to that quota."

He puts his hands in his pockets and laughs, then moves closer to me. He still smells like garlic and thirty years in the school system. "Oh, my dear silly Charlotte, who do you think they would believe? A Professor having an affair with that very student or me?"

He eyes me up and down then and the look on his face makes my stomach churn. He's right, unfortunately. Even if I spend the time finding all the other women that he harassed, and I'm sure there are plenty during his long career - *what had Mo called him? Fletch the letch*. It was him who was going to be believed, it always was.

"Fuck you Frank Fletcher, fuck you!" I turn away from him, I don't want to spend another moment in his company. Besides, I still have an even bigger asshole to deal with - my husband.

Chapter Thirty-Six

Charlotte

Charles and I said nothing to each other in the taxi from the college to his hotel. I want nothing more than to get away from him, but I need to get this over and done with first. I've been texting Ethan telling him I am sorry, that I can explain, to please call me. He hasn't responded and how can I honestly expect him to. I did this to myself. Lauren was right, I should have told him from the get-go.

"Jack on the rocks, and a martini with two green olives and a pickled onion for the lady."

We're sitting at a small table in the hotel bar. It's darker than I would've liked and there's a pianist playing old show tunes in the corner. Not the setting I'd imagined for this conversation, but I'm certainly not going to invite Charles over to mine. He orders for me as usual, without asking what I want. He smiles at the waitress as he pulls down his jacket sleeves, fiddling with his cufflinks, disarming her. He's aged since I last saw him, or perhaps I'm just looking at him properly for the first time in years. The bags under his eyes are heavy and he can no longer cover his receding hairline. His hair has a baby bird like quality; pale little tufts sprout up on his head. His eyes are as intense as ever, like a cold English day. There's a difference now though; he doesn't frighten me anymore. Something in me has changed since I've been here, and I hadn't even realized. I've been thinking of him as a monster that I was running away from. Being with him now though, I can see that he's actually just a pathetic little man. I wonder how much longer he can go on getting women to fall at his feet. There's something faded about him, as if he's an old piece of furniture and the upholstery is rubbing off. I'm familiar with all his little habits that made up his armor, and I watch him go through the motions. He looks around to see if anyone recognizes him. He leans back in the chair and does the masculine spreading out, to make himself seem larger than life. He tilts his head to make it appear as if he's listening.

The waitress brings our drinks back over. We still haven't said a word to each other, he's content to study me, and I him. I take the pickled onion from my drink and place it on the table. I haven't liked an onion in my martini for years. I match his body language and sit back and take a sip. Charles Armstrong is still trying to intimidate me, and he can't.

"What are you doing here Charles? Did you not get the divorce papers and the court order and the one hundred letters from my lawyer?"

He sighs and waves one of his hands about, "Pff, that."

He dismisses me as if I'm being unnecessarily dramatic. He's trying to gaslight me like he's done for so many years.

"I said, what are you doing here?" This time he focuses his glacial eyes on me and for a minute the glint in them brings up that old familiar fear; but I swallow it.

"I'm here to bring you to your senses. You had your fun, my girl, now it's time to come home."

"I am home Charles."

He laughs so loudly that the piano player looks up from her seat. Perhaps it sent a chill down her spine too.

"How do you plan to stay here without a visa? I don't think that little twerp Frank Fletcher is going to extend your contract, is he? I hear you've been a naughty girl."

So, Frank did tell him about Ethan. Of course, he did.

"No naughtier than you've been for the last ten years." I take a sip of my martini and cross my legs. I don't even know who I'm being right now, but it certainly isn't the old Charlotte.

He raises his glass to me, "Touché my darling, touché."

"The difference is I did it after I filed for divorce. I was always faithful to you Charles, even after all those years that you weren't to me. Ethan and I care a great deal about each other and..."

He laughs again "Oh Charlotte, you've been caught with your hand in the biscuit tin. Just call it what it is. Never fall in love with them my dear, that's not what they're for." He knocks back the rest of his drink then signals to the waitress for more.

When she looks at me, I shake my head. I'm not going to have more than a sip of this one. I need to be stone cold sober for this.

"Did you ever love me, Charles?"

He crosses his legs and runs his hand along his jaw, his stubble is patchy like his hair. He's always had trouble growing a beard.

"Does anyone know what love is? I *need* you; is that the same thing?"

"No, it's not."

"You keep me steadfast Charlotte, you have a stabilizing effect on my life. Since you've been gone, my life has sort of been in disarray."

"Don't you have Becks to help you with that?" He looks surprised for a second but recovers his composure quickly.

"Ah, you've been talking to Penny."

"Yes, I have. She was worried about you. She called me to say you were missing, she even phoned the police."

"Were you worried, poor Charlie?" I cringe at his use of the old nickname he gave me.

"I was worried that you might do something stupid, and I was right."

"As you are always, my love. Thank you."

The waitress hands him his glass and he beams at her, she half smiles back then looks at me and puts her head down. Maybe he's losing his touch.

"I'm divorcing you Charles, whether you like it or not and you will sign those papers."

He considers me for a moment. I pull my jacket tighter across my chest, I don't want him looking at that part of me ever again. Between him and Frank today, I feel like I need to take a long shower.

"I wish you could still smoke in these damn places, what I wouldn't do for a cigar." He's stalling.

"Did you hear what I said? I'm divorcing you." I lean forward in my chair and focus my gaze on him. He takes another sip of his drink, then swirls it around in his glass before leaning back.

"I will sign those papers if you come home to England with me."

"Why would I do that?" The idea of going back with him makes me shudder.

"That's the only way you will get an amicable divorce from me. I want it to be known that I am divorcing you for irreconcilable behavior. I will only do it on those terms."

I laugh, "*Irreconcilable behavior, i*s that a fucking joke? After everything you've done to me over the years. Fuck off Charles!" I stand up. I need to find Ethan. I don't want to sit here and do this stupid dance with Charles.

He smiles, "There she is, the passionate Charlotte I fell in love with."

"You were never in love with me. I was just one of your many conquests, fuck knows why you married me."

"My dear, you were the best briefcase carrier I had. I wasn't about to let that go." He raises his eyebrows and places his glass on the arm of the chair. I know what he's insinuating, all those years ago when I was his assistant on trips, and I'd give him blow jobs in the bathrooms of the first-class lounge in airports. I can feel the shame rising in my body as I think about it.

"I just want you out my life for good."

"Then you must come back to England with me, I need to be seen with my wife in public. I want people to think you've come back to me. I need to reject you."

"It's really all about your ego, isn't it? It only ever was."

"I'm a man of some standing, this is important to me."

"How do I know you'll give me the divorce if I come back with you? How do I know you're not just trying to wheedle your way back into my life?"

He studies me for a second, then takes another sip of his drink. "Because this Charlotte, the one in front of me, is not the one who left."

That's the biggest compliment he's ever paid me.

"I will happily come with you to your lawyer in the morning, sign whatever is required to reassure you of my word. I can be out of your life in as little as six months." He runs his fingers around the rim of his glass, it reminds me of a mouse running around the bottom of a cage. "Or you stay here, and I drag it out as long as I can and financially you will have nothing."

"You do know that I practically wrote your last two books for you?"

"And your point is?"

"That financially you actually need me."

He makes a gesture with his hand as if he's shooing away a fly.

"I can always get some eager little ghost writer to help me out, don't think you're anything special." The little spasm in his left eyelid tells me that he's lying. I can get a good deal from this divorce, using the fact that I am the real writer behind his latest books as a bargaining chip. I have more power than I realized.

I sit back down in my chair and cross my legs, "You know what, Charles as lovely as the offer is you just made me. I think I'll stay here." The look on his face tells me that isn't the answer he expected.

He pushes back his baby bird hair and fixes his steely eyes on me, "I'm so honored that they asked me to be a trustee on the college board, it's such a privilege to be able to help these kids."

I shift in my chair, an uneasy feeling rising in me. "You don't give a shit about those kids. It's all about show for you."

"That's where you're wrong my dear. I can actually wield a great deal of influence." He picks up his glass and looks at it, before downing the rest of the liquor. "One word in the right person's ear about your sordid little affair, and your career here and in the UK is over. Also, Ethan will be on the blacklist from any college or university. I will make absolutely sure of that."

"You can't do that! Frank and I had a deal."

He laughs. "Frank has kept his deal. You just didn't factor in your husband showing up." He makes a tutting sound. "Silly old Charlotte, thinking I wouldn't find you."

Suddenly I feel cold. The air conditioning is blasting into my neck, and I shiver. I feel my eyes start to fill with tears, but I blink them away. I will never let Charles see me vulnerable again. If I have to live in a gilded cage for six more months to get my freedom, then so be it. I will get the payment I deserve for writing his books as I'm confident he will be keen to keep that quiet. I have no idea if Ethan ever wants to see me again. As heartbreaking as leaving now will be, there really is no other choice. Maybe I have to lose Ethan for a while, in order to gain him back.

"Okay, I will come back with you, but we *will* go to the lawyers first thing in the morning, and you *will* sign any paperwork I want. In six months, you will be out of my life for good and I never want to see you again. Ever. Do we have a deal?"

He nods his head, and for a minute I think I glimpse a tremble at the corner of his mouth, but then it's gone.

Chapter Thirty-Seven

Ethan

"This is the last place I thought I'd find you."

"Well, here I am." I raise my can of beer to Mo and take a gulp.

"It's a bit early to drink, isn't it?"

"Nope." I toss the rest back and reach in my bag for another one. She takes it off me and places it on the sand beside her. She crouches down and touches me on the arm. I shrug it off. "I'd rather be alone right now."

"Your jeans are wet; did you go in the water?"

I ignore her and stare out into the horizon. The ocean is calm today, but it doesn't match my mood. The current here is dangerous, it can lull you into a false sense of security then sweep your feet from under you before you know it. I don't know why I came straight here after walking out of class. I didn't know where else to go and this beach is usually deserted. It's like my body took over and brought me here. It hasn't really changed in the years since I was last here. The steps are more lethal and the, *'Danger, rock fall'* sign still seems to keep the tourists out. There's no sign of the sea glass that my mom and I used to collect from the shore. Its nature's own recycling - discarded bottles and jars that have been tumbled by the waves over years into glass. *"If only people could be rinsed like that and come out all shiny and new,"* she used to say.

I still don't know what happened in class. How could that man be Charlotte's husband? How could she have kept that hidden from me? She just stood there nodding and smiling with his hand around her waist. I don't know her at all, I knew she had to be running away from something. Nobody tries to start a new life in a different country unless they are. Maybe I didn't ask because I was afraid of what I'd find out. What do I really know about her? I know she'd been a university professor, that she adored her father and had a difficult relationship with her mother. I know that she hiccups when she gets upset and says most things out loud that come into her head. I know she likes her legs rubbed after standing all day in class, and that she has a star shaped birthmark to the left of her belly button.

"I guess you heard what happened." I don't look at Mo as I say it, I'm hypnotized by the sound of the waves washing over the pebbles, it's a constant I can focus on.

"I did."

"News travels fast. Did one of Gina's spies tell Rob?"

"No, I already knew."

I turn to look at her, as she sits back and untucks her feet from under her. She picks up a small pebble and turns it over and over in her hand.

"What do you mean, you knew?"

Her lips are pinched, and she squints into the sun. Her dark hair is tied back, but the wind keeps playing with the strands of hair around her face. "I only figured it out today. I finished reading that book, the one that was in the kitchen when you both had breakfast at our house. I enjoyed it a lot, so I looked up the author online to see what else he'd written. I also thought he was quite handsome, so I wanted to find some more pictures of him."

I've never heard Mo talk about a man like that before, she looks down at her feet as she says it.

"Anyway, I was just lost in this author rabbit hole. I looked him up on Wikipedia and it said he was married to a Charlotte Davenport. Then it hit me, the memory of Charlotte's face when she saw that book in my kitchen. It was like she had the fright of her life. So, I kept looking through the pictures and I came across one from some awards ceremony and you can just see the profile of her sitting next to him. She's turned away from the camera, but it's unmistakably her."

I feel like I've been thumped in the stomach again and I lean forward, with my arms on my knees. Mo puts her hand on my back and rubs it gently.

"I knew it was her last day today, I was planning to catch her after class and confront her about it. Then when I got there, Josie the receptionist told me she'd left already with her husband."

"Were you planning to say it all in front of me too?"

She takes her hand off my back and hugs her knees in. "I didn't know you would be there, you told me you'd been suspended. Josie told me she'd seen you though. I went to look for you, but you weren't at home or the garage. I tried the gym, the last place I looked is here."

We sit together in silence for a bit; I don't want to take any of this in. I want to be alone.

"Do you ever think about what it feels like to drown?"

She looks across at me startled. "No, and you shouldn't either."

I lean back and press my elbows into the sand, "It's all I think about Mo, how mom must have felt, was she at peace or was it violent?"

"Stop it Ethan, you're in a bad place right now and this won't help."

"You know, I watched a documentary once where the swollen body of a dead whale sank to the bottom. Sharks tore its blubber from its bone and little fish gnawed at it, until all that was left of the whale was its rib cage. I have a recurring nightmare about it. Except in my dream, they're the ribs of my mom rolling along the ocean floor."

"I'm sorry, that's horrific."

"I used to come down here after she died and thought about just walking in the water and not coming out. I could never go in though, it was like her ghost was haunting it, preventing me from taking even one step in."

"You never told me that, I wish I'd known."

I look over at Mo, she's hanging her head, now it's my turn to reach out for her hand. "You did everything you could to help me; I couldn't have asked for anymore. You're still looking out for me now; you were prepared to go down to the college and have it out with my girlfriend. You still want to protect me. At some point though, you have to let go and protect yourself." I squeeze her hand; it feels so fragile in mine.

"You went in the water today didn't you; your jeans and your hair are wet."

"I did. I needed to face all the ghosts in there and I needed to cleanse myself of what's happening out here. I was scared at first, I held my breath and let myself go under, the current picked me up and tossed me around for a bit."

"Oh Ethan..."

"No, don't be upset. I needed to do this, I fought for my life there today, Mo. Despite everything, my life is worth fighting for. I needed to be reminded of that. I think you need to remind yourself of that too. You deserve more than just taking care of Rob and me."

She nods, snot coming out of her nose and her face wet. "I am going to make some changes, I promise."

I pull her close to me and kiss her on top of her head, she really is the sister I never had.

"What are you going to do? Are you going to talk to Charlotte."

I don't know if I want to see her, the sense of betrayal is cutting into my chest and at the same time I don't want to let go of her.

"I will when I'm ready."

I look up at the sun, the breeze tickles my face, and the heat feels good on my skin. I don't want to hide from it anymore.

Chapter Thirty-Eight

Charlotte

I bang on Ethan's door; he won't answer his phone and I don't know what else to do. I came straight here from the hotel. I don't even know if he's home. I collapse against the door with exhaustion just as it opens, and Ethan is standing there. He's shirtless and his jeans are wet. His eyes are red, and his face is blotchy. He says nothing, just leaves the door open for me. I stand up and follow him into the kitchen. He opens the fridge and takes out a bottle of coke. Without offering me some, he undoes it, tips his head back and takes a long drink from it; just like the first day we met. He wipes his mouth with the back of his hand and pulls out a breakfast stool. He sits on it, leans his elbows on the counter and puts his head in his hands.

I talk to him softly, "I've been trying to call you."

The look he gives me is icy, like I have ceased to exist for him. The field of long grass is beckoning again, and I want to drift away there, but I must tether myself here. I pick up the bottle of coke and take a gulp. The cold helps startle me back into my body. "I don't know what to say to make things better."

"How about nothing?" He spits out the word nothing as if its poison. One of his arms keeps giving way from under him and I realize then that he's drunk. There's no point having this conversation if he's not going to remember it in the morning.

"Why don't we talk more when you're sober."

'Nah." His head jerks again, he looks like he's about to pass out. I put my bag down and take off my blazer. I wish I wasn't wearing this stiff suit, but I haven't been home to change yet.

"Why are your jeans wet?"

"I went for a swim."

"In the sea?" He doesn't answer me. He gets up, wobbles, then goes to the cupboard and pulls out a half empty bottle of liquor. He drinks straight from it.

"Don't you think you've had enough?"

"Don't you think YOU'VE had enough!" he replies, pointing his finger at me. His hair is a mess and the top button to his jeans is undone. I want to get him out of them, to get him to put something warm on, but I doubt he will let me near him. He's standing facing me with the bottle in one hand and the other resting on the countertop. There's a chasm between us that seems uncrossable.

"I filed for divorce before I left England. I should have left him years ago, but I was too afraid to."

"Oh, poor little daddy's girl, too afraid, awe." He sticks out his bottom lip.

"You know you're being really childish."

"Am I? He swings the bottle in the air as he says it "Well I'm just your student after all, and you were supposed to be *my fucking teacher.*"

I go over to him and take the bottle off him. He sways for a second.

"Mm you smell good." Did you put on that perfume for your husband? Did you beg him to put his dick in you too? *Charlotte loves cock!"* He raises his hand triumphantly and punches the air.

The indignant part of me wants to walk out, but I also don't want to leave him like this. "I think you should take those jeans off."

"I bet you do; you have a one-track mind sister." He winks at me then goes for the bottle of whisky, but I grab it before he can. I sense he is fading, so I take the opportunity to take him by the hand and lead him into the living room, he doesn't resist. He stands by the couch and lets me take down his jeans, holding onto me as he steps out of them. He falls onto the couch and stays where he lands, sprawled out with one leg dangling off to the side. I fetch a blanket from upstairs and when I come back, he's already snoring, I put his dangling leg back up on the couch and roll him gently on his side, before covering him with the blanket. I take a seat in the armchair opposite and watch the rise and fall of his body under it. I feel calm, despite everything. I think I'm still running on adrenaline. I'm sure by the morning, the reality of the situation will hit me, but right now I'm going to pretend I haven't lost Ethan. I can't face the pain of that yet.

I rub my eyes trying to figure out where I am and why I ache so much. Then I remember and I close my eyes, hoping it was all a dream.

"Hey, I thought you might like this." When I open my eyes again Ethan is standing in front of me with a cup of tea.

"Thank you." I take the cup in my hands.

"I'm sorry about last night. I had too much to drink and I was out of line."

"I probably deserved it."

"Still, I was a jerk."

"I'm surprised you can remember anything."

"I remember enough." I nod and take a sip of tea; I can feel the tears threatening to come. I knew this would happen once the adrenalin wore off. I hiccup as I sip.

"Got the hiccups?"

"No." I lie and go to laugh, but instead I cry. I'm crying for every mistake I've made these last few months, and for what I'm about to lose. He leaves the room and comes back with a box of tissues.

"I thought it was about time I got some. I seem to make women cry a lot these days. I should have taken shares in them." I manage a small smile, wipe my eyes, and blow my nose, I'm beyond caring how ugly I must look.

He's wearing his navy hoodie that is so familiar to me, the one he likes to hide in. His five-o clock shadow is already closing in.

"I should have offered you some clothes to sleep in last night."

"You passed out."

"I shouldn't have done that."

"It's probably best that you did." I blow my nose again, it's sore now, it must be red. "Don't you want me to explain?"

"Explain what? You're married, what else is there to say?"

"There's lots to say. I told you last night, I filed for divorce before I left. I had no intention of ever going back to him."

"Didn't look like that yesterday. It looked like you were his wife."

"How do you know? You left."

"I'm so sorry that I couldn't just sit there and watch a strange man with his hands all over you."

"His hands weren't all over me."

"He had his arm around your waist, he kissed you!"

"I was in shock! I panicked and I was scared. That man wore me down for ten years! I went into automatic pilot mode. All smiles just to keep up the show."

"Well, it was a damned good show."

"Yes, but that's all it is! I sent him divorce papers again last week. My new lawyer said he was legally bound to respond."

"Well looks like he did!" He's up and pacing now then suddenly stops. "Hold on, so you were doing all this behind my back? Even after I told you everything about my past, you just sat there and said nothing?"

"I know, I know I should have said something. Even at that moment, I was going to, but the words wouldn't come out."

"Oh, please Charlotte, when have you ever had a hard time saying anything?"

"When it matters the most."

He runs his hands through his hair. I just want to go to him, put my arms around him and nuzzle into his chest.

"Were you just using me?"

"What? No!"

"Was I just a pawn to spice up your marriage? Get your husband to pay you some attention?"

"How can you think that?"

"Well, it certainly didn't take you long to let me into your panties, almost like it was what you were planning."

"Fuck you Ethan, fuck you!" I put my tea down and get up to go, but he takes hold of my arm and for a minute I am there again, in the safety of him.

"I'm sorry, this isn't getting us anywhere." He lets go of my arm and sits back down.

"I know, but where do we go from here?"

"I'm not sure that there's anywhere left for us to go."

I sit back down in the armchair. I wish I wasn't still wearing this silly little skirt and shirt; it feels so inappropriate now. I tuck my legs under me and grab the cushion, holding it in front of me.

"I have to go back to England to get my divorce. He's promised I'll have it in six months if I go back with him. We're going to my lawyers for him to sign something later this morning."

Ethan is leaning forward with his elbows on his knees, he just nods.

"You could come back with me. You could get a student visa, go to art college or something in London. We could be discreet for a bit until my divorce comes through."

I know as soon as it's out of my mouth that it's a stupid idea. Why would he agree to do that? To hide from Charles for me. The shock of what I'm about to lose hits me and I think I'm going to throw up. I cover my mouth. "Is this it?"

He looks up at me from under those glorious lashes." I think it is."

I'm nodding and sniveling and he comes to sit at my feet.

"Don't cry anymore, please don't cry." He kisses my feet, then my ankles, my knees, my thighs and then I'm down on the floor in front of him and we are kissing each other as if the end of the world is upon us and there is nothing left but this. My hands are pulling off his clothes before I even know what I'm doing, his hands are in my shirt pulling one of my tits from my bra, rolling the nipple between his fingers and he's whispering it a tender goodbye. I lick his neck and then I bite into it as if it's my last meal. My skirt is up around my waist and he's pulling my panties off as I roll on top of him on the floor, undoing the zipper on his jeans and scrambling to get them off. He's not wearing any underwear and his dick is erect. All I want is him inside me. I straddle him with my skirt wrapped up around me. I find the tip of his cock with my pussy, then I push down, and his hips shoot up under me as I gasp and lean forward and bite him again on the chest. I want to feast on all of him, like it's the last fucking supper. His arms are around me and I begin to fuck him hard, gyrating up and down on his shaft as we bite and lick each other like wild animals. I entwine my fingers with his and move slowly on top of him. My pussy is slick and wet as I make small figures of eight with my hips so his cock can reach every part of it. Our eyes are transfixed on each other, both knowing this is the last time we will do this, the memory burned into us forever. The emotion rises again in my throat, but I won't allow it. I lay forward onto his chest again and rub my tits against his muscles there, soaking up his sweat. I bring my legs together in between his and push him even deeper inside me, my clit rubbing against his cock. I won't be able to stop myself from coming like this and he knows it. He takes my face and kisses it all over as my pussy drips all over his dick. His lips are on mine and he's whispering, "Oh, Charlotte," into my mouth. I swallow his words so they can keep swimming around inside me. Then his hands are on my ass as he cums and my pussy grips his cock as I orgasm in wave after wave. We rock back and forth like one being, for the last time, together.

We lay on the floor staring up at the ceiling catching our breath, no stars this time, no eternal night. I rest a hand on his thigh. We don't say anything for a while and then he puts his hand on mine. "I love you, Charlotte Rose."

I put my fingers through his, feeling the rough parts one last time.

"I love you too Ethan Delaney. I always will."

Epilogue I

Ethan

The sky is clear tonight and the stars plentiful. A red moon is floating above, or a *Grain Moon* as the locals here call it. I can't believe it's nearly been a year since I sat on top of a mountain and watched the meteor shower with Charlotte. I've never been able to get that night out of my head. Her milky skin, her saucer eyes, her gorgeous body revealed to me for the first time. I think I knew even then that she was more than just a casual fuck. I take a sip of my iced tea, welcoming the coolness in my throat. I made a pitcher and am sitting out on my porch. I moved to Vermont a few months ago and am living in my grandfather's old place. My dad, Arthur, died in February. Rob and I drove up to his funeral then to his small house to sort through his things. It was like walking into a stranger's home.

We hadn't seen our father since we lost our mom. Rob and I talked in the car, him and Mo are getting some therapy and she's moved into my old apartment for a bit. We talked about mom and dad; he opened up about some stuff that happened to him as a kid. We found my grandfather's will in dad's papers. He'd left his property to me for when I came of age; he knew how much I loved this place. My dad never told me. He moved tenants in and lived off the proceeds. I thought what better place to make a fresh start, out here in the middle of nowhere. I had enough money saved from working at the garage, besides towns always need mechanics and I knew I could get work if I needed to. When I got here the place was really run down, the last tenants hadn't treated it kindly. I've been working on the house, talking to local farmers about restoring the land. Old Blue is here, her paint sparkling in the moonlight. Mo was right, she barely made it a few miles down the road. So, I had her shipped out here, I've got more time and space to work on her now. I've been painting these spectacular sunsets and sunrises. I'm converting the shed into an art studio. It would make a great writer's retreat too, something Charlotte could have run.

Did I do the right thing in letting her go? It wouldn't have felt right otherwise, I couldn't be with her knowing that she was still tied to someone else, she needed to figure all that out and I had to get my shit together too. I reach into my pocket and pull out a postcard with a painting on the front of a boy with jet black hair and charcoal eyes, it's called, *'The Lost Boy.'* I turn it over between my fingers like a playing card. It was sent to my old address and Mo forwarded it on. I get up to go inside; the dark is too full of Charlotte tonight. As I climb back up the porch and turn back, something catches my eye. A golden light streaks across the sky, as a star dies and falls to the earth.

Epilogue II
Charlotte

This August London heat is stifling. We will get about a week of this stagnant air and then the moody skies will roll in and summer will be over. It doesn't stop most Brits thinking that the heat wave will last forever as they gather outside on picnic blankets in parks. This time of year, the ice cream vans sell out of ice creams and the hardware stores sell out of fans. I don't even want to think about getting on the Tube yet with all those people stuck together. So, when I leave work I take a walk to Trafalgar Square instead, the pigeons parting like the sea as I walk through them. It's the only way to do it, as if you are walking through a herd of sheep. Otherwise, you'll get stuck as they peck around you for their supper. I've been working at a publishing house for the last six months. I got my divorce as promised just before that. Charles kept his word, my little bargaining chip worked. He bought me out of my half of the house and thanks to London prices, I put a good amount away in the bank. I've been renting a small flat by Hampstead Heath with a willow tree out the front. It's peaceful and I've been writing in the evenings when it's too hot to sleep. It has sash windows overlooking a pond with ducks and Greylag geese. I'm writing a love story about a beautiful boy and an impossible girl.

I can't believe it's been a year since I went to Los Angeles, since I saw Ethan. I wrote to him a couple of months ago. I sent him a postcard, one from the national gallery with the painting of, *'The Lost Boy'* on the front. I had written my address on it and just put, *"Wish you were here."* He didn't write back, not that I thought he would. I'm sure he's moving on with his life now, back at college doing what any twenty something should be doing. I also sent an anonymous letter to the Los Angeles college board detailing information about Frank and his harassment of women. Since then, I have been keeping an eye out to see if anything came of it. Then, about a month ago there was a small piece online in the LA Times saying, *"Dean on indefinite suspension."* Turns out that other women have come forward now too. I wonder if he packed his award when he left.

I like to come to the national gallery after work, it's cool and during the week at this time there aren't many tourists. I sit in the cafe and have a drink, then wander around looking at my favorite paintings or a new exhibit. I'm planning what to do next with my life, I want to get back into teaching and travel again, perhaps do both at the same time again in South America. Lauren and I went on a week's yoga retreat earlier this year. She finally managed to get a part time nanny to help with the kids and her mother-in-law. It was good to spend time together, though we spent most of the time giggling and less reaching spiritual enlightenment. I walk up the marble steps of the museum, I know where I want to go first today. The guard at the entrance greets me with a nod of his head. I am a familiar fixture here now. I take a left turn and go up one flight of stairs, I could do this in my sleep. Then I find the room on the right and go and sit on the bench at the very end where it is darker and narrows. The boy looks out at me from the painting, his eyes trained on mine. I must be familiar to him now. I wonder how long he's been lost. I close my eyes and imagine I'm smelling salty air and a fresh pine forest.

"Charlotte." I open my eyes and there is a man in front of me blocking my view of the boy, he's tall with midnight hair and a blue-black beard. It takes me a second to register who it is.

"Ethan?" His beard is full, and he's grown his hair, it sits just above his shoulders, which look broader. The t-shirt and hoodie are gone and he's wearing a white linen shirt.

"What are you doing here? How did you find me?" He reaches into his back pocket and pulls out the postcard I sent him.

"I went to the address you wrote on the back of this. Your downstairs neighbor said to try looking for you here. I figured this painting might be a good place to start."

My mouth opens and closes, like a turtle coming up from a pond for air.

"I came to wish you a Happy Anniversary." I'm still not registering that he is here. Lately he has sort of merged into my dreams and I've questioned whether he was ever real or not.

"Anniversary?"

"August the 18th, one year to the day we met." I stand and reach up to his face, my fingers tracing the topography of his beard until I find the zig zag on his chin. I inhale the sweet-smelling earth of him.

"I remembered."

"You didn't forget me then?"

"Never." I take him in, my heart feels like a songbird soaring out of my chest. "How long are you staying?"

"I'm not."

"Oh."

"I'm not staying, because I've come to take you home with me."

I swallow, trying to take in what he just said.

"I live in Vermont now, at my grandpa's old place. We can sit on the porch and look at the stars every night. There's a place for you to run writing retreats if you'd like that."

"Is this a dream, or are you really here?"

He throws his head back and laughs, "No, it's not a dream."

I look at his hands, tiny streaks of paint have replaced the oil smudges. I don't say anything for a minute, and he gently tilts my face up to his.

"If you don't like the sound of that then we can live where you want."

"Vermont sounds lovely, but can we just take it one step at a time? We rushed things the first time around and…"

He puts his finger to my lips, "I don't care where we live Charlotte, as long as we're together."

He leans in and kisses me. I close my eyes, and the lost boy fades into the background behind us.

The End

Didn't Get Enough?

Want to spend more time with Ethan? Subscribe to my newsletter and you'll get instant access to a bonus scene from his pov.

www.corablacksen.com

RUBY'S REVENGE
A Suspense Romance

When Ruby Wilder returns home for the first time in ten years, her childhood sweetheart Cole Harrington is the last person she wants to see, especially after what happened that fateful night before she left.

She wants to forget the ghosts of the past, but they refuse to be buried and all paths lead to Cole.

Will Ruby finally discover the truth of that night, or will her love for him turn out to be the most dangerous thing of all?

COMING SOON
Sign up here for release date
corablacksen.com

About Author

Cora Blacksen is a hopeless romantic. She grew up on the English coast where the north wind blows and the sea is wild. Her favorite love story is 'Wuthering Heights.' Her characters are flawed, passionate and on the dark side.

She lives in California with her husband, cat and dog. She writes from home, in an office formerly known as the broom cupboard.

You can find her at www.corablacksen.com

Enjoyed the Story?

Thank you so much for reading! I sincerely hope you enjoyed *When Stars Fall*. There will be a sequel coming out later this year, but in the meantime, if you thought Charlotte and Ethan were a couple written in the stars, might I encourage you to write a review?

Both traditional and indie authors alike rely on reviews to spread the word of their work, so they can keep on writing and putting out books that hopefully entertain you. It helps us out immensely. If you have the time, and you're excited about a sequel to Charlotte and Ethan's love story, then please head on over to Amazon and write a short review for *When Stars Fall!*

Made in the USA
Columbia, SC
24 September 2023